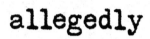

allegedly

allegedly

a novel

tiffany d. jackson

KATHERINE TEGEN BOOKS
An Imprint of HarperCollins Publishers

Katherine Tegen Books is an imprint of HarperCollins Publishers.

Allegedly
Copyright © 2017 by Tiffany D. Jackson

For information address HarperCollins Children's Books, a division
of HarperCollins Publishers, 195 Broadway, New York, NY 10007.
www.epicreads.com

Library of Congress Control Number: 2016935938
ISBN 978-0-06-242264-4

Typography by Erin Fitzsimmons
17 18 19 20   PC/LSCH   2 3 4 5 6 7 8 9 10
First Edition

For my Mother and my Grandmother
who never let me feel an ounce of pain.

chapter one

Excerpt from Babies Killing Babies:
Profiles of Preteen and Teen Murderers
by Jane E. Woods (pg. 10)

Some children are just born bad, plain and simple. These are the children that don't live up to the statistics. One cannot blame their surroundings or upbringings for their behavior. It's not a scientifically proven inheritable trait. These children are sociological phenomena.

This type of child is perfectly depicted in the classic 1950s film The Bad Seed, *based on the novel by William March. It is the story of an eight-year-old girl, sweet and seemingly innocent, the prize of her picture-perfect family, who her mother suspects is a murderer. The adorable Rhoda, a blue-eyed, blond-haired princess, skips around the film in pigtails*

1

and baby doll dresses, killing anyone who won't let her have her way.

The film was horrific for its time, a villain played by a young girl, appearing as innocent as any other. People couldn't conceive of a child being capable of murder. Even in present day, the act is unfathomable.

This is how Mary B. Addison became a household name. Mary is Rhoda's story, personified, begging the question: was there something that made her snap, or was the evil dormant all along?

A fly got in the house on Monday. It's Sunday and he's still around, bouncing from room to room like he's the family pet. I never had a pet before. They don't let convicted murderers have pets in the group home.

I named him Herbert. He's a baby fly, not one of those noisy horseflies, so no one notices him until he zooms in front of your face and lands near your orange juice. I'm surprised in a houseful of delinquents, no one has killed him yet. I guess he has survival skills, like me. Keeps a low profile, never begging for unnecessary attention. Just like me, he wants to live a quiet life, nibble on some scraps, and be left alone. But just like me, someone is always coming up behind him, shooing him away with the back of a hand. I feel for Herbert. Being a chronic unwanted guest can really suck.

At night, Herbert sleeps on top of the crooked molding that frames my closet, home to the few items of clothing I own. Three pairs of jeans, one pair of black pants, five summer shirts, five winter shirts, one sweater, and a hoodie. No jewelry. Just one of those ankle bracelets given by the state so they can follow me around like the sun.

"Mary! Mary! What in the hell are you doing? Get down here now!"

That's Ms. Stein, my . . . well, I don't know what you'd call her, and hopefully you'll never need to. I climb off the top bunk and Herbert wakes, following me into the bathroom. I'm the youngest, so of course I get the top bunk. That's the rules of the game. In one month I'll be sixteen. I wonder if they'll do anything to celebrate. That's what you're supposed to do, right? Celebrate birthdays, especially milestones like sixteen. I was still in baby jail on my last milestone, my thirteenth birthday. They didn't throw me a party then either. My birthday gift, a black eye and a bruised rib from Shantell in the cafeteria, just for breathing in her direction. That chick was mad crazy, but I'm the one with words like "rage tendencies" all over my file.

Anyways, I've been in this home of seven girls for the past three months and not one birthday has ever been mentioned. Guess birthdays don't mean nothing in a group home. I mean, it kind of makes sense. Hard to celebrate the day you were born when everybody seems to wish you were never born at all. Especially after you come into this world and fuck it all up.

I can name several people who wish I was never born.

Some chocolate cake and ice cream, maybe even some balloons would be cool. But that's what the stupid girl I used to be wishes for. I keep reminding myself she's dead. Just like Alyssa.

"Mary! Mary! Where the hell are you?"

The showerhead is a slow drizzling rain cloud. I hate showers. In baby jail, I only got to take one five-minute shower every other day, the water like a fire hose, whipping my skin like towel snaps. I never took showers before, always baths, playing in bubbles made from lemon dish soap in white porcelain tubs.

"Mary! Goddammit!"

I swear that woman can drown out water. Herbert buzzes around my wet hair, drawn to the gel that helps slick my brown 'fro back into a curly ponytail. Wish I was a fly. Like be a real fly on the wall, staring with kaleido-scope eyes at particles floating in the air, trash blowing in the wind, singling out snowflakes and raindrops. I do that now anyways. I can spend hours entertained by my own fascination of nothingness. It's a trick I learned in the crazy house, to look like I was stone-cold dead to the world so they would stop asking me so many damn questions.

But I can't be a fly, not today. I have to prepare. Be on

high alert and focused. Because in a few hours, the most dangerous, most diabolical, most conniving woman in the world is visiting me:

My mother.

Transcript from the December 12th Interview with Mary B. Addison, Age 9

Detective: Hi, Mary. My name is Jose. I'm a detective.

Mary: Hi.

Detective: Now, don't be afraid. Your mom said it was okay for us to talk to you. Can I get you anything? You hungry? Would you like something to eat? What about a cheeseburger?

Mary: Uhhh . . . cheeseburger.

Detective: Okay! Great, I love cheeseburgers too. Now, don't be scared. Just want to ask you a couple of questions about what happened last night. You'll be really helping us out.

Mary: Okay.

Detective: Great! So now, Mary, how old are you?

Mary: Nine.

Detective: Nine! Wow, such a big girl. Do you know how old Alyssa was?

Mary: Momma said she was three months old.

Detective: That's right. She was a very tiny baby. What did you do when you helped your mommy take care of her?

Mary: Umm . . . I fed her and burped her . . . and stuff.

Detective: Okay, so now, Mary, can you tell me what happened last night?

Mary: I don't know.

Detective: Your mommy said you were alone in the room with Alyssa. That she was sleeping in the room with you.

Mary: Ummm . . . I don't know.

Detective: You sure? Your mommy said she was crying.

Mary: She wouldn't stop crying . . . I couldn't sleep.

Detective: Did you try to make her stop crying?

Mary: I don't remember.

I'm on kitchen duty today. That means I have to scrub and wash until Ms. Stein can see her fat white face in every pot and pan. Ms. Stein doesn't know how to clean but she sure knows how to criticize.

"Mary, does this look clean to your dumb ass? Clean it again!"

It took the state six long years to realize I wasn't a threat to society before they ripped me out of baby jail and put me with Ms. Stein. From one prison to another, that's all it was. Understand, there's a big difference between baby jail and juvie, where the rest of the girls in the house come from. Juvie is for badass kids who do stuff like rob bodegas, steal cars, maybe stupidly try to kill someone. Baby jail is for kids who've done way worse, like me.

Anyways, some social worker dropped me off and said, "This is Ms. Stein," and left right before I met the real Ms. Stein. Most of my life, no one has bothered to explain anything to me. It's been one "'cause I said so" scenario after another. I stopped asking questions and in six years I have not run into one adult who would do me the common

7

courtesy of explaining why something is happening to me. I guess killers don't deserve respect, so I've stopped expecting it.

Ms. Stein limps into the kitchen, her bowlegs fat and swollen. You'd think someone would change their diet after they reach over two hundred pounds. But not Ms. Stein. She still eats an entire box of Entenmann's crumb topped donuts a day.

"Mary! You move as slow as molasses. Why does it take you so long to wash some damn dishes?"

I don't know why God sent me to Ms. Stein. I don't know why God does a lot of things. But Momma always told me not to ask questions and to keep praying. Even for fat, mean white ladies like Ms. Stein.

"I still see grease on that counter! If I can see it, why can't you?"

That is the only advice Momma ever really gave me. Keep praying. God will work everything out. It never occurred to her that maybe she should try to work some things out for herself. Sometimes I wanted to shout, "God's a little busy, Momma! He can't find your keys for you all the time!" She was always lazy like that, expecting everyone else to do everything for her.

God and I share the same problem.

Tara, one of my roommates, drops more breakfast dishes in the sink. She's big, and black as tar, so I call her "Tarra." But only in my head, because I don't talk to anyone.

Talk gets you into trouble and these girls are looking for trigger words to be set off. As far as everyone is concerned, I'm a mute.

"Clean it up, psycho," she grunts and bumps into me with the hardest part of her hunchback shoulder. Tara tried to kill her boyfriend. Stabbed him ten times with a pen Scotch taped to a ruler. When asked why she didn't just use a knife, she said, "Knives are too dangerous." Seventeen but has the mental capacity of a five-year-old. She, no lie, still colors in coloring books and counts on her fingers, using her knuckles when the number goes above ten.

Kisha comes stomping, slippers scratching against the floor, with her nail file in one hand and curlers still all up in her hair.

"Oh my God, this place is so wack! I'm mad bored! Ain't nothin' out here! You know that's why they got us here, right? To keep us all trapped and shit."

She isn't really talking to me. She's just talking out loud with an audience. Kisha is from some projects in East New York. I've never been there. I've never been to a lot of places in Brooklyn. Momma said everywhere else outside our home was too dangerous. Kinda funny how our home wound up being just that.

"Dumb bitches won't catch me slipping," Kisha mumbles, checking her eyebrows in the microwave. This is a girl who threw a desk at her math teacher, paralyzing her from the waist down, just because she didn't answer a question right. Most of the crimes the other girls in the house committed are like that. Crimes of passion, "snapped" moments, and good ole-fashioned wrong place–wrong time situations. My crime was more psychotic. I was the nine-year-old who killed a baby.

Allegedly. That's the word they always used.

Everyone in the house knows what I did. Or thinks they know what I did. No one asks though, because no one really wants to hear how I killed a baby. They don't even want to know why I killed a baby. They just want to pretend they know for knowing's sake.

Excerpt from <u>People</u> magazine article "Girl, 9, Charged with Manslaughter in Baby's Death."

An unnamed nine-year-old girl faces manslaughter charges in the death of little Alyssa Richardson. The case is generating controversy and tough questions about blame. Who should decide the outcome—the criminal courts or mental health experts—and can such a young defendant be judged competent to stand trial?

The girl, who is the daughter of the babysitter charged with Alyssa's care, is currently in state custody, due in court at the end of March. If found guilty as a juvenile, she could face the maximum eleven-year sentence, locked in a state penitentiary until she is twenty-one years of age. A second option would be to keep the child in a juvenile facility until she is twenty-one, at which point a judge could consider sentencing her to an adult prison for the maximum term.

The group home is always muggy, like we live in an old shoe, smelling like corn chips mixed with roach spray. I never call the group home "home." It's not a home. No house where you fear for your life can be considered a home. It's in Flatlands, by absolutely nothing. From the outside, it looks like a two-story brick-face house. There are four bedrooms, two bathrooms, a living room/dining room, kitchen, office, and a half-finished basement. The sitting room looks like a doctor's waiting area. It's for visitors like family, social workers, or parole officers.

"Mary! Quit your goddamn daydreaming and mop them floors! Here, make 'em shine."

The mop. A stringy black wig attached to a faded yellow pole. She pours a mixture of bleach and Pine-Sol on the warped floor, the burning stench inching down my throat like a knife forcing me to gag, eyes leaking.

"What's wrong with you! You pregnant or something? You better not be pregnant!"

The yellow linoleum becomes blacker, years of dirt bleeding back into the floor. I wonder how many girls used this same mop before me. Stupid, because no matter how much she makes us clean, it doesn't stop the army of mice and the swarm of roaches from visiting us in our rooms at night. Dust covering our lungs like plastic, sitting in cat-piss-soaked furniture, with dark panel walls leaving the house in a constant shadow. Let's just say I've lived in better conditions. Then again, I've also lived in worse.

The doorbell buzzes. It's not a friendly buzz, more like an angry dryer finishing its load.

"Reba! Get the door!" Ms. Stein hollers next to my ear.

Ms. Reba is security, Ms. Stein's second in command, also known as her sister. She's the taller, thinner version of Ms. Stein, with greasy gray hair and giant breasts, wrapped flat so she can pretend she doesn't have them.

"Alright. Alright," she hollers from her post on the living room sofa. She wears black wrist guards and one of those weight belts that sits right below her bulging gut, yet I've never seen her work out or lift anything but food to her mouth.

The front door has seven bolt locks, one key lock, and a bar that takes her at least five minutes to open. "It's for safety," they say. But it's really to make sure we don't run away in the middle of the night. Not that I've ever thought of it.

You can hear her whimpering before the door even opens. It's the new girl.

I shuffle by the kitchen doorway to get the first look at her. Mousy-looking white girl with dark pink lips and long, tangled brown hair, clutching a familiar state-issued bag of new clothes. Winters, my parole officer, escorts her in.

"Morning, Judy. Reba. Meet your new guest, Sarah Young."

He passes her file off, then pats her on the back as if to say "good luck." New Girl is crying. Real sobbing, snot-nosed tears. I'm jealous; I haven't cried in six years. The tears are frozen inside with the rest of my emotions. She probably doesn't think she did anything wrong. I was that girl too once.

"Thanks, boss! We getting any more?" Ms. Reba asks, pressed for more minions to rule over. Ms. Stein signs his clipboard like he's a UPS driver delivering a package.

"Not sure, can't say."

"Well, come on, child. Let me show you your room," Ms. Stein says before hobbling down the hall, the mousy girl following behind her.

"Thanks, boss. We won't let you down," Ms. Reba says.

He nods and adjusts his belt. From what I heard, he used to be in the army until he got shot in the leg or something, so he always walks with a limp.

"Any problems?"

"Not on my watch. No sir." She tucks her thumbs into her pockets and stands like Superman, smiling with teeth the color of corn, sharp enough to eat through rock.

Winters smirks then glances down the hall in my direction and nods.

"Addison."

I nod back.

Winters had zero patience for me from the moment we met. "You're gonna give me problems, Addison, I can tell," he'd said. I'd wanted to ask why, but he'd looked like he wasn't in the business of explaining himself to anybody, especially not to teenage girls.

"Staying out of trouble?" he asks.

I nod.

"Any problems?" His eyes dart to Ms. Reba then back at me. Ms. Reba turns, giving me a sharp look, a warning. One wrong answer could land me on bathroom duty for months. I shrug.

"Humph. Alright then, I'll leave y'all to it. Social services here tomorrow, yeah?"

"Yup, yup! I'll walk you out, boss!"

I go back in the kitchen, finish mopping, and head to my room. My bedsheets are piled on the floor in the hallway, sneaker footprints like tire tracks. The usual. I dust them off, remake my bed, and grab the Harry Potter book off my dresser. That joke of a bookshelf downstairs has the same crap they had in baby jail I've inhaled three times over and I'd kill for something—anything—new to read. But I'd never say that out loud. I'm a killer after all; they'd probably think I'd really do it. Figures of speech are luxuries convicted murderers are not allowed to have.

I sit and read about magic spells, waiting for the demon I was spawned from to arrive.

Dawn Marie Cooper was born in Richmond, Virginia, in 1952. The oldest of five children, she was forced to drop out of school at age fifteen to take care of her growing brothers and sisters.

"I was always taking care of babies. All my life."

Her youngest brother, Anthony, died as an infant. The coroner ruled the cause of death as sudden infant death syndrome. Her brother's passing inspired Dawn to become a registered nurse. It is unclear where she received her training, but she worked exclusively in a neonatal care unit for many years.

Dawn moved to Brooklyn, New York, with her youngest sister Margaret Cooper. Margaret wanted to pursue a career in the fashion industry and Dawn was worried about her living in a big city alone. Dawn found work as an elderly caretaker. She met her first husband, Marc Addison, at a bus stop on Flatbush Avenue. Although Marc was twenty years her junior, they fell in love and were married within three months. Marc was killed on his way home from work by a drunk driver. Shortly after, Margaret died of HIV-related complications. A devastated Dawn went into hiding.

Mary Beth Addison was born in October. Dawn testified that she had given birth at home, only bringing Mary to the hospital to get a birth certificate. She was forty-one.

When describing what happened that day, she stated, "It

was a cruel and painful birth. I knew something was wrong with her from day one."

"Yo, I can't believe this dumb shit. There ain't no trains, no White Castles, no corner stores. Some bullshit!"

Kisha complains about the group home every single day. She could go out, but chooses to stay inside, combing and straightening her hair every ten minutes like she's about to see someone new. Momma is like that too. Hair always has to look right, permed and hot-combed perfect. She would get all dressed up in heels to go to the corner store and never left the house without her lipstick, cranberry brown. Smells like crayons.

"And it fucking stinks in here," she says, trying to open a window to let out the stench of rotting food. Ms. Reba pokes her head in our room.

"Mary, your mom's here."

Like clockwork, Momma arrives at 2:35 p.m. every other Sunday, right after church. This has been her commitment to me ever since I was locked up. I'll always remember what she said in the courtroom. "I'll come see you every week. Well . . . on second thought, maybe every other week. Every week may be a bit too much for my pressure."

And sure enough, every other Sunday, she would be in the visitors' center at baby jail, cheerful and bright as cotton candy. One of the officers working my cell block said she deserved mother of the year, for all the love she showed a little psychopathic killer like me.

Mother of the year? Hilarious.

"Baby!" she squeals in the sitting room, arms extended wide, waiting for her hug. Her hot-pink skirt suit is paired with a matching bag and shoes that could almost blind you. Her cream church hat is centered, a regal crown. Momma is all about appearances.

I walk into her hug and she wraps her arms around me as tight as she can, kissing my face like always. I pull away, the remnants of her burgundy lipstick burning my cheek. She smells like my childhood: pepper, pomade grease, and laundry detergent mixed with that purple lotion from Victoria's Secret one of her boyfriends gave her.

"How's my baby girl doing?"

I have to give it to the woman. She puts on a show, through and through. Even when no one's watching.

"I'm fine," I croak out. My voice is scratchy and feels funny from not talking for so long. I can't keep up the silent treatment with Momma. She'd nag me to death until I spoke at least five words.

"Well, come on, baby, let's sit. Talk with your momma for a while."

We sit on the old blue couch. Everything in the room is a hand-me-down, thrift store finds. It's like me and Momma's first apartment, except warmer. Momma wraps her arm around my shoulder, smiling ear to ear. She was always so happy. All my life, she was the happiest person I'd ever met. Inside her bubble, nothing or no one could get her down. She smiled during evictions, smiled after Ray would beat the shit out of her, smiled when we were dead broke, and even smiled during my manslaughter sentencing ("See, baby, it's not so bad. At least it's not murder!"). She's the most optimistic person on earth. Even when she's visiting her daughter in a group home.

"Baby, your hair is getting so long," she says, looping her finger into my kinky curls, pulling at the ends like a bouncing spring. "You may need a trim soon."

"It's fine," I snap, shooing her fingers out of my hair.

She folds her hands in her lap with a closed-mouth smile, glancing around the room, bobbing to some mystery music in her head. She is waiting for me to ask about her. I'm an irrelevant factor to these visits, she's here to make herself feel good.

"So . . . Momma, how are you?"

Her eyes light up and sparkle big like stars, as if she was waiting her whole life for someone to ask her that question.

"Oh, I am so blessed, baby girl. Just so blessed! I wish you'd been at church today. Boy, pastor had an amazing service for our truly awesome God. Oh, and last week, we had . . ."

I stop listening and stare, counting the wrinkles on her face, trying to find pieces of myself in her. She has dark skin, small brown eyes, big lips, a wide nose, and a sharp pointy chin. Her black hair never grew past her ears. I have light skin, big hazel eyes, a narrow nose, and a round face. My dark brown hair has always been long and curly, lightened in the sun. She says I'm the spitting image of my father, but I've never seen a single picture of him to prove it. And while I rarely do it, when I smile, I see her smile. That has always scared me.

". . . And the youth ministry is putting on a play next week for the church's fiftieth anniversary. Oh, and baby girl, they're so excited! They asked me to make the refreshments and I told them only if they behave 'cause they just about fought over my banana pudding at the . . ."

The day after they locked me up, Momma jumped into the deep end of the Baptist church and was born again. "The devil tried to get to me through my daughter and I wouldn't have it!" The church took pity on her, of course. No good decent woman like her would ever be responsible for raising such a monster. "That devil must have came from her daddy's side."

"So, young lady? Aren't you gonna ask about Mr. Worthington?"

Mr. Troy Worthington, my new stepdaddy, owner of a soul food restaurant and apartments in Brooklyn. They met at church of course; he's one of the deacons. She married this one only six months after my sentencing. They honeymooned in Hawaii. She brought me back a seashell.

I've never met him and don't really need to either.

"So how is—"

"Sit up straight, baby. You always look better when you sit up straight."

"SO MOMMA, how is Troy?"

"Mr. Worthington. And yes, baby, he's doing just fine. We went out the other night to this beautiful . . ."

Momma did it. She finally married rich, so she could be what she has pretended to be for years. Mr. Worthington has money. I know by how Momma dresses. Never in the same outfit twice, diamonds in her ears as big as marbles, shoes in every color. Never been in her car, but I've seen the key chain, a BMW. Meanwhile, I've been in baby jail for four years, seven months, sixteen days, nine hours, and forty-three minutes before dumped in this group home the past three months. And she has never bought me a single thing. Ever.

"And then he said, 'Well, we shouldn't let good wine go to waste.' Ha! Lawd, that man is just too much. He so funny and smart . . ."

She's still talking about Troy but I know what will shut her up quick.

"Sounds great, Momma!" I smile and cozy up to her. "Hey, you think I can come to church with you sometime?"

Her face drops and she wipes it away with a nervous smile.

"Well, now, baby . . . Let's not get ahead of ourselves. You need permission and it's—"

"But we could ask, and Troy could—"

"Oh baby, I plum forgot," she says, glancing at the watch she isn't wearing. "I was supposed to pick up Mr. Worthington's dry cleaning. You know he needs his suits for his . . . well, the place closes in an hour."

She jumps up, straightening her skirt, pulling a marked-up Bible out her purse.

"And I still need to drop these flyers off for the church picnic next weekend. But before I leave, scripture for you. Ready? It's from 1 Peter 5:8. It reads, 'Be sober, be vigilant; because your adversary the devil walks around as a roaring lion, seeking whom he may devour: Whom resist steadfast in the faith, knowing that the same afflictions are accomplished in your brethren that are in the world.'"

Still trying to cast that devil out of me, I see.

She smiles and puts her Bible away.

"Now, I will see you in two weeks. Same time now, okay?"

She kisses my other cheek, leaving the same war paint mark against my skin before rushing out. And that's it. Her fifteen minutes is up. Like clockwork.

"Why the hell did you use my deodorant, you dumb bitch?"

"I didn't use anything, you stupid *puta!*"

21

Marisol and Kelly are fighting for blood in the hall again. Almost once a week Kelly is fighting someone. She's a real monster, with the bluest eyes and the blondest hair. If she stands still and doesn't talk, she looks like Barbie. I heard she was captain of the cheerleading squad at her high school before she ran into two girls in the school parking lot with her Range Rover, something to do with them missing practice.

"*Ay, coño! Quítate de encima*, stupid! I didn't touch your shit!"

The tussling blond and black ball of hair ram into the wall, dust flying. Another hole, another doorway for the mice. That's fifteen on the second floor alone with ten downstairs.

"Yes, you did! Get her, Kelly!" That's Joi, Kelly's shadow. She is the gossiper, knows everything about everybody's business. Skinny as a straw, her nappy hair can't grow past an inch with bald patches where the perm burned her. Joi pushed a girl into a moving train for talking to her boyfriend. Except he wasn't really her boyfriend.

"I didn't use it," Marisol says in her thick Dominican accent. "The new girl did!"

Uh-oh. Poor New Girl. Not even six hours in the house and is already being blamed for something. Kelly lets go of Marisol's hair and storms into the bedroom, looking for New Girl.

"Where is the little bitch?"

Kelly drags New Girl off the top bunk and into the hallway while she screams. I watch from the safety of my own top bunk.

"No, please! NO!"

"Shut up, you little cunt!"

"Get her, Kelly!"

She drags her down the hall by her hair, the others cheering like it's a football game. I go back to my book. Mind your business and you won't get hurt. That has always been my motto.

"What's going on?" Ms. Reba screams from the bottom of the stairs. That's the kind of "enforcer" she is, always a good ten minutes late to the party. Just like in baby jail, the COs were never around when I needed them.

Ms. Reba breaks up the fight (or the pummeling, however you want to look at it), and brings New Girl down to the kitchen to get fixed up. Ice for the black eye, Band-Aid for the cut forehead, aspirin for the pain.

An hour later Ms. Reba returns New Girl to her room, next to mine. Hearing her cry into her blanket through the walls reminds me of my first night in the group home.

Except I didn't cry. I never do.

chapter two

Excerpt from <u>What Happened to Alyssa?</u>
by Star Davis (pg. 34)

The New York juvenile court retained jurisdiction, despite intense public pressure to try her as an adult in hopes of a death sentence. Mary was held in the children's psychiatric ward at Bellevue Hospital under close surveillance.

With the circumstantial evidence mounting, as well as inconclusive testimony from three separate child psychologists, Judge Maggie Brenner allowed a plea bargain, sentencing Mary to a period of up to ten years in an adult state correctional facility, where she would be kept in isolation as opposed to a lesser restrictive private treatment program. Ms. Cooper-Addison was, willingly, stripped of her parental rights, making Mary a ward of the state until she comes of age.

The institution of choice was kept a closely guarded secret, given her age and the multiple death threats that have accompanied this case. Brenner ordered state officials to devise a long-term, comprehensive treatment program.

Even as her future was being determined around her, Mary never said a word.

"Ayyy, he so beautiful! Have you ever seen someone so beautiful in your 'ole entire life?"

Marisol flips back her long silky black hair, staring up at the pictures and posters of Trey Songz surrounding her bed like wallpaper. He stares down at her, lust in his eyes, even while she sleeps. He stares down at me now, on the floor by her bed waiting for Ms. Carmen, our social worker, to finish room inspection. Short, skin roasted by a Spanish sun, she goes through my stuff like one of those sniffing police dogs.

"He's gonna be on *106 & Park* tomorrow. I want to go, but I can't skip work."

Trey Songz. That's all she ever talks about. His CD is on repeat again, singing about sex. That's all he ever sings about, like he knows nothing else.

"Ayyyy, but if I was there . . . all he need to do is take one look at all this and it'd be a wrap, yo. I'd have his baby. His son!"

She pushes her chest at his picture with a kiss and he sings back. Marisol is so gorgeous that she may be right.

He may take one look at her thick ass and huge tits and be sprung. If he were smart though, he'd stay clear. She's only seventeen and is always in love. That's how she ended up in here; in love, doing stupid things for stupid boys.

"You like boys?"

I shrug.

"Me neither. I like men. REAL men. Real men take care of you."

Ms. Carmen stops to look at her and says something in Spanish. Marisol rolls her eyes.

"Mary," Ms. Carmen snaps at me. "Why do all your underwear have holes in them?"

I shrug and flick a clump of dirt off my sneaker. She curses under her breath and calls Ms. Stein as Trey Songz sings "Panty Droppa" in the background. Marisol laughs.

"Judy, have you been giving Mary her allowance? All her panties have holes in them."

Ms. Stein holds up a pair, sticking her fat fingers through the rips and glares at me.

"Why haven't you bought some underwear? What did you do with all your money?"

I shrug.

"Who cares?" Marisol says. "Not like she has a MAN to see them."

Ms. Carmen nips at her in Spanish again.

"Damn it, Mary," Ms. Stein flusters. "You can't walk around with holey underwear. Now, don't you feel stupid?"

Not really. It only bothers me a little when Ted sees them.

"Make sure she buys underwear next week," Ms. Carmen says. "If someone sees these, they'll say we're mistreating her or something."

They leave the room, complaining about how stupid I am. As soon as they're out the door, Marisol shoves me away from her bed.

"Disgusting *puta*! You smell like pussy through your holey panties."

I straighten my side, then put my money, cell phone, and pocketknife back in their hiding spot.

There is a lot that goes into reforming a teen felon. I'm reminded of this every morning when I look at my weekly schedule. As part of our parole program, we have fitness on Mondays and Wednesdays, and group therapy on Tuesdays and Thursdays. On Fridays, we're given our weekly allowance of thirty dollars, which goes toward any personal items, like tampons, underwear, MetroCards, and lunch during the week whenever we're not at the home. Sundays are for educational field trips that we never go on and visitations. Our only day of freedom is Saturdays, after we finish our chores, but we still need approval to leave before checkout.

I also have to prepare for the GED, pick a trade, and go to vocational school. It's Ms. Carmen's job to advise me on my options. I think she is my eighth social worker, but I'm not sure. I've lost count. The other social workers I've had stopped by baby jail once a month, if they could remember, dropping off animal coloring books, reading and math work sheets, and crossword puzzles. I'd eat through them like air. They'd also leave board games and cards, but for what? There was no one else like me. There was no one for me to play with. Baby jail was what they called my cell block, but I was the only baby there.

"So, Mary," Ms. Carmen asked in a dead voice during my first week at the group home, fiddling with her rosary like a candy necklace. "What do you want to be when you grow up?"

At first, this gave me hope. No one had asked me what I really wanted to do in years, but I knew the answer: I wanted to be a teacher. When I was little, I used to line my toys up in front of an imaginary chalkboard and give reading lessons. I'd even sit Alyssa on my lap and teach her the ABCs. Momma would say, "She's too little, baby. She can't even talk yet." But I didn't care. Alyssa was going to be smart. I was going to see to that.

When I wrote *Teacher* on a piece of paper and showed it to Ms. Carmen, she'd chuckled but wasn't actually amused.

"Well . . . I don't think that's a good idea."

Ms. Carmen is one of the names on a long list of people who don't really like me. Which seems ass-backward, since she's responsible for my well-being. I think it's because she is super Catholic and I killed a baby or something.

Allegedly.

She made it very clear I would never work with children, that no baby killer would ever be able to work with children. Ever. I'd scratched out *Teacher* then wrote *Nurse*.

"Welllll . . ."

Oh right. The pills. Can't touch those either.

After an hour of discussing what is left to do with my life at the ripe old age of fifteen, it was then determined that the safest career path for a psychopathic baby killer is cosmetology. That is what she chose for me. Another brilliant decision made by a government official. So I sit in GED class for two hours pretending to know nothing, then learn about perms and curling irons for another four hours.

Checkout is a pain in the ass. Ms. Reba has to write down the date and time we leave, where we're going, and a description of the clothes we're wearing. But she writes slow as shit and can't spell worth a damn.

"Gray sweatshirt, blue jeans, gray sneakers, pink smock. Uhhh . . . wait, how you spell *smock* again?"

Every day, we have to be checked back in the house by nine, or they'll call the marshals, track us by our anklets that won't let us go more than a three-mile radius away, and throw us in juvie. No questions asked. Ms. Reba calls it AWOL, when girls don't come home on time. Don't really know what that means though.

Another part of my parole is twenty-five hours of community service a week. They assigned me as a candy striper at Greenview Nursing Home, where I change pissy sheets and feed diabetic ice cream to the dying. It's actually the most peaceful part of my week. No one bothers me and I'd rather be surrounded by the semi-dead than what passes for the living at the group home.

There are five floors at Greenview: first floor, assisted living, for those who still have their senses but can't be bothered with the real world. A hundred-dollar cable bill would give them a stroke. Second floor, old and tired, for those whose batteries are dying, becoming slow-moving toys no one wants to play with. Third floor, hospice, for those literally knocking on heaven's door, waiting for someone to answer. Fourth floor, purgatory, for those slowly losing their sense of self; and the fifth floor, hell. Otherwise known as the dementia ward, for those possessed by demons who took over the bodies of the people you once loved. I prefer the fourth and fifth floors. Familiar circumstances.

It's five o'clock, time to meet Ted.

The dining hall at the nursing home smells like baby jail; like old cafeteria food, piss, and moldy flesh. He is at our table under the vent, bobbing his head to some music. He jumps up and glances around before kissing me, his lips lingering. I fall into his hug, wishing I could stay folded in his arms forever. There is literally nothing better in the world than his hugs.

"Hey," he says.

"Hey."

"Class was fun?"

"Fascinating."

He chuckles and we sit down to eat. Turkey meat loaf, mashed carrots, chicken broth, and a white roll.

"Babe, you missed it," he says. "Lady from 207 rolled up on the lady from 110 for flirting with her boyfriend."

"By rolled up, you mean . . . in her wheelchair?"

"Yup! They were about to throw blows before Ms. Legion stepped in."

"I thought he was messing with 420?"

"Nah, that was last month. She caught him pinching some nurse's butt in the TV room. Now she can't even remember his name. And he got 121 sneaking him cupcakes when he knows his blood can't take all that sugar."

"Damn, 211 is a pimp."

Ted's smile fades and he slides an extra milk on my tray.

"Still no period?"

I sigh.

"Still no period."

My period is now ten days late. We both know what it could mean but refuse to acknowledge it. Life is hard enough as it is.

The first time I ever saw Ted, wheeling a woman from the second floor into the community room, all I noticed was his knuckles, cut up and scarred like he'd been punching through brick walls all his life. He reminded me of a Hershey's Kiss with his rich, smooth, dark chocolate skin, slick with Vaseline that glowed under his pink scrubs. Pink meant he was a candy striper from a group home, like me. You'd have to be stupid to volunteer for this type of work. Our eyes locked for a moment too long. I'd buried my hot face back in my book because I'd felt them, the butterflies Momma always told me about, terrifying but exciting.

"Anyways, I got you something." His voice snaps me back to the now as he digs into his book bag, pulling out a black plastic shopping bag, placing it in my lap. It's square, thick, and heavy.

"What's this?"

"Something you wanted."

I slide the bag half off. A book, *Kaplan SAT Strategies, Practice & Review.* My smile is so wide it feels unnatural. I make sure no one's watching before I kiss him.

"Thank you."

His rough hands caress my face, eyes soft and searching. He always looks at me like that, like I'm the most amazing thing he's ever found. He is sort of amazing too. Who knew I would find the one person who understands me, no words necessary, among the half-living.

"You know your feelings are showing?"

He grins.

"I know, right. My bad."

I kiss him again, the sparks addicting, and his hands rub against my thigh under the table. I can feel the new Band-Aids on his fingers, probably from school. Ted is studying to be an electrician, out of juvie six months for a crime he won't tell me about but swears he didn't do. I don't pry; don't want him knowing what I've done either.

"So," he says, nuzzling behind my ear. "What's it like being the baddest chick in the old folks' home?"

"The baddest?"

He laughs, eyes widening.

"Calm down, babe! Baddest, like the hottest. Like, beautiful."

"Oh."

"I'm saying, I don't wanna have to fight 211 over what's mine."

My face burns and I shy away from his stare.

"I'm sure you can take him."

I flip the book over. The price, thirty-nine dollars and ninety-five cents.

"Whoa, how'd you get this?"

Ted rolls his eyes.

"Don't worry about it, aight. You need it, don't you?"

Ted's allowance is like mine. There is no way he could afford a forty-dollar book and still live.

"But, where'd you get the money?"

"Baby, just—"

"Did you steal it?"

He sighs, playing with my hair.

"You really wanna know?"

Thoughts wander but I don't flinch at them.

"No. Not really."

We finish dinner and head to the elevators, standing side by side like a pair of parallel lines. He moves his hand an inch closer, brushing his knuckles against mine. My eyes close; the slow static shock stings my fingers, leaving me warm and breathless. Doors open. Ms. Legion, the nursing home director, steps out and we part like the Red Sea.

From the Deposition of Ms. Ellen Rue— Mary Addison's Fourth-Grade Teacher

The best way I could describe Mary is gifted. She was one of the brightest, most brilliant students I ever had. She could read at an eighth-grade level and excelled in mathematics. I once gave her a math test fit for a sixth grader. She finished it in thirty minutes, scoring a 90 out of 100.

There are 756 pages in the SAT prep book. If I study fifty pages a week, I'll be ready to take the exam by December. That's if the mice don't eat my book first. They've already nibbled on the edges.

Ted and I have a plan. Since he's older, he'll be off parole before me, hopefully by the time he finishes school so he can get a job and an apartment. I won't be released until I'm nineteen, maybe longer. Until then, I'll take half of my allowance each week and save for school. That is fifteen dollars a week for fifty-two weeks, which comes out to $780. Times that by four years, I'll have $3,120 by my first semester. Ted will take care of us while I go to school and study business. Then we'll open up our own hardware store, get married, and put the past behind us.

I wrote the plan out in my cosmetology notebook.

In order for colleges to potentially overlook my conviction, I have to fall in the ninety-eighth percentile, 200 points less than perfect. Verbal I can handle with no problem. I read the whole dictionary one time because I didn't have anything better to read. Math will be tricky. Sure, I'm real good at counting in my head. I always counted out the rent money Momma kept in the coffee can above the stove. We were always short and Momma would yell at me for counting it wrong. I counted right; we were just short. But the SATs have these graphs, shapes, and formulas I've never seen before, and my GED class only covers the basic stuff. I'll have to learn the rest on my own. On top of all that, I don't want the girls or Ms. Stein knowing what I'm up to. They'll only screw up my plan. So this all has to be in secret.

"Aye! What you doing?"

Damn, I really hope Tara isn't talking to me. But the room is mad tense and quiet, so I know something is up.

I keep my back to them, bedsheet like my own personal tent, and continue flipping pages. Maybe if I just ignore her, she'll go away.

"Aye. Psycho! I said, what you doing?"

She yanks the sheet and the book falls off my bunk, slapping the wooden floor. I can't untangle myself fast enough to jump down and grab it before she does.

"What's this?"

The whole room is staring at us but I can't focus on anything else besides the book Ted gave me in her fat, greasy hands. It's like she's touching him, my Ted. Just the thought of that makes me itch from toes to fingertips. My tongue detaches itself from the roof of my mouth and pushes out some words.

"Give it back," I mumble.

The whole room freezes and Tara's mouth drops. They've never heard my voice before. Someone in the background whispers an "Oh shit," and Tara grins.

"Or what?" RIPPPP! She tears the cover.

"Give it back," I say, wishing I could talk louder or at least sound dangerous.

Laughing, she rips the first pages, crumbling them into balls on the floor.

I grab for the book and she holds it over her head, knocking me right on my ass. RIPPP! Another page. That itch in my toes sends a shock through my whole body and I launch at her feet. She topples over slow, like a black domino, screaming. The house shakes when she lands.

"Fight! Fight! Fight!" the girls scream, giggling. But this is a David and Goliath type of battle I have no chance of winning. So I jump up with the book and run out of the room toward the stairs, Tara clambering to pull herself up and chase after me.

"Fucking bitch! I'm gonna kill you!"

I tuck the book under my arm and race down the stairs. Tara comes thundering down the hall after me, each step like an earthquake. I can't stop fast enough before slamming into the front door. Locked. It's after nine; the door is bolted shut for the night. Tara trips down the stairs with a scream. I buckle back, jumping over her, and race to the back of the house. With all this noise, where is Ms. Reba?

Tara is at my heels. I duck into the kitchen, throwing a chair in her way. She falls again. Shit. She's really mad now and I'm trapped. I claw at the window but the lock won't budge. Where the hell is Ms. Reba? The noise had to wake her up by now. I know she's always ten minutes late to the party, but damn! Tara gets up, madder than mad. It hits me that I'm hiding in the kitchen, near all the knives. Not the smartest move but Tara isn't bright enough to even consider that. This was the same girl who taped a pen to a ruler for Christ's sake!

"Fucking bitch!"

Clutching the burning radiator pipe, I cower in the

corner, chipped paint splintering up my nails. I pull myself into a little ball on the floor and squeeze my eyes shut. Tara yanks at my shirt, trying to shake me off the pipe, banging on my hands to loosen my grip. Screaming, she gives up and starts beating me, fists slamming against my back like a raging gorilla. I clench the pipe and start to pray. The last time I prayed this hard, Alyssa wasn't breathing.

Why won't you breathe, Alyssa!

The lights come on and the fists stop. I look up and Ms. Reba has Tara in a chokehold, all out of breath from trying to beat me to death.

"Calm down! Calm down!"

Ms. Stein comes limping in.

"Jesus Christ, what's going on?"

The book, sandwiched between the pipe and me, topples over as I let go, falling on my back with a gasp. Pain rips through me as I stare at the ceiling, catching my breath. Herbert flies over and for one insane moment, I wonder how he is surviving in this place while I'm the one being batted down like a fly.

Ms. Stein bends quicker than I thought she ever could and picks up my book, examining it like a Rubik's Cube. I sit up and lean against the stove, the movement unbearable.

"What's this?"

The floor is full of dust and belly-up water bugs. I don't say nothing. Ms. Reba drags Tara into the living room, trying to calm her down.

"I'll kill you! I'll fucking kill you!"

"I said, what is this, Mary?" Ms. Stein barks.

I'm fighting to breathe and losing. Breathing hurts my lungs, which hurts my back.

"It's . . . it's a book."

Ms. Stein's eyes go wide and her head snaps to Ms. Reba. They've never heard me talk before either.

"Wa . . . wait. What did you say?"

"It's a book," I mutter again.

Ms. Stein doesn't know how to react, thoughts all jumbled and thrown off by a few words. She frowns then blows out a huff of hot smelly air.

"I know that, dummy! What the hell you need a SAT book for, Mary? All this fighting and carrying on, waking folks up in the middle of the night over some book for a test you too stupid to take!"

A knot rolls into my throat and I try to swallow it back.

Don't snap, Mary. Don't.

I wouldn't go to baby jail if I killed Ms. Stein. I'd go to prison, a real prison. I'd never see Ted again.

"You're never gonna get into college! They don't take killers in college!"

Don't kill her, Mary. Don't. Kill. Her.

Ms. Stein flips the book over and looks at the price.

"Where'd you get this?"

"It . . . it was a gift."

"Bullshit! Ain't no gift. Who bought it for you then?"

39

They can't know about Ted. No one can know about Ted.

Ms. Stein puts her free hand on her hip. "Well?"

I guess I'll have to lie. I hate lying but I've been doing it all my life. No sense stopping now.

"I bought it."

"You BOUGHT it? You bought a forty-something-dollar book? You expect me to believe that? Okay then. Where's the receipt?"

I can't think. My back hurts too much to think.

"I . . . I don't know. I . . ."

"Rule number five, Mary! Anything you buy, you have to show proof. And that means a receipt. We can't have you stealing shit and bringing it in here."

She stands smirking at me and my mind goes blank.

"So you don't have the receipt?"

Eyeing over her shoulder, the entire house is in the kitchen, watching. New Girl looks straight frightened. There is no way out of this. There is no way I'm going to get my book back. I shake my head no.

"You steal some book you too stupid to read and cause all this goddamn commotion!"

"I didn't steal it," I mumble toward the floor.

"Oh really? Well, I'm just gonna hold on to this. And when you find that receipt, you can get it back."

Ted finds me in the walk-in freezer, leaning my back against the icy wall. He pulls me out and takes me to one of the empty rooms on the third floor where a patient died this morning.

"Let me see."

Wincing, I lift my arms and he slowly removes my smock and my undershirt. He unhooks my bra and turns me around. A quick breath whistles through his teeth and I'm happy I can't see his face.

"Shit, baby . . ."

"I'm okay."

"Your back is purple."

I sigh and it hurts. The room smells stale of diapers, old shoes, and death.

"Just . . . lay down," he says. "Hurry, we don't have a lot of time before Ms. Legion comes looking for us."

I climb into bed, whimpering with every movement, and collapse on my stomach. He runs out, returns minutes later with a few ice packs and gently places them on my back, covering them with a damp towel. The cold stings like hell, but it's better than nothing. He slides into the small twin bed with me and our noses kiss. Having him near me, I start to heal.

"You aight?"

"She took my book."

He frowns, but doesn't pry. It's what I love most about us. No questions, no explanation needed. He rolls on his back and pulls me on top of him. Chest to chest, I breathe with him, his heart a drum in my ear. He sits his chin on top of my head and plays with my hair.

"It's okay to cry, you know. You can cry in front of me."

"I don't cry."

His fingers graze my cheek.

"You a bad liar, Ma."

I exhale a calming breath and close my eyes.

"If I was, I wouldn't be here."

Two days later, Ted finds the receipt at the bottom of his book bag. He didn't steal it after all. Which makes me wonder how he afforded it in the first place, but I don't ask. I get to the house before dinner and slap the receipt on Ms. Stein's desk. We stare at each other. Now would be the time for her to apologize, but she doesn't. Instead, she opens her drawer and hands back my tattered book. I snatch it and walk straight to my room. Maybe Ted and I need a new plan, because I have to get the hell out of here. Soon.

The unfinished basement is the exact size of the visitors' room above it, with a storm door leading to a junky back-yard. Dark, damp, and always cold. I hate it down here. I hate therapy.

"Hi, ladies!" Ms. Veronica says in a nasal voice. She always reminds me of the lady on that show I used to watch with Momma, *The Nanny*. She looks like her too, mad tall, long black hair, and super white skin with lots of makeup. We sit in a circle of metal folding chairs while she runs at the mouth.

"How was everyone's weekend? What did you ladies do? Who wants to share? Anything exciting? Well, I had a really nice dinner with my hubby on Saturday. We had Indian for the first time."

First, let me tell you about Ms. Veronica. She is straight up the most un-relatable person to have ever entered the group home. Ever. She doesn't belong here. But every Tuesday and Thursday she leads us in group sessions about anger, trying to make us discuss our feelings in order to find what she refers to as "peace."

There is no such thing as "peace" in a group home.

Why is she so un-relatable? Because she is too damn happy all the time, mad optimistic. Thinking that everything will turn around with a snap of a finger and we'll all live happily ever after. Sweet, but unrealistic. Some of these girls still use their fingers to count.

"Okay, ladies, let's take out our journals. Who wants to be the first to share?"

Our "feelings" journals; notebooks we're supposed to write in three times a week about our "feelings." No one writes in them. No one has feelings in here.

Ms. Veronica starts talking about sadness and what it means to be sad and how sadness makes us do terrible things. I overheard Ms. Stein talk about her once. She is from Staten Island, married young and rich, so this little therapy job is sort of a joke.

"So, does anybody want to talk about a time they were sad? I mean, really, really sad?"

No one says anything for a while, then China raises her hand. She is always the first person to speak.

"My moms . . . she kicked me out when she caught me with my first girlfriend. Pretty little light skin thing with curly hair . . ."

She glances at me and I stare at the floor. Kelly rolls her eyes and mouths "Ew."

China is the manliest person in the house. She wears nothing but boy clothes, even boxers, which seems like overkill. Momma would be disgusted at the "nasty lesbian" I'm living with. She hates anything that is not in the Bible, which seems like everything.

"How long you been a rug muncher for?"

"Joi! Inappropriate," Ms. Veronica says in a shaky voice.

Joi rolls her eyes and the others snicker.

"Anyway though, she kicked me out the house and I was, you know, on the streets for a little while before I linked up wit my crew."

"Don't you mean your 'gang,'" Kelly corrected.

"Blood or Crip?" Kisha asks.

"She's a Blood."

"WAS a Blood. Not no more."

The room goes silent. Ms. Veronica, wide-eyed, nods for her to continue.

"Anyways, I linked up wit my crew, and started getting into things. Then, like a couple of months later, I ran into my boy who lived on my block. Said Moms was in the hospital. So I go to check on her and she was in this room wit all these machines and stuff hooked up to her. She looked real bad. Doctor said she had cancer. When she woke up and saw me, she started screaming, 'Get that bitch out of here. I don't want to see her!'

"It's like, damn, yo. She didn't even want to see me on her deathbed. She died like a month later. Didn't have the right insurance to keep her. It hurt, you know? 'Cause I was always the one taking care of her. She wasn't that smart so she didn't keep a job for too long. A week after she died, I got caught."

"What did you do?" New Girl asks and the whole room stares. It's the first time she has opened her mouth. I think she even shocked herself.

"China likes slashing people's faces for fun," Kelly snickers.

"Yo, why don't you mind yo' fucking business!"

"Make me, you dyke bitch!"

"Whoa, whoa, whoa, ladies! Language! What did we talk about?"

The room erupts and I stay still, thinking about how I took care of my momma. She needed watching after. Especially when she was having "a day."

• • •

I was falling off a building.

Or that's what it felt like. Falling to my death off my bunk. But I didn't fall, I was yanked. My feet hit the floor, balance off, eyes still closed. I can barely stand up straight before I'm dragged out of the room.

"Get in there now!"

Ms. Stein grips my arm so hard she leaves half-moon imprints with her nails, blood throbbing to break through the skin. She throws me in the bathroom, eyes still crusted with sleep, a black mop in one hand and a hairy, rusty sponge in the other. The sun hasn't even got up yet.

"Well, don't just stand there," she snaps from the hall-way. "Clean up!"

We stare at each other, because she knows I'm on kitchen duty this week. She knows I shouldn't have to clean the bathroom. But this is punishment. She had to do something. She couldn't let me get away with outsmarting her. Not in front of the other girls.

"Hurry up! I want that toilet shining!"

My hand tightens around the mop, ready to shove it in her fat mouth. But then I remember the cement blocks of my cell in baby jail and slowly lift up the toilet seat. A ring of shit splatter circles under the rim. I dry heave the moment the stench hits my nose.

"Ohhh, quit your bitching! It's your own damn food! Here, put a little bleach on it."

She dumps some bleach in the bowl and it splashes on my pajamas. I can taste last night's dinner in the back of my throat, hot dogs and broccoli. My back stings as I hunch over, wiping the shit with a sponge. Small chunks fall into the water, pieces splattering on my hand. My eyes are so watery from the coughing and heaving that I'm almost blind. It's too hot . . . I need air.

"Wash off that sponge. It's still good to clean the tub. And take out that garbage too. It fucking stinks in here! Hurry up, Mary, I ain't got all day!"

The garbage reeks of old rolled-up pads with dry period blood and Kisha's empty Noxzema jars. The smell hits the bottom of my stomach and I heave so hard my chest aches. SPLAT! Pink and white vomit covers my bare feet, slime seeping between my toes, even as chunks still hang off my lips.

"Eww! Mary, that's disgusting! Well, you gotta clean them floors anyway. Here, use some of this bleach. Make them floors shine!"

Interview with Correction Officer at Bedford Hills Correctional Facility: Anonymous

A little black girl who kills some little white baby? Man, that kid was famous, face all over the fucking news! And that was the problem. She couldn't stay in the youth detention center or she'd be eaten alive and she couldn't be with the adults, 'cause they no better. So what do you do with a kid who murders a baby? Where do you put her? What do you feed her and when? No one knew. And you can't have some ten-year-old little girl skipping around the yard, now can you? So yeah, she spent a lot of time in the hole, but if they didn't know what to do with her, how were we supposed to know? It ain't like she could go crazier than she already was. You ask me, we were doing her a favor.

Dinnertime. It's Kraft macaroni and cheese day, made from powdered cheese and water. Reminds me of the first meal I had in baby jail. Served with a side of peas and carrots on a square plastic blue plate, like a TV dinner. I'd never had TV dinners before, or Kraft mac and cheese. I'd seen commercials for the stuff between my cartoons after school, but Momma would "humph" and say things like, "That stuff is so fake. All them preservatives and chemicals . . . you like your momma's mac and cheese, don't you, baby girl?"

Momma made the best mac and cheese. The best fried chicken, the best collard greens. I miss her food more than her. She cooked almost everything and was always ranting about "fake food." Problem was you had to have money to buy "real food," and she'd rather us starve than eat a pack of ramen noodles. So we did a lot of starving.

After dinner and cleanup, everyone runs to the TV room to watch reality shows. I'm no therapist, but it doesn't seem like a good idea for girls with raging tempers to watch grown women fighting on TV. My favorite show is *Law & Order: Special Victims Unit* but no one else in the house likes it.

"Shit is mad fake. Cops don't care like that!"

"And those trials are mad fast. I didn't get offered no deal like that!"

But I think it's real, it has to be. Detective Olivia Benson, the lady cop, seems so, I don't know, smart and mad nice. She can always tell when someone is lying. Always making friends with the victims and doesn't stop until she gets the real bad guy. Sometimes, I imagine what life would've been like if she was the person on my case. She would've said, "Mary, it's okay. I know you loved that precious little girl. My gut tells me you didn't kill her. And I promise you, I won't stop until I find out the truth." Then a week later I would be free, because her gut is never wrong. Maybe even stay at Benson's house, because she likes me so much and wants to protect me. Would she adopt me? Could she? Damn, my life would've been so different if I had Benson and not the man who gave me that cheeseburger.

In the shower, I find another freckle. Or beauty mark, I'm not really sure. That makes twenty-three. So pale and bony, nothing about me screams "black child." I don't mind though, just makes me wonder if my daddy is white. Whenever I tried to ask about him, Momma would act like I was crazy and say, "What are you talking about? Ray is your daddy."

Ramon, "Ray," stepfather number two, was a five-foot-three Dominican. Even Momma was taller than him, but he'd beat her down to his eye level all the time. His skin like honey wheat toast, he wore glasses that would fall off his face and break whenever he came home drunk. He was also missing about four of his front teeth. I looked nothing like Ray. And thank God for that.

But my real daddy, he is out there, looking for me. No one wants to be that kid in the orphanage, waiting to be rescued by her real parents, like in *Annie*. But some nights, I dream about him. In my dreams he is a big, tall, rich, handsome white man. He'd pull up in his limo, walk through the door, wrap his arms around me and say, "I've been waiting my whole life to meet you." Then, he would save me from this place, and Momma.

There are two computers in the corner of the basement we're allowed to use for thirty minutes at a time. This is where I find New Girl hiding out in her pajamas. Do I say something? Maybe? It's only us and she is a wet noodle compared to the others.

"What are you doing?"

She yelps, jumping from the chair and turning off the monitor in one swift motion, backing away, eyes wide and white as lightbulbs.

"Listen, I'm not gonna hurt you," I chuckle. "You're too old for me to hurt anyways."

Her eyes grow wider, hands shaking like I'm a cold wind. I have scared what little color she has right out of her. Bad joke, I guess. I shrug and walk to the opposite side of the room, giving her space. I'm used to being a leper, so my feelings aren't hurt.

She waits until I'm seated at the other computer before returning to hers, fingers flying fast across the keyboard. They didn't let me take computer classes in baby jail. I don't know why. I bang on the mouse, but the screen stays black. Thought you just moved it and it would turn on? Maybe it's broken? But New Girl's is working.

"Um . . . you know how to . . . turn this on?"

New Girl's mouth drops, eyes blinking a few times. "You never used these before?"

Why she got to ask like that, like I'm stupid or something?

Still, I can't meet her eye, it's mad embarrassing. She hesitates before creeping over, clicking a button on the back of the black box.

"Thanks," I mumble as my screen comes to life. She scurries back to her seat, still eyeing me like she doesn't know what to think while I click on the Google logo. I've seen Ms. Carmen on it before. She would type in something and all this information would pop up, so I punch the letters *S A T* with one finger.

51

"I . . . uh . . . Googled you," New Girl says, a tremble in her voice. "I remember. I was ten when you . . . when you killed that baby."

I let out a sigh before turning to her.

"Allegedly."

She swallows hard, eyes returning to her screen. Honestly, I've never thought about looking myself up before. What did she see? The stories, the TV shows, pictures . . . maybe pictures of Alyssa! There are probably tons of pictures of her on Google. They wouldn't give me a picture in baby jail. I was put on cell restriction for even asking. Matter of fact, I was always on cell restriction. The COs were never eager to open my cell. They'd rather keep me locked up all day, staring at the gray cement, thinking of Momma and Alyssa. It's easier to keep an animal in a cage than to play with it.

But I'm not in baby jail anymore. All I have to do is type my name, and then I can see her! I delete *S A T* and type *M A R Y A* . . .

"There was a lot about you though. About how you did it."

How I did it? Did what? Oh right.

I didn't mean to throw her.

"Are you . . . Googling everybody?" I ask.

"No. Just you. You're the celebrity. That's why they hate you."

"Who?"

52

"The other girls."

"Oh."

I thought the whole world hated me. They probably do, like the ones in front of the courthouse. All those people, yelling and screaming, Alyssa on big posters and T-shirts . . . there will be pictures of them too. Backspace. Backspace. Backspace.

"They all seem crazy. The others. Don't they?"

I know crazy. I've lived with it for a long time. But none of these girls are crazy. They're just stupid. They made stupid decisions for stupid reasons. I guess you could say I'm stupid too.

"I guess."

"Do you ever think about . . . that night?"

My eye twitches and I sigh.

"Every day."

Excerpt from the Final Autopsy Report of Alyssa Richardson:

Description of Patient: 12-week-old Caucasian female. Brown hair, blue eyes. 13 pounds 5 oz.

Time of Death: Approximate time of death between 7:30 and 9:30 p.m.

External Examination: Bruising on forearms, upper right thigh, and center forehead. Ecchymosed bruising under the left eye.

Cause of Death: Asphyxia due to strangulation.

Stomach Contents: Colostrum's lactate (Breast milk), Methylphenidate (Ritalin), and Clonidine.

Manner of Death: Homicide.

The moaning through my thin walls wakes me up. Momma and Ray, sexing again. Why does she have to be so loud? When he's done with her, he'll come for me, I know it. *He's coming, he's coming, he's coming . . .* the tremors start, body shaking from my toes to my ears. I should try to hide again, but I'm too afraid to move. How bad will it be if he finds me this time? Where's bear? I reach for him, feeling for his stiff clump of fur, but find I'm alone, my sheets rough and scratchy. This is not my bed, this isn't my room.

Where am I?

The smell of Tara's stank feet brings me back to the group home, but I still hear moaning. Marisol's bed is empty; she must be next door with China, another night visit to her bunk. Poor New Girl has to witness it.

"I told you it ain't my fault!"

"I don't want to hear it! You know the rules!"

I roll over, away from the door and cover my head with a pillow, but I can still hear Joi and Ms. Stein screaming downstairs. It must be really late, because lights-out was at least two hours ago.

"But there was a fire on the tracks at Union Square. All

54

the trains were stopped! I was waiting for almost an hour. How else was I supposed to get home?"

"You expect me to buy that? It's one in the morning! Check-in is at nine! Where the hell were you?"

"I told you! I was waiting for the train."

"Fine, you don't want to tell me, then tell the marshals."

"But I came home!"

"You're late! You went AWOL!"

"Yo, I didn't!"

"And you changed your clothes," Ms. Reba adds. "That's not the outfit you had on this morning."

"I . . . it . . . it got dirty."

"Strike two, Joi! You're on house restriction for the rest of the month. AND bathroom duty."

"WHAT! Yo, that ain't fair! I didn't do nothing!"

Damn, house restriction is the worst. It's like real house arrest, you can't leave for nothing except school and even then they escort you back and forth like COs. I was on house restriction for a month when I first got to the house. Once they figured out I wasn't a threat, they gave me a MetroCard, subway map, and pointed me in the direction of the bus. Kisha said we lucky; she'd been in another group home where they were on house restriction all the time.

Marisol moans louder; China must almost be done with her. Joi is hollering for her freedom. I pin the pillow tighter to my ears, nauseous and feeling anything but lucky.

"You know, I was thinking," Ted says, his arm wrapped around my waist, sitting on some crates in the low light of the janitor's closet. "We should get out of Brooklyn."

Snuggling under his arm, I lean into his chest, breathing easy. I can imagine us like this, in the apartment Ted always talks about getting for us once we're out.

"And go where? The Bronx or something?"

He laughs. "Nah, like leave New York. For good. Get you in a school some place out of here. Maybe down south. Or California. They ain't got no snow out there."

I don't know what to say. I mean, all we know is Brooklyn. We can't just leave all we know.

He peeps my face and shrugs. "Mad tired of this place. Always something. What's wrong? You scared? You think I'd let anything happen to you?"

I'm not scared. I know wherever we go, if Ted is there then I'm safe. But . . . what about Momma? How could I be so far away from her? What would she do without me? Or would she even notice I'm gone.

"We'll be straight, Ma. Just you and me," he says and kisses my forehead.

I swallow, thinking of my missing period, hoping it really will just be him and me. But maybe going away would be good. The farther we are, the less likely he'll find out that I killed a baby.

Allegedly.

"Oh snap, I almost forgot." Ted pulls a crumpled piece of yellow paper out of his pocket and irons it out. "They having a practice test at Brooklyn Tech on Saturday."

FREE SAT PRACTICE!!!
Saturday, September 26th
Come practice for the real thing!
Brooklyn Technical High School

"You should go," he says.

I stuff it in my pocket with a shrug. I am about a third of the way through my book. The vocab isn't too hard, though I can always learn more words. The math isn't too bad either, since it turns out I'm pretty good at geometry, but there is still a bunch of stuff I don't know.

"What if I fail?"

"It's just practice, right? And you ain't gonna fail. You mad smart."

"But what if I fail," I say again, without looking at him.

"You won't. Chill."

He eases me onto his lap, tickling the back of my neck with kisses.

"I don't even know where Brooklyn Tech is."

"I got you, babe. I won't let you get lost, no need for an Amber Alert."

I laugh. Ted remembers everything, like how I hate being lost, afraid I'll never be found. He keeps me safe, warm and grounded, even when I want the earth to swallow me up.

During that first week at Greenview, I could feel Ted watching me. In the halls, in the kitchen, and patients' rooms, staring, heat in his eyes. I mean, I was curious about him too. I kept thinking, is this what boys do, make you feel naked with all your clothes on? And the way he smiled at me, like he was honestly happy to see me, reminded me of a time when someone wanted me. I would have given anything to have that again.

The next week, in the dining hall, he planted himself at my table without asking, slurping up soup and crackers. His presence was like a space heater, the feeling confusing. Too nervous to hold a spoon steady, I rubbed my feet against the carpet, desperate to run and hide. This went on for a week, every day him sitting next to me, calmly eating his food, me frozen in terror. Maybe it was the way he didn't push me to talk, but by the next week, my muscles, tense and hardened from baby jail, began to ease. I started eating again, enjoying his silent company, no questions, just the comfort of knowing he was there and didn't want a thing from me. Then one day, he slid his milk onto my tray without looking up and said, "I love your eyes."

It was the nicest thing anyone had said to me in years . . . and I panicked. Always alone in my cell, I didn't know how to talk to people. I mean, how do you tell someone you're a mute for Christ's sake? But for some reason, with him, I couldn't just say nothing either. So I stared at his knuckles and blurted out the first thing I thought of.

"What did you do?"

I'd slapped my mouth shut, horrified. Shit, what a stupid thing to say!

He'd smiled and said, "So how long you been out?"

And then my whole universe had opened up and he became my sun.

Saturday comes fast. I leave the house at six thirty in the morning to meet Ted at the station. I lied and told Reba I volunteered for extra hours so she'd unlock the door for me. We take a bus to the L train, transfer to the C train, and get off at Lafayette.

Ted holds my hand as we walk down the brownstone-lined block, under giant trees toward the park. Momma told me only millionaires live in these brownstones. I didn't believe her. Why would rich folks want to live in Brooklyn? But it's so pretty and clean over here, the houses so huge. No crack heads, no bodegas, not even a liquor store. Just wine shops. So maybe she's right.

Brooklyn Tech is big. I mean, it takes up a whole city block; it's the biggest school I've ever seen. The roof touches the clouds. The windows, maybe a thousand of them, are covered in mesh metal . . . no escape. There are other kids, like me, walking through big metal doors that slam hard behind them. My chest feels funny. I try to pull my hand away but Ted grips it tighter.

Big like hospitals . . . Big like baby jail . . . White rooms . . .
Don't leave me . . .

"I have to throw up."

Ted lets go of my hand as I rush in between two parked cars and puke everything out of my stomach. I recognize the blueberry muffin and cranberry juice I had on the train ride over. Two dollars and twenty-five cents. I wipe my mouth with the tissue in my bag and rub my hands with sanitizer, free from the nursing home. Ted watches, his face a stone. I know what he's thinking. Still no period.

Ted clears his throat. "Maybe . . . we should come back another day."

chapter three

It's Tuesday. Now twenty-five days and still no period, so I'm pretty sure I'm pregnant. I've never missed before. Never even been a day late. It always came on time. Punctual. Just like Momma.

I didn't tell Ted I used my savings to buy a pregnancy test. Thirteen dollars and forty-nine cents for a generic one at Duane Reade. But the only private place to take it is in one of the patient's bathrooms at the nursing home.

The lady in room 408 sobs in the corner, talking in circles. I close the door so no one would hear and change her piss-soaked sheets for the third time this week. Poor lady is not ready for the fifth floor just yet.

Before Ted, I didn't know anything about sex but what it sounded like. Momma had lots of sex with Ray and a bunch of other guys. She used to make all these wild noises, like someone was hurting her. Ray would talk to her in Spanish, she would holler back in English. Our last neighbor, Mr. Middlebury, was the worst of them. Sweaty, lumpy, and smelled like he bathed in Head & Shoulders shampoo. Soon as he'd walk in, I'd run in my room and close the door before the smell could seep in. He'd scream like a girl in Momma's room and the whole house would stink for days. Every time I saw his wife, I'd wondered how she could stand it.

Ted and I talked about sex a lot. He kept saying I didn't have to do anything I didn't want to, but I was ready to chase the numbness away. And I wanted Ted to be my first. If it had been up to the devil, I would've lost my virginity to Ray a long time ago. But I fought back. And that made me crazy, impulsive, and my favorite misdiagnosis, "hyperactive." Go figure.

We decided to do it during dinnertime, while the nurses were busy making sure no one choked. The only free bed was in a room share on the second floor, with a patient that never ate in the dining room. So we waited, made sure he was asleep, snuck in, and pulled the curtain closed around us. Ted had been with girls before. But the way his big eyes searched my face, gently moving, making sure I was okay, made it feel like it was his first time too. His lips soft, sweet like pancake syrup, skin smelled like cocoa butter and soap, his arms locked around me like handcuffs; I never wanted to escape his prison. I was better than okay.

Not like I am now, in this bathroom.

It took four minutes to confirm what I already knew with two blue lines. I wrap the test in 408's pissy sheets and throw them in the trash so no one will know either of our secrets.

For the rest of the day, I avoid Ted, hiding on the fifth floor. The look on his face when I threw up in front of the school . . . I don't know how he's going to react. Other than Alyssa, I haven't kept anything from him. I'm sick just thinking of telling him that secret too.

What if I just got rid of it? He would never know.

But an abortion would make me a baby killer. Again.

New York Police Department First Responders Report—Officer Ricardo Hernandez— 67th Precinct, Brooklyn

On December 11th, at approximately 19:17 hours, I was dispatched to 330 E 18th Street in reference to a home disturbance. As I arrived on scene, I observed a woman, later identified as Dawn Cooper, screaming in the front yard. When questioned, she said a baby wasn't breathing.

The smell of eggs frying in butter makes my stomach heave. I run, but can't make it to the toilet before throwing up last night's dinner in the sink. Morning sickness. This is it. I really am pregnant.

"Kisha, hurry it up or you'll be late," Ms. Stein barks downstairs. "And where's Mary?"

"She still upstairs."

"That lazy brat! Mary! Mary! Reby, go get her."

Shit!

I scoop up the chunks and slime with my hands quick, shaking them off in the toilet. Reba knocks on the door.

"Mary!"

Flush, down my secret goes. I use half a roll of toilet paper and wipe the sink clean.

"Come on, Mary! Let's go! Now."

My forehead is wet, hair sticking to my neck. Ain't no air in here to help me breathe right. I wash my hands, change for school, and head downstairs.

"Hey, what's wrong with you?" Ms. Stein snaps. "Why you look like that?"

One whiff of the girls eating fried eggs, sucking and mashing on them like cows, and I hurl by the stairs. SPLAT!

"Ew, Mary! That's disgusting! What's wrong with you?"

The girls scatter like roaches. I drop to my knees, frantically sopping up chunks with a rag, like I can make it all disappear. But it's too late. They've already seen.

"Are you pregnant?"

Shit.

Ms. Stein is the last damn person I want to know. I shake my head.

"Are you lying?"

"No?" I say.

"Get in here now!"

I follow her to the half bathroom, the girls whispering behind us. She pulls out a pregnancy test, the mad professional kind, and makes me pee in front of her.

Five minutes later, she confirms what I already know.

"See. I knew it! Dumb little girl can't keep her damn legs closed. Get to school! I'll deal with you later."

Continued—First Responders Report— Officer Ricardo Hernandez

I was led to a back bedroom in the house. Upon entrance, I found a Caucasian female infant wearing a pink onesie and lying face up on a bed. I asked Cooper the baby's name and she identified her as Alyssa. Cooper stated the baby was not hers. I alerted dispatch, brought the baby into the living room, and began CPR.

Ted is mopping in the community room on the fifth floor, his back to the patients. I watch from the door, my chocolate prince. Should I really ruin his life with this? Could I be this cruel?

Ted turns, but is unrecognizable. Under his dark skin, a black eye is forming. His lip is split open and it looks like a cheese grater cut across his cheek. I run across the room.

"What happened?"

"Long fucking story," he snaps, pushing my hand away, his eyes another shade darker. I flinch. Same way I used to when Momma got mad at me.

Alyssa . . . he knows? But how?

Blood rushes to my feet, heart pumping the life out of me while Ted barely looks at me. I don't know this Ted; he's never snapped at me before. I feel like a moon drifting farther away from my sun, lost and growing colder. He pinches his eyes closed and with a groan drops the mop, wrapping his arm around me.

"Sorry. I didn't mean that," he whispers. We rock slow for a minute and he kisses the top of my head. "I always feel better when you're around."

"Me too," I say into his chest, relief washing over me. And it's true. He dulls the pain of missing someone who doesn't want me.

It's okay. He's not Momma. He won't hurt me.

Letting my heart slow down, I focus on his sneakers. Once blue, now blackened from wear, the laces frilled at the ends.

"I'm pregnant."

Ted stops breathing and freezes. I was afraid of this. If this is the last time he'll ever speak to me again, I want to remember and touch every part of him, so I hold him tighter. He untangles himself, stepping back with this tense stare, his hands cupping my face.

"It's okay, babe. Aight, we'll . . . figure it out."

I relax and melt back into his arms. He inhales deep.

"Don't worry. You'll make a great mom. You won't let anything happen to our baby."

I stare back down at his sneakers, at the dried mud crusting around the bottom.

If he only knew the real me.

Continued—First Responders Report— Officer Ricardo Hernandez

Shortly after moving the baby, Officer Robin Blake arrived on the scene. A young girl wearing pink and white pajamas with no shoes, later identified as Cooper's daughter, Mary Addison, ran into the living room from the back entrance of the house. I observed her running toward the infant's room. The front of Addison's clothes appeared to be wet and covered in black mud. She was visibly shocked to see us. Brooklyn EMT arrived and took over CPR. They pronounced the child dead on scene.

On the bus ride back to the group home, some kids jump on near the high school and I pretend to be invisible, dipping lower in my seat. Normal teenagers. Boys in baseball hats, baggy jeans, dreads, short cuts, and boots. Girls in expensive sneakers, purple book bags, straight hair, long braids, and pink lips. They're loud, talking about some football game they just came from, midterm projects, and music. Eating Rice Krispies Treats, drinking soda, laughing and smiling. Going home to their mothers or fathers, maybe both. They don't have to worry about cells with no windows or COs raping them. They probably never had to worry about money for soap or deodorant or taking pills until they can hardly taste the rat shit slipped into their oatmeal. They don't have to worry about group homes, fat foster mothers, or turning eighteen. There are no social workers hating them, roommates trying to kill them, or parole officers looking for any excuse to throw them back into baby jail. And they don't have to worry about having a baby at sixteen. Wish I could be them, but I'm not.

I'm gonna have a baby.

And Ms. Stein knows, which means everyone is going to know soon enough. This makes my stomach turn. Where the hell am I going to live with a baby? The group home? It's too dangerous. Strollers, diapers, baby food . . . where am I going to get money for all of that?

I'm gonna have a baby. A real baby . . . like Alyssa.

It's going to grow and come out of me. I'll be its momma and can make all the rules. I'll be able to do all the things I couldn't do with Alyssa; hold her, feed her, change her diaper, read to her, play with her all the time, all day long, whenever I want. Ted and I, we'll be real parents, like Alyssa's momma and daddy. They were the best parents. I used to wish they were my parents. If they were, then maybe I wouldn't be here.

One of the kids starts talking about the SATs and my ears perk up. It's the one thing I have in common with them, the only thing that keeps me normal and separates me from the animals. I can't help but smile.

I'm gonna have a baby.

When I get back to the group home, social services is parked out front. Right on time. Ms. Stein is an award-winning snitch. Ms. Carmen and Winters are in the visitors' room, waiting. I sit and take one hard look at Ms. Stein, who pretends not to notice.

"So," Winters starts. "How the hell did this happen?"

This doesn't seem like the type of talk I can keep quiet for but I shrug anyways.

"Ha. Sure. You have noooo idea," he says.

"Do you even know who the father is?" Ms. Carmen says, rolling her eyes.

This is a tricky question. Ted is eighteen. I'm fifteen. I shake my head no.

"Of course not," Ms. Stein mumbles. "So . . . what do I do with her?"

"What do you mean?" Ms. Carmen snaps. "You keep her, until the baby is born! You'll have to move her to a bottom bunk though."

Ms. Stein purses her lips. She wanted to get rid of me.

"We'll start the adoption proceedings immediately,"

Ms. Carmen says to Winters. "Make this quick."

"Adoption? Someone's going to adopt me?" I blurt out. I'm surprised at how quickly the thought sparks hope in me. Like, me, adopted, someone actually wanting me.

Winters does a double take then leans back in his chair, the wind knocked out of him. Ms. Carmen, momentarily shocked by the sound of my voice, turns my way, irritated and disgusted, as if she forgot I was still in the room.

"No, no, adoption for your baby."

There is a brief pause as the world comes crashing around me. Windows break, buildings collapse, people screaming and drowning in the rising sea, and yet somehow I still hear Herbert, buzzing nearby.

"What?"

"Mary, you are still a ward of the state, which means your baby is now a ward of the state. Both Winters and I have the final say in what happens to your baby. And given your crime . . . we cannot in good conscience put another life at risk."

A tightness pinches around my lungs, face hot and tingly. My baby, my Alyssa, they want to take her away from me?

"You don't get to keep your baby in prison," Winters says.

Is this prison or a group home? I guess they're one and the same. But I didn't do anything. I've been good! That's why they let me out, right?

"But I . . . I've been—"

"Now, we can't make you do anything you don't want to," Ms. Carmen says. "If terminating the pregnancy is something you'd like to explore instead, we can schedule that. But if not, we will have to make adoption arrangements."

I'm dizzy from holding my breath for so long, maybe for years. And something ugly, hidden deep inside me is threatening to erupt. I can't hold it back anymore. How do I make it stop before it's too late?

"Well, Mary? What you got to say for yourself?" Ms. Carmen asks.

I open my mouth, but nothing comes out. My lungs are about to bust, body shaking.

"What is it, Mary? Spit it out."

The hot stingy sensation on my face makes my head hurt, the buzzing louder. I can't keep my baby? All 'cause of Alyssa? But Momma said . . . damn, should I tell them? No, it's too late. You can't! But it's MY baby. It's me and Ted's baby, NOT theirs. They can't do this. It's not fair. It wasn't my fault.

I didn't mean to throw her . . .

"I didn't do it."

"Didn't do what?" Winters snaps.

A dam opens and I realize what the sensation is. Hot tears, dripping down my face, eyes a leaking facet. I am crying. I never cry. And everything clinched up inside me releases before I say her name out loud for the first time in years.

"I didn't kill Alyssa."

Winters scoffs. "I'm sure."

No one moves or says anything, but their faces all say the same thing: they don't believe me.

"Mary, would you excuse us? I'd like to talk to Winters and Ms. Stein alone," Ms. Carmen says.

Still can't feel my legs, but somehow I walk out, every breath wheezing. I stand in the hall and listen.

"Well, this is a fucking mess," Winters says.

"That girl has been trouble from the start! I told you it was too soon to let that animal out," Ms. Stein barks.

"You were supposed to be keeping an eye on her!" he screams.

"Don't tell me how to do my job! You don't think I know—"

"Would you calm down," Ms. Carmen snaps. "Nobody is blaming you!"

"So what do we do?" Winters asks. "I have to report this, obviously."

"You can't make her get an abortion?" Ms. Stein asks.

Winters laughs. "She ain't like the others, Judy. She ain't stupid."

"What about the baby?" Ms. Stein asks.

"What about it? You heard what I said," Ms. Carmen scoffs.

"But you can't just take a child away from someone, can you?" Ms. Stein asks.

Ms. Carmen chuckles, evil like a witch. "With her record, parental rights aside, she'll be delivering that baby straight into ACS's hands. I'll make sure of it."

From the Deposition of Charles Middlebury— Dawn Cooper's Neighbor

Mary . . . that Mary . . . such a weird little kid. She never blinked. Never made a sound, but stared with those cold-blooded eyes of hers. Her momma was always screaming at her, she was always getting into trouble.

I was watching my programs when my floodlights came on in the backyard. I get up to look, 'cause sometimes boys be cutting through my yard on the way to the ave., only it's Mary I see out there. She was outside by the big tree, digging. I tell you she was trying to dig up a grave for that little baby. Digging like a dog trying to hide his bone.

Poor Ms. Dawn. Shame she had such a bad little thing. People always want to blame the parents, but Ms. Dawn's the sweetest lady you'd ever meet. She'd never even hurt a fly.

There was this girl named Ariel, like in *The Little Mermaid*; had the smartest mouth in baby jail. Very small, but very pregnant. Once she got too big to walk, they kept her in my cell block for safety. But when her water broke, safety didn't mean shit. She was lying on the cement floor, screaming and begging for hours. I watched it tear her in two, the floor covered in gooey water and blood with that funny metal smell. The COs didn't care. They took their sweet time letting her out. She ended up giving birth in the infirmary, handcuffed to the bed. They took her baby right away and she was back in her cell two days later, crying for weeks.

"They're not supposed to do that," she said. "They're not supposed to just take him away like that. I didn't even get a chance to hold him!" But that was the scariest part. They CAN just do that. They can do whatever they want.

So at two o'clock on Sunday afternoon, I am doing something I've never done before. I am eagerly waiting for Momma.

Herbert flies in circles around my head, a little slower than usual. Maybe he's getting old. I have no idea the life span of flies, but Herbert's a survivor. He'll be okay. We'll be okay.

At 2:35, I hear Ms. Reba greet Momma at the door, searching her bag for any weapons or drugs before leading her into the room.

"Baby! Isn't this a surprise?"

I have to act fast. I only have fifteen minutes before she disappears.

"Hi, Momma!"

I run into her hug, almost toppling her over.

"Lawd! What has gotten into you?"

She backs away, smoothing down her dress. It's a royal blue church suit today, black trim with a black hat. Her ugly green Bible clashes, but she'll never stop carrying it. It was her mother's. I pull her over to the couch and yank her down.

"Momma, do you love me?"

"Well, of course I do, baby, you know I do."

"Well, I'm sorry, Momma, but it's time. You have to tell the truth."

"The truth about what, sweetie?"

"You have to tell the truth about what happened to Alyssa."

She stiffens with a hard blink, her smile fading. She opens her crocodile purse and pulls out a tube of hand lotion, thick and white as frosting. Her hands are always rough and dry. She can take hot cake pans out the oven without flinching.

"I . . . I don't know what you're talking about."

"You know what I'm talking about. The night Alyssa died. You have to tell them . . . your plan. I just can't do it anymore."

"What d'you mean?"

"Momma . . . I'm pregnant."

She blinks hard. Nothing but pure blankness. This isn't a good sign. Tense and rigid, she stands and walks to the window, staring out into the sun.

75

"They're gonna take my baby away if you don't tell them the truth!"

Nothing. She looks gone. She can't be gone though. I need her here.

"Momma, please say something."

Nothing. The woman is frozen and my heart can't take the waiting. Then, without a word, she picks up her purse and heads for the door, as if I said nothing at all.

"No, Momma, stop!"

I jump, grabbing her sleeve, pulling her back. She spins around and slaps me, hand like lightning. The grease of her lotion sticks like oil to my flaming cheek.

"Now you listen to me, little girl," she says, finger in my face, voice seething. "I know the devil got inside you and made you kill that little girl, but I didn't raise no 'ho! You know better than to open your legs up and let some boy inside you!"

The devil got inside me? She's lost it. She's absolutely lost it.

"Now, I have to go. You've upset me. My blood pressure must be sky-high and Mr. Worthington will be all worried sick about me."

I grasp at her sleeve again, struggling to hold her.

"Momma, don't do this to me! I've done enough for you. You *have* to!"

"There ain't nothing for me to do! I didn't do anything wrong. You're gonna have to accept the consequences of your actions, Miss Missy!"

She breaks free, eyes glaring. Then she snatches one of the visitors' magazines, rolls it up, and before I can stop her . . . SMACK! Herbert is a smudge of legs and wings, plastered to the wall. My heart sinks to my feet.

"Pesky little thing," she mumbles, throwing the magazine away.

And with that, she straightens her hat, storming out. All I can do is watch, accepting the consequences that I let her go free. Again.

chapter four

From the Deposition of Connie George, Chief
Nurse Officer of the Neonatal Intensive Care
Unit, Kings County Hospital, Brooklyn, NY

*Dawn Cooper, wow, I haven't heard that name in years.
Yeah, she worked here, long ago. Level one neonatal unit,
was great at showing new mothers how to breast-feed and
swaddle. She loved them babies, almost a little too much, you
know. Not saying there's anything wrong with that, but she
was always a little too . . . attached. Real touchy and kissy,
took her time bringing infants to the mothers. I caught her
feeding and rocking one to sleep in an empty room once. Odd
but harmless.*

*Her husband died and she took some time off, but when
she came back, she was never the same. Forgot to fill out*

charts, blanking out in delivery rooms, getting really agitated with the new mothers; she even started singing and praying hard over the preemies in intensive care. Parents were uncomfortable. I had to let her go. The last time I saw her, she came in with her daughter. I was glad for her. She seemed happy at least. And, I'm not gonna lie, I've been working here for close to twenty-five years and I've never seen a new mother look so, well, regular, after giving birth. She was glowing. Good for her, I thought. Seemed like having her little girl was helping her get back on track.

Momma calls herself a healer. Says she has powers to heal people, like Jesus. She always used to talk like that when she was having "a day."

"My prayers are powerful! I can heal the blind, bring the dead back to the living. God made me this way. But I save my special prayers for you, baby girl."

She prayed for Alyssa too. Now look where we are.

Ted takes my hand, but I can hardly feel it. I've been numb all week. I feel nothing as he drags me inside Brooklyn Tech, the steel doors slamming behind us. The building reminds me of baby jail, with its hollow blue halls and bright hospital lights. Stench of cafeteria food and sweat from the gym baked into the walls makes my stomach hiccup. I stop moving.

"Chill," he laughs, pulling me. "You'll be aight."

I hold his hand tighter.

We should go, this place is dangerous. Doesn't he see that?

There are a lot of kids here. They don't know me and I don't know them, but they look like the ones in baby jail. Eyes dead of life, heartless, cold-blooded; smelling the fear I stank of like dogs. They line up at a table outside the auditorium for another practice SAT. Ted insisted I take it, even though I don't see the point anymore.

We stop at the end of the line. Ted tries to let go of my hand and I don't let him.

"Chill," Ted reminds me, squeezing away.

I move in the line with slow shuffling steps, looking every three minutes at the corner where Ted is waiting. He nods and smiles back. A girl behind me notices and rolls her eyes.

"So fucking sprung," she mumbles and I stay forward, eyes down at my sneakers. Gray with blue Nike stripes, the laces black with dirt. A girl in front of me has on pink sneakers with turquoise laces and jewelry hanging off the tongue. She could eat dinner off of her shoes.

"Name?"

The lady at the table looks like she grew up in the projects; that's what Momma would've said if she saw her. Tan skin with short, bright red hair, a gold chain, bracelets, and rings with hoop earrings to match.

"Um, Mary Addison."

"School?"

"Don't go to one."

She looks up at me for the first time, like I said something strange. She isn't as young as I thought.

"Home school?" she asks.

"Umm . . . yes."

I guess.

"ID?"

"0031496."

"What?"

Wait, where am I?

"Hello? Your ID! I need your ID."

"I . . . I don't have one?"

She rolls her eyes.

"Didn't yuh read di flyer? Go stand over there!"

I stand aside with a pocket of kids that look as homeless as I feel. Ted watches from the corner, his face hard like he is about to hit someone, but he doesn't move.

0031496. My ID in baby jail. Momma played the number all the time, never won though. Even if she did, I doubt she'd have given me any of the money.

When they are done with the regular registration, the same lady calls us pack of misfits back over.

"Yuh all lucky dis is just a practice test and not di real deal. 'Cause next time, they won't let yuh take di test. Yuh need to get yourselves an ID. Do it now before it's too late."

I look over at Ted and he nods. Then she gives us a form that asks for our name, number, and address. That's the last straw. I put the paper down and walk away.

"Aye! Gyal! Where yuh going?"

The lady chases after me and I stop a few feet from Ted.

"Where yuh going? After yuh wait all dis time now."

For the first time, I notice her thick accent, like she is from an island.

"I can't put my address."

"Why not?"

"'Cause."

She blows out air. "Meh trying to help yuh. We won't—"

"I don't want them . . . anyone . . . knowing I'm here."

The lady keeps a straight face, but I think she knows what I'm talking about. She looks at Ted then back at me.

"Listen to me, 'ere, chile, don't ever let anyone stop yuh from bettering yourself. Yuh scared of people knowing, yuh scared of change? Good. Change is scary. Get used to it! But nothing comes from nothing."

My head drops like it always does when I'm being lectured. I stare at her shoes. Plain black. Looks like they've been worn a while and . . .

"Look at meh when meh talk to yuh! Don't put your head down, nothing to be ashamed about! Why yuh give up so?"

Because it's easier this way, to give up, walk away and avoid the fight. That's a rule in baby jail, don't bother trying. Why break that rule now? But the way she's yelling, makes me feel stupid.

She huffs, hands locked on her hips.

"Yuh know what, yuh can pick up your scores from our office. Meh write down the address. Come next week. Meh name Claire. Yuh can ask for meh when yuh get there."

Ms. Claire, I say in my head. Momma always told me to call adults Mr. or Ms. I do it to everyone except Winters. He's too much of an asshole to pay respect to.

"Yuh got your pencils?"

I dig in my bag and pull out a pack of brand-new number two pencils from the dollar store. One pack, one dollar and nine cents.

"Your calculator?"

I pull out the calculator Ted stole from the office. She snatches it out of my hand.

"Dis little ting 'ere? Yuh need a proper graphing calculator."

I have no idea what that is.

"Come now. They starting."

Continued Deposition of Ms. Ellen Rue—Mary Addison's Fourth-Grade Teacher

She said she wanted to be a teacher, just like me. Was always my little helper! She would clean the boards, straighten the classroom, and sharpen all the pencils. Used to tutor her classmates during lunchtime too, that came easy to her because she was so much ahead of everyone. I reported her progress to the principal and we had her tested. Turned out, she could skip at least two grade levels. But when we told her mother, she flipped out. Threatened to sue the school for unauthorized testing! She thought Mary would think she was better than other people, that she was "too good" for regular school. It was bizarre. Most parents want their children to advance and would be thrilled. It just didn't make sense to leave her in a class where she wasn't challenged. Poor Mary. She was just so bored.

"You walked out of that room like a zombie," Ted says, handing me a hot dog. We sit on a bench at Fulton Street Mall, what they call a street mall. There's a Macy's, a Jimmy Jazz, a Foot Locker, and a bunch of jewelry shops. The streets are always packed with vendors selling oils, books, gospel CDs, bags, and cell phones.

We pool our money together for two hot dogs and a can of Coke. I'm glad Ted took me here. I'm not ready to go back to the house; my mind is still recovering. The test took forever with words I don't remember ever seeing in the dictionary and math problems as long as the alphabet. The other kids had those calculators Ms. Claire was talking about. Black and bulky, not like my puny little white one.

"I need an ID. And a calculator." They are the first words I've spoken since we left the school.

"Calculator shouldn't be hard. But how you gonna get an ID?"

"Do you have one?"

He pulls out a plastic ID from his wallet. I smile at his picture.

"Oh, you laughing," he says, tickling me.

"You look so young."

"That was me, three years ago. My moms brought me to the DMV with my birth certificate."

"Oh."

Now I see. I don't even know if Momma ever had my birth certificate. She's never been great about keeping stuff like that. Maybe my white father has it. Maybe he'll take me to get an ID when he comes.

We sit for a long time in silence, just people watching. It's an Indian summer day, I once heard a CO call it. When it's super warm even though it's supposed to be cold. I unzip my hoodie and arch my head back, letting the sun beat my face. A couple of flies bounce around a trash can on the corner. Herbert's family. Thinking of him makes me think of Alyssa and how I couldn't save either of them from Momma. Damn, I think about her so much she has become a mood, an emotion. I am Alyssa-ing over a fly.

"What happened to your brother?"

I snap back up. Ted never asks about family stuff. I forgot I even mentioned I had a brother. He stares off at the people passing, expressionless, and my body tenses up, ready to run. Why is he talking about this now?

Oh God, maybe he knows.

Maybe he Googled me like New Girl did and he knows about me. He knows about Alyssa.

He can never know about Alyssa.

I start to breathe funny before he places his arm over my knee, massaging my calf. I love when he does this. I love whenever his arms are around me in any way. Even though the thought of him knowing scares me, it makes me start talking.

"I was . . . six when my momma had him. Ray Jr. He was tiny, a preemie or something. He looked just like Momma, brown skin, big eyes, but with the tiniest little fingers and toes. I always wanted to be a big sister, I just never thought it'd happen, you know, 'cause Momma was . . . well, Momma. But when she brought him home . . . he was so cool."

Ted smiles.

"So you've always liked babies?"

"Yeah. I guess. Maybe 'cause of the way they smell. You ever smell a newborn? It's so different . . . just new. They're like these tiny, brand-new humans that don't know who you are, or what you've done, or anything. But they love you anyways."

"See! I knew it! This ain't no mistake." He rubs my stomach. "It was meant to be."

I swallow, Alyssa-ing, guilt coming over me.

"Anyways, one night, Momma put Junior to bed and he didn't wake up. That was it. She was sad. Ray beat her pretty bad after that. He lost his firstborn son and blamed her."

"But was it her fault?"

All the feeling in my face is gone. It's like he can see right through me, all the way into my mind, into our history.

"What d'you mean?"

"Did she do something wrong? You know, like did she forget to feed him or something?"

Now I've lost feeling in my legs. No one has ever thought of holding Momma accountable. For anything. The smoke from the roasted nut cart on the corner turns my stomach over. Or maybe it's the conversation. I shrug and sip the last of the soda.

"I don't know. Who really knows what they're doing with a baby?"

Ted shrugs.

"You came out aight though."

That is true, I survived. Well, if you call this surviving.

"What happened to Ray?"

"He's dead."

Ted looks like he wants to ask how, but doesn't. Does it matter how he died? He's dead. I know how, I just don't feel like saying. I don't feel like talking about it.

"Do you love your moms?" he asks.

He is going in a direction I need him to come back from. He is going down back roads filled with thorny bushes and poisonous fruit. I touch his temple with my index finger.

"What you got cooking up in there?"

He smiles and holds my hand. Even with a busted lip and bruises all over his face, he's still beautiful.

"Nothing, just thinking."

"About your mom?"

He nods.

Ted's mom lives in the Linden Houses, over in East New York, not too far from his group home. But he hasn't seen her in years. She's never visited him in juvie. Not even on holidays or his birthday. I don't know what's worse. My momma visiting to make herself feel better or his mom not visiting at all.

"Do you love your moms?" he asks again.

I don't know the answer to that.

"Do you?" I ask.

He sits up, playing with the tight curls in my ponytail.

"I guess. Ain't I supposed to? Moms bring you into this world with one job, to love them, right?"

I shrug. "I guess."

He rubs my shoulder, grazing his thumb against the scar on the back of my neck.

"You never told me what happened here."

Momma happened. She hit me with the wrong end of

her belt. The buckle cut out a chunk of skin like an ice cream scooper. I should've got stitches, but that would've meant hospitals, questions; Momma in trouble and me left alone with Ray. So I wrapped it up in toilet paper and baby Band-Aids instead. It healed all wrong. Now it looks like the inside of a belly button. I brush his hand away.

"Nothing happened."

Ted looks at me, but doesn't ask anymore. He knows all about scars. He has mini moons up and down his body where his dad used to put out cigarettes. But Momma's not a monster like that. She just doesn't know what she's doing sometimes.

At least that's what I'd like to believe.

"What does it mean when you love and hate someone at the same time?" I ask.

He laughs. "It means they family."

From the Deposition of Ms. Rachel Edwards— Third-Grade School Counselor

Ms. Cooper-Addison came to my office at the beginning of the school year to talk about Mary. She said during the summer she had some issues with her hitting and biting people. I recommended she see child psychologist Dr. Reuben Jacobs. Two weeks later, Dr. Jacobs called to tell me about the visit. He was concerned. Said that Mary was silent the entire time, never said a word or colored a picture. About five minutes before the session was about to end, he asked Ms. Cooper to join them. She asked Mary, "Why aren't you saying anything?" Mary turned to her and said, "You told me not to talk about Ray." Ms. Cooper was apparently very angry and quickly left with Mary. Dr. Jacobs called and tried to convince her to come back for another session, but Ms. Cooper became irate, accusing him of trying to steal her money. I tried to schedule a meeting with Ms. Cooper but she kept dodging me so I called social services. They went by the house and said everything was normal, which was bull. I don't even think they talked to Mary. After that, Mary was out of school a few days, then I got wrapped up in some other cases, weeks went by and then . . . it happened. I should have followed up or something, but I was new. And I never would have thought . . . she was just such a good kid.

The basement erupts with applause. Kisha, standing in the middle of our circle, closes her feelings book and takes a bow while the girls cheer. Ms. Veronica wipes a tear out of her eye.

"That was a beautiful poem, Kisha. Nice work!"

"Yo, Kish, that was dope," China says. "You should put that in a book or something!"

Kisha nods, pretending to be modest in a room full of starstruck fans.

"Hey, psycho," Marisol says to me, her long black hair curly today, clothes so tight she might turn blue. "Why you no clap for her, aye? You think you better than everybody? *Estúpido!*"

I'm the only one not clapping.

They can't be serious? They really don't know?

Kisha sits and stares at me. I stare back. She shifts her eyes away, smile quickly fading because she knows. She knows I know.

"Whatever, she stupid anyways," she says, cutting her eyes at me.

She knows I know the poem. I know it because it was in the book Alyssa's mother gave to Momma that she never read. *The Complete Works of Maya Angelou.*

"That's why she ain't gonna go nowhere! Trying to get into college and shit. She don't even talk none," Kisha snaps, her voice growing louder.

"Nah, I hear her talk with her momma," Joi says. "She sounds mad white! That's why she thinks she's better than everybody. Mulatto bitch!"

The girls cackle. Ms. Veronica claps her hands.

"Girls! Cut it out!"

They high-five each other, bonding over their mutual hatred for me.

"Now, today, I want to focus on some of the positive moments from our past. It could be anything. Let's start with something, like, what's your favorite childhood memory?"

This is the brilliant question Ms. Veronica asks a bunch

of social outcasts; a group of convicts and products of broken homes. She wants us to relive our terrible childhoods and give her the one point in our life that didn't suck. Now I'm sure they found her off a street corner.

"Oh, come on! Someone has to have one," she urges.

Tara raises her fat hand.

"Okay! So I got, like, four brothers on my mom's side and two on my dad's. So one day, my brother Ty Ty came home with a busted lip, 'cause he got in a fight with this kid at his school. So my brother Kells, he just got out from doing a bid, calls up my other brothers and all seven of us went to pay this boy a visit. Yo, he was mad shook when he saw us walking down the street, in line, like an army, coming for his ass. We beat the shit out of that nigga. After that, we went to IHOP and got a stupid amount of food, then skipped out on the bill. I think that was the only time all of us ever got together. Best day ever!"

Ms. Veronica nods, struggling to smile. That wasn't the kind of story she was hoping for.

"O . . . k! Good story! Ummmm . . . everyone, how about you write your stories in your feelings book. Okay?"

I open my book and write one word: IHOP.

When I was little, Momma and I used to go everywhere together, but the place we went the most was church. Sunday school, Sunday service, Saturday service, Wednesday Bible study, Fish Fry Fridays, and every single gospel concert, we were there, dressed alike. They would call us the "Addison Twins." Sometimes after Saturday service, we'd stop at IHOP for breakfast. She would let me get extra whipped cream on my strawberry pancakes; that was my special treat. Then, we would take the bus home, playing "I spy with my little eye," just the two of us. I thought I made her happy. But I guess children don't really fill the loneliness in your heart. At night, I could hear her crying through the wall.

That was even when she wasn't having "a day."

Then, one day, she put on her red heels, did her hair all fancy, made up her face, and sat me in front of the TV.

"I'll be right back, baby," she'd said and left. Four hours later, she'd come back with Ray and he never left. She'd said he was the ray of sunshine she had been waiting for. We stopped going to church since Ray didn't believe in God. Momma is a follower, not a leader, so no more trips to IHOP. No more extra whipped cream, no more "I spy," no more being twins after she dropped my last name and started only calling herself Cooper, as if she didn't want to be mixed up with me anymore. Plus, Ray had sucked her bone dry until we only had pennies for the collection plate, and Momma would rather die than be embarrassed in front of all those people in the house of the Lord.

I'll take my baby to IHOP. If they let me.

Interview with Anonymous Inmate at Bedford Hills Correctional Facility

The kid's a fucking genius. And that ain't a good thing, know what I'm saying. She's too smart. Them COs . . . Lawd, they hated that child. They never like to let her out the cage 'cause she was always getting her ass beat. Them other young girls, they picked on her bad. She was once in the nurse's office for like a whole month with some broken ribs. So the COs just kept her in the hole. Probably stayed in there 'bout few years. But when they let her out, you can just tell she was thinking. Ever seen those people who just think too much? Yup, up to no damn good.

Ms. Stein sent me to the clinic with a note. I'm pretty sure she is supposed to come with me. Or maybe Ms. Carmen, but I don't feel like asking. The clinic is in Bed-Stuy, off Fulton Street and Kingston Avenue. It's where all the group home kids go, and everyone else who don't have insurance.

Not one seat left in the waiting room. Not even on the windowsill. So I stand by the door, against the chalky green wall, making room for the incoming and outgoing strollers and walkers. There are babies busy crying and coughing up germs into the hot air. The TV is muted on some talk show right above a fan sitting in the corner. A girl, who looks about my age, sits on the opposite side of the room with her swollen belly and tangled hair. The lady next to her looks like her older twin. I can't tell if it's this waiting room that makes her look so pissed, or the fact that her kid made the same mistake she did a few years earlier.

Momma never liked taking me to the doctor's. One time, I got real sick eating some spoiled tuna, starving because we didn't have anything else in the house. I puked and puked and Momma still refused to take me to the hospital.

"Bunch of crooks, them doctors. Always finding something wrong with you, so they can take hard-working people's money."

But Momma had no money to give. Ray took it all. The coffee can above our stove was always empty.

"I guess he needed it more than we do, baby girl," she would say. My cramping stomach disagreed.

That was all before Ray's other girlfriends came banging on our door. Before he moved us to Ditmas Park, to the big house he sublet from a friend. Before we met Alyssa's momma. Before Alyssa. Life would've been real different without Ray. But it's a waste of time thinking about that now.

"What the fuck is taking so damn long," the girl's mother groans. "I can't believe this fucking shit. What did I tell you? Ain't I tell you that nigga ain't shit? And you go and fuck him . . . uggghh. Where he at, huh? He ain't here, like I told you he wouldn't be!"

The girl doesn't respond, just stares at the floor. Acid creeps up from my stomach to my throat.

"So fucking stupid," the mother mumbles. The girl and I share a look that makes my skin go cold. Why does it feel like we're both getting the same talking to?

Minutes tick by to an hour. My knees hurt, tired of supporting me. The girl's mother is at the front desk now, taking her anger out on the nurse who doesn't give a damn. The girl holds back tears. Don't blame her; I wouldn't want my momma here either. And the two of them in the same room . . .

The door opens again and Ted walks in. I almost didn't recognize him with his hoodie pulled up. He scans the crowd until he spots me on the wall.

What is he doing here? He can't be here! They'll know!

"Sorry I'm late."

I shake my head, pretending not to see him.

"You shouldn't be here."

"I ain't letting you do this alone."

I catch the girl and her mother staring at us. The girl lets her tears fall and quickly looks away. The mother rolls her eyes and mumbles more curses at her daughter. Every muscle tightens around my stomach.

That could be me. That was me.

I glance back up at Ted, grateful, and don't argue. I'd risk being caught just to be near him, just to breathe easier. He holds my hand, palms sweaty in the funky heat, and leans against the wall watching the waiting room like a foreign film, English barely spoken.

"You scared?"

I don't want to tell him what I'm really afraid of. Ms. Stein, Winters, Ms. Carmen, all the people employed by the state to help me; the people who only want to take the one thing that actually belongs to me.

"Do you really think we should keep it?"

He stares, drinking me in. "Do you want to?"

"No."

He is silent for a moment, then chuckles. "You a bad liar."

I look up and smirk. Kind of hate how he knows me yet doesn't know me at all. Guess I love it a little bit too. Ted is so tall the top of his head almost touches the welcome sign a few inches above him. His eyes are so pretty and brown, a shade lighter than his skin, but always mellow, loving, and calm. He never looks at me the way everyone else has the last six years. He looks at me like he's happy I'm alive. Like Alyssa used to. I could stare at him for hours if we ever had the time. He squeezes my hand and looks away.

"You know I love you, right?" he says.

I know this, but it makes no sense. How could anyone love me after what I've done?

"You know I won't let anything happen to you," he says, real serious. "Or our baby. You know I got you."

His face darkens with resolve. He is thinking about the

girls in the house. But they aren't the ones he should be worried about. I'm the one who killed a baby.

Allegedly.

"Addison," a nurse calls from the door, aggravated and annoyed.

"I know," I mumble and let go of his hand.

My white smock has tiny dots on it. Blue ones; I've counted two hundred and twenty-three so far. Momma made me a dress just like this for Easter. During dinner, I dropped a spoonful of cranberry sauce in my lap and it seeped deep into the cotton. Momma beat me only because Ray told her to. She did everything he said.

"Get in that corner! NOW!" she'd said.

Sometimes, I think Momma used to forget who I was when she beat me. Or maybe she was just a whole different person altogether. Her eyes would go blank, face almost unrecognizably mashed up in rage.

"Take off them clothes! You gonna feel every bit of this!"

I'd strip down to my underwear and back into a corner, my whole body trembling, waiting for her to finish her belligerent rant.

"How many times I got to TELL you. Lawd Jesus. How many! Huh? You don't listen, you just don't listen! Father God, why did you send me this little wretch?"

She'd beat me with whatever was handy. Her favorite

was the dirt brown extension cord she kept hanging on the refrigerator handle, a ready threat. It would crack in the air before biting my skin, leaving welts the size of fists all over my legs, arms, and ass.

"Mami, don't hit her face," Ray would say with a smirk, sipping on the brown liquor he bought with Momma's money. "You leave marks and those nosy bitches come and be all in your shit."

I thought maybe if I didn't scream so much she would stop, but she never did. It's like she wanted Ray to hear me beg for my life, to make him happy. She'd grunt and curse over me, working up a sweat, while I tried to block the blows. Then later, she'd complain about her arm hurting, blaming me for making her hurt herself. When the beatings started to get worse, when it was harder to explain the welts, cuts, and bruises, I thought about running away.

But then who would take care of Momma?

"Are you still taking your medication?" the doctor asks. His name doesn't matter, since he won't remember mine. He is another overworked government employee and has the same look of annoyance as the rest of them have when they see me. He does his exam with zero enthusiasm, touching me only slightly if he has to.

"Are you still taking your medication?"

Oh right. The pills.

"No. I'm not."

The doctor scribbles some notes. He hasn't looked me

in the face the entire time I've been in front of him.

I shouldn't have been on those stupid pills in the first place. You would never think it would be so easy to drug up a child. But Ray and Momma had found a way. For the fifth time, Ray had come into my room and tried to get into my bed. His musky cologne and stank underarms had woken me up before I felt his hairy hands, creeping, pulling back my Hello Kitty sheets, pushing my teddy on the floor, rubbing up my thighs. This time, instead of crying and kicking like a wild animal, I'd bitten down on his arm and drawn blood. Ray had left the house. Momma was so mad she wouldn't speak to me for a week.

He was back two nights later; I'd heard them talking about me in the kitchen.

"Mami, I was just checking on her to make sure she was asleep. You know me, baby. I treat her like she's my own. And she go ahead and bite me. I got teeth marks, baby. She loco. We got to get her help."

Next thing I knew, I was in a doctor's office, a "friend" of Ray's, who threw around big words like hyperactivity, neurobehavioral, comorbid, and oppositional defiant. Momma hadn't known what any of those words meant. But she had heard one word that she could relate to: medication.

"Look, baby girl, see, we both gonna be taking medicine every day now," she'd said.

I'd tried the pills, thinking maybe it'd make her happy.

Maybe she'd even kick Ray out. But all they did was make me slow, sleepy, and achy. Almost too slow and sleepy to watch out for Ray. I'd spat them out like sunflower seeds. No amount of beatings would make me take them. Momma had just given up. Soon after that, she'd stopped taking her own pills. Things went downhill from there.

They gave me more pills in baby jail, five in total. Those pills I didn't fight. The numbness helped me breeze through prison life. But I stopped taking the pills the day I met Ted. He made me want to feel again.

"Do you know who the father is? Do you know anything significant about his medical history?"

"There is no father."

The doctor rolls his eyes.

"Oh, sure there isn't. Here."

He scribbles on a pad and rips off a piece of paper.

"Walk down the hall and get an ultrasound. Go to the drugstore and pick up some prenatal vitamins. No smoking. No alcohol. Make an appointment with the women's clinic for next month."

He ushers me out and I do what I'm told, like always, and walk to my ultrasound. An older nurse looks me up and down when I walk in the room, then checks her clipboard.

"Mary Addison?"

I nod. She said my name like she knew it, which only makes me think of Alyssa.

"Date of birth," she says, taking her time standing up.

"October thirteenth."

"Hm. Okay, change into this. Then up on the table."

The nurse scans around my belly, then jams a stick up my insides. It's cold; the stick, the jelly, the room, and the woman running the machine. When she is done, I change back into my jeans while she scribbles on some paper.

"Here," she says, passing me a folder. "Take this to the front. Oh, and happy birthday."

"Thanks," I mumble, not meeting her eyes and rushing out the room.

Ted is waiting outside the discharge door, grinning. I stop by the booth and another nurse hands me an envelope.

"Take this. Give it to your guardian. Results in a week. Appointment in four weeks."

Inside is a bunch of paperwork where the most important figure stands out: I'm eight weeks pregnant. Stapled to the report is a fuzzy black-and-white picture of my ultrasound. Ted looks over my shoulder.

"Wow," he says, taking the photo out my hand. We stand outside the clinic, studying the picture, the fall wind blowing through my hair.

"It looks like a kidney bean. Red beans and rice!" he says.

I laugh. "I was thinking more like a jelly bean."

Ted is in some type of trance, but happy. "It's there."

"Yeah. It's there."

"Our bean."

He smiles and stuffs the picture in his hoodie. We walk down Fulton while I tell him about the appointment.

"That's it? Vitamins? What kind?"

"Prenatal."

"Aight, let's go get you some then."

We walk two blocks up to a Duane Reade pharmacy and Ted stops at the counter.

"Yo, my dude, where you keep them vitamins?"

The young sales guy glances at me, then at him.

"In the back, against the wall."

Ted turns to me. "You thirsty?"

I nod.

"Aight, I'mma get you some water. Meet me in the back."

I walk through the aisles to a towering wall of vitamins. There is an entire shelf for prenatal vitamins. More pills. But these pills are good for me, good for Bean, so I should take these. I grab the first bottle I see. Seventeen dollars and ninety-nine cents. I only have five.

"Can I help you?"

The sales guy from the front startles me. He looks my age, skinny and pimply faced, grinning in his red smock, with dry-looking cornrow braids.

"Are you looking for something specific?"

I don't say nothing. Just stand there with the bottle in my hand and I don't know why, but he makes me feel uneasy. Maybe it's the way he's smiling, like he's up to something. And he is so close. Too close.

"Maybe I can—"

"Yo! The fuck is you doing?"

Ted walks behind him and he scoots away.

"Yo, you pushing up on my girl, son?"

Ted jumps in his face and Sales Guy shakes his head hard. Ted's voice sounds like a giant, the store feels smaller with him in it.

"Nah, man! I was just . . . helping her and . . ."

"Then why you all up in her fucking face for?"

Ted is inches from his nose. Sales Guy looks scared. I'm scared for him.

"Back the fuck up!"

He bucks and Sales Guy jumps back a foot. Ted glances at me and I freeze.

"Why you look like that? Come here."

I don't move. I can't move, but I want to run away. Ted, my sweet Ted . . . is a monster. Like Dr. Jekyll and Mr. Hyde, that story was mad crazy.

"I said, come here," he says roughly, pulling me by my hoodie. I whimper, bracing for a smack. Instead, he leans down and kisses me, his tongue slipping inside my mouth. He tastes like fruit punch, lips greasy with Vaseline. His angry voice, the Sales Guy, the world, all forgotten because he has never kissed me like this before. He backs me against the vitamin wall, hand slipping around my waist. That's when I feel him grab one of the bottles and slide it into my coat pocket. He cuffs my face, eyes glowing, and gives me another kiss before turning to Sales Guy.

"The fuck you looking at?"

Sales Guy chews on his words. He knows Ted is up to something, he just can't figure out what. Ted grabs my hand and pulls me through the aisle.

"Yo, hold up a minute," Sales Guy nervously calls after us. Ted walks faster. He drags me out the door, through the alley, and across the street. We're five blocks away before he slows down.

"Sorry. Shouldn't have done that with you."

I laugh, out of breath from our escape. Is this what regular kids do? Do they feel this rush? This love? Ted grins and is back to himself, like nothing ever happened.

"You hungry?" he asks.

We walk into a Burger King down the block and he sits me by a window. I try to give him five dollars, but he doesn't take it. A few minutes later, he returns with a tray of two Whoppers with cheese, fries, and a Coke. All that running and kissing has me mad starving. I finish my burger, licking the sauce off my fingers. Ted laughs.

"You want another one?"

I do, but I don't want to be greedy, so I shake my head. He smiles but it fades fast, folding his hands on the table. His fist looks like a cat used his knuckles as a scratching post. I can see why Sales Guy was nervous.

"Baby . . . I gotta tell you something."

The burger and fries drop to the bottom of my stomach.

"Remember when we first met, you asked me what I did. And I didn't tell you, 'cause . . . I didn't want you looking at me . . . different."

Oh no. What if I'm dating a murderer? A real murderer.

He gives a long sigh. "When I was fourteen, I was a wild boy, man. Out partying and drinking like I was a grown-ass man. Most of my crew was older than me. So I just did what they did. And did what they say. They say to kick someone's ass, I kicked they ass. They say stick up that bodega, it was handled. I was in and out of juvie, small stuff, nothing major, all year. My file was thick. Social worker came to my house, told my mom my nine lives are almost up and I better straighten up. But I wasn't at the house that night, I didn't know.

"I was with my boys, drinking and shit on my homeboy's stoop. This girl walks by. My boy talked her into drinking with us. She got real drunk. We were all drunk, mad faded. My boy brought her inside, we all followed. She passed out, I guess. Then . . . he had her on the couch, he lifted up her skirt . . . after the second guy, she woke up and started screaming, and my boy told me to hold her arms down."

Ted shifts in his seat a little, eyes on the table.

"They covered her mouth, ran a train on her . . . I was mad scared and . . . I let go of her arms. She kicked the last

106

dude out and ran off. My boys blamed me for letting her go. When the cops came, later that night, they arrested all of us. Charged us with rape. The girl was thirteen."

He finally looks at me.

"But I swear, I didn't rape her!"

He didn't rape her, but he sure held her down for others to. How could he be so stupid? He reaches for my hands in a panic.

"Baby, I was scared and drunk . . . I . . . I didn't know what I was doing! But with that and my other charges, they sent me upstate, bumped out at seventeen. My boys I was with, they blamed me for us getting caught. 'Cause I let go of her hands. I ran into some of them the other night on the way home. That's where I got all this."

He points to his busted lip and black eye.

"But I swear on everything, I didn't rape that girl. I would never do that. I didn't know what I was doing. I was just a kid."

That was the defense my lawyer tried to use. The "she's just a kid, she didn't know what she was doing" plea. But when you're caught red-handed trying to hide the evidence, it means you had some idea of what you were doing.

"So?" I finally say.

"So. I just wanted you to know. That's all."

I relax and let him touch my arm again. How can I judge him; I've done way worse.

Allegedly.

"But hey . . ."

He scoops a hand from under the table and sets down a Hershey's chocolate pie.

"Happy birthday," he says hesitantly, staring at me as if to say "is this okay?"

He remembered. I knew he would.

"Thank you." I giggle and read the box. Chocolate mousse, whipped cream, with a cookie crunch. He grins and relaxes.

"It ain't much, but next week, I'mma take you to the movies. Just didn't want the day to go by . . . and nothing."

I smile at him, at my pie, at our day. No one else is happy I'm alive except Ted.

Ted takes out the ultrasound picture, studying it hard. His smile could light up a pitch-dark room.

"So, right, if we have a boy, what you want to name him? No junior though!"

I scoop a spoonful of the pie. It's delicious.

"Hmmm . . . Benson."

"Okay. What about a girl?"

I think of Alyssa, but swallow back her name.

"Olivia."

He laughs and stares at the picture again.

"Yo, this is so dope."

Making Ted happy is the best birthday present of all. A present I don't deserve because if he knew the truth about what I did, he'd hate me. He'd break up with me and then

I'd be alone. No Ted. No baby. No Momma . . .

My eyes feel heavy again. Ted looks up at me.

"Aw, baby, don't cry."

He switches to my side of the booth, wrapping his arm around me. This is the second time I've cried in less than a month. Now I'm sure it's the pregnancy.

"It's aight, babe. It's gonna be okay," he whispers in my hair, smoothing my back.

It's not going to be okay, but I can't tell him that.

chapter five

Notes from Dr. Alex M. Spektor, Chief
Psychiatrist at Bellevue Hospital, NY

Upon arrival to Bellevue, Mary was prescribed two antipsy-
chotics: phenothiazine, to control the reported aggression, and
Tegretol, to stabilize her mood. She was also put on a con-
tinued regiment of Ritalin, in order to treat her previously
diagnosed Attention Deficit Hyperactivity Disorder.

However, Mary never demonstrated or showed any signs of
a learning disability, least of all hyperactivity or impulsivity.
School records give no mention of disruptions or violence in
the classroom. Every progress report highlights her attentive-
ness, thoughtfulness, and ability to follow direction. In her
eight months of residency, although she never spoke a word,
she demonstrated cognitive awareness, a sharp memory, and

follow-through of tasks given, like coloring inside the lines or writing complete sentences. We requested the official documentation and reports from her original diagnoses, but no one could provide the information. This led us to question whether she was ever tested at all.

The Learning Center is way downtown, right by Brooklyn City Hall. One more train stop and we'd be in Manhattan. That's where Ms. Claire told me to go. I forgot all about the test until Ted reminded me.

"Let's stick to the plan. Just 'cause you having a baby, don't mean you can't go to college," he said.

I halfway disagree. I have so much more to worry about, like how to keep Bean and stay out of baby jail. But, maybe if I get into school, they'd see I'm better and stop all this adoption crap. So we went first thing Saturday morning after chores and checkout.

The center is big, bright, and new, like they just finished building the furniture this morning. We stand in line at reception.

"Nice place."

"Expensive place," I correct him, losing interest by the second.

Ted smirks and kisses my temple. Ms. Claire steps out of an office and hands some packets to the receptionist. She is dressed different today, slacks and a striped button-down. No jewelry, but her hair is still flaming red.

"More applications, Candace. Make sure these go out tonight."

She turns and spots me.

"Ah! Yuh came. Good, come. Leave him there."

I look at Ted and he nods, taking a seat in the waiting area.

Her office is a tiny box, not even a window, just bare bones. A desk with stacks of papers, two chairs, and a small bookshelf of SAT and college books. She shuts the door behind me.

"Give meh time to find it."

She shifts through stacks of hundreds, finding mine at the very bottom.

"I want to talk to yuh 'bout dis 'ere."

I sit, because bad news is always taken better when sitting.

"Yuh got a 690 in critical reading, 520 in math, 660 on the writing."

I shrug.

"What is dis ting yuh do wit your shoulders? Yuh know how good that is? That's excellent! Compared to everyone else, yuh aced it!"

She is grinning hard, waiting for a reaction. I try to give her a real smile, but give up.

"Only reason why yuh math may haf been so low is 'cause yuh didn't haf the proper calculator."

The calculator. Right. I have to buy one of those.

"Are yuh in a prep course?"

"No. Studying on my own."

"Well, how yuh gonna learn anything new if yuh not taking the proper studies?"

"I didn't read the whole book yet."

She nods.

"Well, we have a prep course that yuh can take," she offers.

"I can't."

"Why not?"

"No money."

That is usually the end to most arguments, but she doesn't look convinced.

"But yuh close . . . yuh can't get the money nowhere?"

I shake my head. She taps her chin, as if she is thinking.

"Hmmm . . . when yuh plan to take the test?"

"December."

"December? Chuh, that's too soon! Why yuh in such a hurry? Why rush?"

Because I need to get out that damn house. Because I'm pregnant and they're going to take my baby away and I don't have time to waste, I want to scream. But it's not her fault. She'll never understand what I'm dealing with. She sighs and moves some papers around.

"Yuh know, when people rush tings they make more mistakes, see? Haste makes waste! Come now, take your time. Push it back to January, or even March. Are yuh free on Saturdays?"

I shrug. I guess.

She reaches behind her and grabs a couple of small handbooks and a flyer, throwing them on the desk in front of me.

"Come to meh workshop. It's every other Saturday in Flatbush."

She writes down an address on a piece of paper.

"Yuh can sit in. We go through text, lessons, and tips, take a full exam. Practice makes perfect. Di more yuh take di test, di better yuh get."

She holds out the paper and I don't take it. Didn't she hear me? I said I have no money.

"Take it! Meh not looking for your little money."

Then what is she looking for?

"And dis 'ere too, take these work sheets. Yuh two weeks behind."

I hesitate before grabbing the work sheets and she holds the other side, looking at me real serious like.

"How old are yuh?"

"Sixteen."

"Hmph. Yuh hav' di eyes of a forty-year-old."

I don't say nothing. I don't like this woman for some reason. She can see inside me, leaving me naked and exposed. The only other person I know like that is Alyssa's momma. I fidget just thinking of her, ready to run into the comfort of Ted's arms.

"Anyway, remember what I told yuh. Let nothing

keep yuh from your dreams."

I nod and rip the paper out of her hand.

Continued Transcript from the December 12th Interview with Mary B. Addison, Age 9

Detective: Mary, do you have any brothers or sisters?

Mary: Yes. I mean, no.

Detective: You sure? You don't seem too sure.

Mary: I used to have a brother.

Detective: Really. What happened to him?

Mary: He died.

Detective: Oh, I'm sorry to hear that. Do you know how he died?

Mary: He was sleep and he didn't wake up.

Detective: I see. I'm sorry. Did you help take care of your brother?

Mary: No. I was too little.

Detective: That's right. But you're a big girl now. And since you're such a big girl, you were helping your mommy take care of Alyssa, right?

Mary: I'm tired. I want to go home. Where's Momma?

Today they've decided to be creative. Not only is all the bedding ripped off and thrown in the hall, but my clothes are piled there too. My roommates giggle as they watch me put my life back together. I hate them. They make me miss my cell; at least I had some sort of peace in there. I head to the basement, knowing in an hour I may come back to the same mess and have to do it all over.

New Girl is at the computer again. She doesn't leave the basement and I don't blame her. It's the safest place for her. She scrambles away when I reach the bottom of the stairs.

"It's just me."

She blinks, then exhales. "I thought you were . . . never mind. Doesn't matter. They all hate me."

Can't see them hating anyone more than me. Unless . . .

"What did you do?" I blurt out.

She strangles the ends of her sweater with a blank face. "Nothing."

"No one is in here for nothing."

Her eyes widen for a moment and she blows out air

with a nervous sort of laugh.

"It was something stupid and everyone . . . overreacted. They didn't even give me a chance to explain. Not that they would believe me. They only believed my mom. And she's never really liked me to begin with."

For someone so different, I can't believe we have something so painful in common.

Misjudging my silence, she stammers out, "BUT this is them trying to teach me a lesson. I'll be out of here soon."

New kids always think this is just temporary; the rest of us know this is the end. I almost feel bad for her, but I'm in no better position. She needs to pull it together and realize that this is what she signed up for when she did whatever it was she did.

Allegedly.

I pull a piece of paper I scribbled on out of my pocket.

"I need to find one of these."

She looks at it, then at me.

"Wow, you really are trying to take the SATs."

"How'd you know?"

"That's the only reason anyone really needs a graphing calculator. I took them last year."

"What'd you get?"

"I got 1500."

I hold back a smirk. I'm smarter than New Girl.

She taps the keys and pulls up the calculator. There it is, just like what the other kids had, a mini black box computer.

"That's the TI-84. It's the one you need. It comes in pink, if you want."

I don't care about colors. But the price . . . $199.99!

"Is that really how much they cost?"

"Yeah. They're pretty expensive."

"Can I . . . get that from a store, instead of online?"

"Yeah. We can go together. I can help you pick one out."

Together? I hold my face still. But I guess it couldn't hurt, since she took them before. She knows what to look for. I nod and see her smile for the first time since she has been in the house.

"We should run away."

Ted and I lay tangled up in each other in bed on the third floor. I nuzzle against his neck, touching his pulse with my lips. I don't want to think about the real world right now. Sex makes me forget the real world. Ted is so strong, he has muscles everywhere, throbbing out of his skin. Sex with him relaxes me, brings me to a place of peace. I can hold him, wrap my legs around his waist and squeeze him like a lemon until I see stars, real stars. And when we're done, I'm light-headed, my lungs exhausted but begging for more. I breathe different when I'm with him. I'm high in space, among the stars, flying into the sun.

"Run where?" I whisper.

"I don't know. Anywhere. Down south maybe."

A patient sleeps next to us, dying slow. His machines beep softly, counting down the seconds.

"With what money? And how are we gonna get these things off?" I ask, pointing to my ankle bracelet. Sometimes I wonder if it knows when we're having sex and if whoever is watching us knows too. I'm shy when I think of others knowing. I want this to just be our world, our secret.

"That ain't nothing. I know someone who takes them off. We'll be straight."

I rub my cheek against his arm. His skin is so soft and smooth. I hope our baby has his skin. I'd never want to stop kissing and cuddling it.

And that one little thought brings me back to earth. I shouldn't even be thinking about our baby when they're going to take it away. Ted doesn't know yet and I don't want to tell him. He has been so excited. Started talking baby names with the cooks, and even asked Ms. Legion about a full-time position. He is doing everything a soon-to-be father should be doing. Except there won't be a baby to do it for.

"I don't want to be on the run, Ted. Not with a baby."

"I don't want you in that house no more. Not with *our*

baby. We got to do something."

I wiggle a little out of his hold. Ted looks at me but doesn't say nothing, which makes me shiver. I'm always nervous when he stares at me like this because I don't know what he sees. There wasn't a mirror in my cell or in the bathrooms, so for a long time I didn't know what I looked like. I had to see myself in other's eyes, the same people who told me when to pee, eat, and shower. The ones who cursed at me for killing a little baby. To them, I was a monster with horns, red snakeskin, and yellow lizard eyes. Momma just kept saying I wasn't taking care of my hair, scolding me for the nappy tangles I didn't even know how to deal with. Then one day, a few weeks after my birthday, I walked in the visitors' room and Momma went pale, staring at me like she hadn't seen me in years. After a while she said, "Boy, you look . . . so grown-up."

When I finally found a mirror, I went cold. Do you know how much time, how much you have to go through, to not recognize your own self? Four years, that's how long. I was fourteen and a stranger. Same me in a whole new body, taller, thinner, with breasts, hips, and fuller lips. My hair was a thick mess of curls down to my lower back. The only part of me recognizable was my eyes. I tried to cry, but couldn't. Stayed away from mirrors ever since.

"I am going to do something," I say.

I just don't know what yet.

We get dressed and I walk out of the room first to get

back to my floor before anyone notices. The elevator dings on the first floor by the lobby. Heading for the kitchen, I pass the main office when I hear her voice.

"And there's no one here she's more friendly with than others?"

My stomach drops down to the basement. I take two steps back and almost faint in the doorway. There she is. Ms. Carmen. Standing behind the receptionist desk with Ms. Legion. She notices me hovering by the door and grins. What is she doing here?

"Hello, Mary," Ms. Carmen says, her voice calm but icy. "Just picking up your time sheets so we can compare it to checkout records. You know, make sure you are where you say you are."

Ms. Legion smiles. "Mary is one of our best volunteers here. Very gentle with the patients."

"Is that right?"

I can't move. Having someone from the group home, in the one place I have peace, brings back the type of fear I haven't felt since Ray was still alive. How do I get her out of here before . . .

The elevator dings down the hall. Ted backs out a woman from the fourth floor in her wheelchair and I stop breathing.

No! She can't see him.

"Well, Mary seems to have a lot of free time on her hands to get into . . . trouble. Maybe she can volunteer some more hours," Ms. Carmen says.

Ted spots me and smiles, pushing the patient in my direction. My legs go numb.

"We could always use more help," Ms. Legion says with a laugh.

We lock eyes and I must look terrified because Ted stops short, his smile dropping. He straightens defensively and frowns. "What's wrong?" he mouths at me and I don't know what to do. My heart is beating so fast it's bruising my chest. I stare straight at Ms. Carmen. This can't be happening.

"Good. I'll make sure her counselors know," Ms. Carmen says, grinning.

Without looking at him, I shake my head slightly.

Go back, Ted. Go back.

From the corner of my eye, Ted hesitates but quickly turns the patient in the opposite direction, pushing her down the hall.

"Mary?"

Ted glances over his shoulder but keeps moving.

"Mary? Do you want to give Ms. Carmen a tour?"

My mouth drops, but no words come out. I look down the hall, desperate to run into the comfort of Ted's arms. Ms. Carmen raises an eyebrow, eyes darting at the hallway. She circles around Ms. Legion, walking toward me. My muscles are squeezing so tight I might pass out.

Ted, please, run!

She swings the half door open, heels clicking as she picks up speed. The room begins to go dark. She brushes past, stepping into the hallway just as Ted turns and disappears into the dining hall. She whips around, scanning in both directions. Nothing but patients, slowly rolling around in their chairs. Ms. Carmen glares at me, the hunt not over.

"Ms. Legion, does Mary have a boyfriend here?"

Ms. Legion is shocked yet amused by the blunt question.

"Well, Mr. Thomas has a little crush on her," she laughs. "But he has a crush on everyone."

Ms. Carmen's eyes narrow and I can tell she's annoyed but knows she can't lose her temper in front of strangers. Might raise suspicion. Momma used to do the same thing.

"Well, I have to get back to the office," Ms. Carmen clips. "Thank you for your time."

I walk away before being dismissed, straight to the second floor, my lungs on fire as I collapse on the bed with 204.

"And by then, I could sprint four miles in twenty-six minutes and was benching something like over a hundred pounds!" Ms. Reba says. She rocks back on her heels, all impressed with herself.

"Oh. Is that so?" Winters mumbles by the front door while signing some paperwork.

"Yeah, the best years of my life were in Junior ROTC."

He spots me by the stairs, lurking like Ms. Reba's cat. "Addison."

I give him a nod.

"I keep telling the girls, the army can really make a man, I mean, a woman, out of you. Discipline, knowledge, free education. How long did you serve again?" she continues.

"Thirty-five years."

"Wow, that's something! And then, you were off on disability?"

He pauses for a moment, then shakes a thought away.

"Yep, something like that."

He signs the last documents and gives them to Ms. Reba while the rest of the girls head upstairs from therapy. My stomach feels funny and I really have to use the bathroom.

"Man, that's awesome. Wish I had the chance to, you know, go the distance. But, I was needed on the home front," she says.

Winters lets out a tired sigh, clearly bored. He glances over in my direction again. "Addison, can I help you with something?"

I fidget with the bottom of my shirt, thinking of the right words to say. "I . . . have questions."

They look at each other, dumbfounded.

"Okay," he says, slowly.

We three stand there in silence. I don't want to do this in front of Ms. Reba. She'll tell Ms. Stein and then everybody will know.

"Well, Mary?" Ms. Reba snaps.

He glances at her and takes a hint.

"I think she wants to talk to me alone."

"Oh, yeah. Sure thing, boss."

"Come on, Addison," he says, longing to be anywhere but here. "This way."

We walk into the visitors' room and he closes the door behind us. Since I'm never in here at night, it looks sort of funny with the lights on and the blinds closed. The walls look extra gray, the fake plants extra fake, and the sofas crusty and worn down.

"What is it, Addison? I'm sure my wife would like me home at a decent hour for once."

He has a wife! I never knew that. I can't imagine anyone being married to him. He's stiff as concrete.

"Well, Mary?"

"Um . . . Ms. Carmen said I was a ward of the state. What does that mean?"

He crosses his arms.

"Oh, so you *can* say more than three words at a time," he snickers. "Why don't you ask Ms. Carmen that?"

Because she doesn't like me! You don't like me either but you're the less of three evils.

"Mary, I ain't got all day. Now, what do you need?"

Maybe I'm going about this all wrong. What I need doesn't matter anymore. It's what Bean needs that matters most. Bean needs to be protected, from the others.

"Are you gonna come by here . . . more often?"

"What for?"

"'Cause."

He frowns and takes a deep breath.

"Do I need to come by here more often?"

There is a creak and a thump by the door. Probably Ms. Reba, listening in. My stomach knots up and I fall silent.

"Well?"

Or maybe it's not Ms. Reba. Maybe it's Kelly. Or Tara. Or Joi. My throat clinches tighter. First rule I learned in baby jail, snitches get stitches.

"Mary, quit beating around the bush and spit it out!"

But he has to know, right? Doesn't he see the cuts and bruises on everyone? Doesn't he read Ms. Stein's incident reports? He can't be this blind.

"I . . . need to talk to the lawyer."

"What lawyer?"

"The lawyer . . . Mr. Harris."

He looks at me for some while until it dawns on him what I'm really asking.

"What for?" His voice grows louder.

"'Cause . . . I didn't do it."

He rolls his eyes.

"Mary, I don't have the time or the patience for this! Look, you already served your time. You're in here now until the courts see fit. You got yourself pregnant—"

"But I didn't do it!"

"Mary," he warns, pointing a finger in my face, just like Momma. "You're about to stir up a pot that's better left unstirred. You start down this road, it's gonna lead you to trouble."

What kind of trouble is worse than what I'm in now? He shifts to his good leg and grunts.

"Look," he says, his voice softening. "Folks wanted you dead for killing that little girl; they won't be so forgiving if you keep on fooling around and lying like this just so you can have your way."

But I'm not lying. How come no one believes me? This is all a big mistake.

I didn't mean to throw her. I didn't mean to throw her. I didn't mean to throw her . . .

"I . . . I . . ."

"Now think hard about this, Mary. 'Cause you start down this road, there's no turning back. And you may wind up somewhere not as nice as here."

Nice? Is he serious?

"And if you're not happy here, why on earth would you want a baby here?"

"Well, why do *you* want my baby?"

It came out. This unrecognizable voice, low and deep, from that place inside me I keep hidden, taking us both by surprise. Winters coughs and gathers himself.

"You don't have that lawyer anymore, Mary. You have

the state. That's it. And ain't nobody wanting that damn baby but you! You want a lawyer, then get one. See what you can afford with that allowance of yours."

My stomach bubbles. I'm screwing this all up.

"Can you just talk to my momma? She knows what really happened."

"What do I look like, a detective?"

"But she knows the truth."

"Mary, I—"

"Please!"

Winters pauses to stare at me, pleading. He takes a long, tired old man sigh.

"I'll . . . see what I can do."

I think that means no.

I head back to my room and the girls are all quiet. My sheets are in the hallway again. But this time there are holes cut in them; my flat sheet is a slice of Swiss cheese. Someone must have heard me talking to Winters. That doesn't bother me. What bothers me is who else has a knife in here besides me.

chapter six

Excerpt from the <u>New York Times</u>: "Arraignment of Nine-Year-Old Girl Who Killed Infant"

Hundreds of protesters lined up outside the Brooklyn Criminal Court awaiting the arraignment of the unidentified nine-year-old girl who killed three-month-old Alyssa Richardson last December. The angry mob, dressed in T-shirts with pictures of the infant, demanded the child be tried as an adult, arguing the juvenile penalty is not harsh enough for the crime. Many of the protestors were women, some pushing strollers with toddlers holding signs that read, "How can you kill a baby like me?" while others chanted "Six years, not enough!" One arrest was made of a woman who threw pacifiers at the van carrying the young girl to the courthouse.

Protestors traveled from all over the country to participate in the rally. The organizers, Justice for Alyssa, have collected over 50,000 petition signatures. "We drove here from Tennessee to support baby Alyssa," says Paula McDermin, mother of four. "It's just a slap on the wrist, that's all this kid will get. She killed a baby! She deserves to rot in jail for the rest of her life!"

Civil rights activists are concerned that the African American girl will not have a fair trial, citing that race could play a major part in the outcome and her safety. Already, the child's name has been spread across online conservative groups and there have been reported death threats to the young girl's mother, Dawn Cooper, who was babysitting Alyssa at the time of her murder. Cooper has since moved from her home and has gone into hiding.

"There would never be this type of outcry if the baby was black. Period," says Tamika Brown, public relations rep at the National Action Network. "Doesn't matter what you say about racial equality, you've never seen white families storming the steps of city hall demanding justice for a little black baby. They're pushing for the death penalty and don't even realize executing this little girl is no different than murdering that baby."

I have a date with Ted.

A real date. It's Saturday, so we can spend a few hours together without anyone expecting us to be someplace else.

He's taking me to the movies, promising we'll get popcorn and soda, maybe candy. I haven't been to the movies since I was seven.

After a shower, I stare at myself naked in the mirror. My new stomach looks funny on me, real out of place. Will Ted still love me when I'm fat? I think so.

You're supposed to dress up for dates, like in the movies, so I comb my hair down and put lots of gel in it so that it slicks back into a low ponytail. I bought some lipstick at the drugstore on the way home from school. Wet n Wild in pinktastic, one dollar and forty-nine cents. It makes my lips look like pieces of bubble gum.

The one dress I own has history. A social worker gave it to me before a parole hearing. Black with little white, yellow, and pink flowers. It's tight around my stomach and too short, so I put my jeans on underneath. I wanted to buy something new, but that calculator I bought with New Girl took a huge chunk out of my savings. At least I got it for half the price at the pawn shop. It's a little dinged up, but it will get the job done.

I crack the bathroom door open slowly. If I walk out and bump into any of the girls looking like this, it'll mean nonstop teasing for weeks. They'll know, and I can't have them knowing my business. Thank God the hallway is empty. I slip out and tiptoe downstairs. They're in the TV room watching a movie with Ms. Reba. I'm supposed to check out before leaving, but that's like walking into gunfire. I'd rather take my chances going AWOL; Ted is worth it. I creep past the room and open the front door. Momma is standing there with her hand held up as if she was about to knock.

"Momma?"

She smiles so wide it hurts to look at her. It's like looking into the sun. She's dressed like a teacher today instead of queen of the Baptist church. Brown skirt with a tan shirt and black flat shoes. She looks almost normal, almost how I remembered her.

"BABY!"

She charges toward me with a hug. I don't hug her back.

"What are you doing here?"

"Well, I'm here to see my baby girl, what do you think?"

She's a whole week early! Something's up.

"I figured we'd spend the day together. Like old times, just the two of us, right? We can go to the park?" She says it like it's a question. "You used to like the park, right?"

"The WHOLE day?"

I haven't spent more than fifteen minutes alone with Momma in six years.

"Don't you have to go to church, or a picnic or something? Where's Troy?"

"Mr. Worthington. And he's out on business and won't be back till tomorrow."

Momma can't stand to be alone. Not for a single minute. She used to stand outside my bathroom door if I was taking too long in the tub. She'd fuss if I tried to be in my room alone, finding something for me to do with her, like cleaning the oven, refolding the sheets, or holding the dustpan. And when she wasn't following me around the house, to every room, every corner, she was following behind Ray to every bar and mistress's home. Ray was evil, but I appreciated him for getting her off my back.

"Now, come on! I'll buy you some ice cream. Strawberry, that's your favorite, right?"

Car sickness slams me, because I don't know this momma. I don't want to go with her, I don't even want to be alone with her. She's like the stranger I was told never to talk to.

"I don't know—"

"What's wrong with you? You sick?"

Am I sick? Damn right I'm sick. I'm pregnant! She knows that and comes over here like nothing happened. Standing with this dumb grin on her face, eyes all loopy like someone knocked her over the head with a baseball bat.

"Well, I—"

"Hey, what's that on your face?"

Oh no. I forgot about my lipstick. My outfit.

My date.

"I was just—"

"Where you off to, Miss Missy?"

Remembering how hard she slaps, I back away from

her, out of reach. I don't know what to say. Momma caught me playing with makeup, sneaking off to be with a boy. This is one of those embarrassing teenage moments I didn't think could exist in my real life.

"N-n-nowhere, Momma. Just . . . let me just go change."

She raises an eyebrow and nods. I run upstairs, rub off my lipstick with toilet paper, and change back into my T-shirt and hoodie. I call Ted on my secret phone and tell him what's happened. He asks if I'm okay and I lie.

On the way back down, I stop dead in my tracks. Momma is sitting on the bench by the door. She has that look on her face, like her body is still here but her mind is a thousand other places at once. I recognize the look before she spots me and tries to hide it with a grin.

She is having "a day." She is not taking her pills.

"Well, Miss Missy. You ready?"

There is a small narrow park near the group home by the elementary school, where the weeds are overgrown and the grass is soaked with dog piss. Momma links our arms like we're close, talking nonstop about the hair salon and her choice of hair color, chestnut brown with a hint of red. Talking fast is also a sign she's having "a day."

I can remember one of the first times this happened. It was before Junior, even before Ray. I couldn't have been more than three or four. Momma was on the floor, on her hands and knees scrubbing spots that weren't there.

"This house is so filthy!" she'd yelled, throwing a rag at me. "Mary, what you waiting for? Get down here and help!"

"But I don't see nothin', Momma."

She'd slapped me so hard I'd hit my head on the radiator pipe. I hadn't cried. I'd just gotten on the floor with her and started scrubbing, eyes watering from the bleach.

"No, not there! What are you, blind?"

I'd started to believe I was.

"Momma's sorry, baby girl. I'm just . . . having a day."

That's what she'd called it. But "a day" turned into weeks and months.

Another time, when I was about seven, she'd just stayed in bed. Wouldn't talk, wouldn't get up for anything. I'd eaten peanut butter and water crackers for three days until we ran out.

"Momma, please get up. I'm hungry."

"Not now, baby girl. Momma's just . . . having a day."

Then the lights had gone out. The food in the fridge had started to rot until the whole apartment had smelled of spoiled chicken and the mice had come looking for their dinner. I'd fumbled around the dark for the coffee can, counting out sixteen dollars and twenty-nine cents by the window under the streetlights with my icy fingers. I'd known it wasn't enough to pay the bill, since I'd paid many times before. But I'd figured maybe it could buy Momma some medicine, so she could get better and get out of bed. I'd gone to a neighbor, hoping she could tell me what to buy. Instead, she'd taken Momma to the hospital.

That's when she'd come back with the pills and things got better. At least for a little while.

"You didn't get all that stuff off your lips," she says, staring at the kids playing on the jungle gym in the schoolyard as we walk by. "That's a bad color on you. Makes you look cheap."

I unlock our arms and rub my lips on my jacket sleeve.

"Ain't today just so nice," Momma says, looking up at the trees. "I love this time of year. Remember when we used to go to the park?"

I do remember the park. Prospect Park. Momma would take me to the swings and I would soar up to heaven. Then we would lie in the big field and share a rainbow icy. Those were good days. Those were the days when she was still taking her pills.

"Remember, you used to pick them flowers?"

"Flowers? I never picked any flowers, Momma."

She waves me off like I'm the crazy one.

"Yes you did, now you just bein' silly! You used to bring them daisies and black-eyed Susans back to the house and put them in the old Coke bottle in the kitchen. Remember?"

She is talking about someone else now. Sometimes I wonder if she had a daughter before me, but she never talks about anything before me.

"Momma, I need my birth certificate."

"What for?"

"'Cause."

"''Cause' ain't no answer, chile. And I knows you my child, you came from me. Don't need no paper to tell me that. I was there."

This is going to go nowhere. "I think they need it . . . for my paperwork."

Momma mulls this over, biting the corner of her bottom lip.

"Well, why don't they ask me then? Nobody ever asks me nothin'. Just carry on like I ain't got no say in nothin'."

She goes on like that for a while. We stop by a kid's sprinkler, turned off for the winter, green with mildew. The breeze kicks at us. She pulls out her compact, checking her makeup, making sure her hair is still in place. Then she looks up through the thick trees, grinning.

"My God, the Lord is amazing, isn't he? He can make the prettiest blue sky and the prettiest little girl in the world, all at the same time. Don't forget, baby girl, the Lord has a special place for you by his side in heaven."

She looks down at the ground, fiddling with her fingers.

"You think you going to heaven?" she asks with a smirk, like she already knows the answer.

"Do you?"

She stays quiet for a minute then laughs nervously.

"Well, of course I do, silly girl!"

She is lying. I know she thinks I'm going to hell. Does she really think she'll be anywhere different?

"Just remember, baby girl, Jesus is the only way to heaven. You must honor him, 'cause whosoever believes in him has eternal life! That's Acts 4:12."

"You mean John 3:36."

She frowns, side eyeing me, and waves a pointing finger.

"Well, he ALSO says honor your Father and MOTHER, so that you may live long in the land the Lord your God is giving to you. Remember that too, Miss Missy. Exodus 20:12."

If only I knew who my father was.

"Momma, about the other day—"

"What about it?"

"I really need you . . . to tell the truth now."

She smiles, all sweet-like. "Well, I did, baby girl."

Delusions. That is another part of her having "a day."

"But you heard me. I'm having a—"

"Oh, we need to forget about all this nonsense! I tell you what we really need. We need to do something fun. Just me and you."

Fun? I don't have time for fun.

"No, Momma. We need to talk about Ray and Alyss—"

"Lawd, chile, you still have that stuff on your face!"

She takes a tissue out of her purse and rubs my lips like she's shining silver. Rough, like the way she used to rub the sleepy seeds out of my eyes in the morning before school. She stops and stares at me, cradling my cheek.

"Boy, you always had your daddy's eyes," she whispers, her own eyes glassing over.

I think Momma really used to love my daddy. She was always staring like this, not looking at me, but looking for him. I touch Momma's rough, dry hand, crusty and cracked from all the houses she used to clean for white people, and stare back; searching for me in her, pretending for a moment that she could change and be the kind of Momma I wish she would be. The kind of mom that Alyssa had, the kind that could really love me.

"Oh! Wait a minute," she shouts, stealing her hand back from mine. "I got a great idea!"

Excerpt from Identifying the Real Killer by Craig Fulton (pg. 43)

One of the first traits of a psychopath is narcissism. The term comes from the Greek myth of Narcissus, the boy who fell in love with his own image in a pool of water. Note that the boy doesn't fall in love with himself, but with the actual image reflected back at him. This is what psychologist Theodore Millon describes as "compensatory narcissism." When people feel insecure, they create a grand self-image in an attempt to compensate for what is lacking internally. They present this façade to the world in order to hide the emptiness they feel, thus falling in love with the idea of themselves. But, if you threaten their self-image—threaten to expose the thing they love most, themselves—they will react, often in a hostile manner.

"Now, smack your lips together like this!"

I follow Momma's instructions and rub my lips together like hands trying to get warmer. The sticky gloss smells like candy, my lips coated a bloody red.

The lady at the MAC makeup counter in Macy's chose pink, but Momma insisted on red.

"It suits her better," she'd said.

It's the final touch to my new face, painted with unfamiliar things like mascara, eyeliner, shadow, and glittery powder.

"There! Beautiful! And maybe if we just let your hair down a little . . ."

She yanks the tie out of my hair and combs out my curls, rough handed as always. Every Sunday when I was little, she'd sit me between her legs with a tub of blue grease like she was going to war, fighting with the knots, slicing through my hair with a black plastic comb like a pizza cutter, mumbling "Goddamn . . . shit," under her breath before braiding and twisting my curls into sections, finishing them with a bow. She always let me pick the bow color; that was my special treat.

"Now, you have to blot. Take a piece of tissue like this and bite down with your lips. Like me."

Momma clamps her brown lips on the tissue. I watch, then follow.

"Perfect! See, baby girl, there's some things only a momma can teach you how to do!"

The MAC lady giggles, offering help when she can, but Momma's in charge, showing me how to curl my lashes with the funny-looking metal thing, how to pucker my lips when I sweep on blush, and how to line them with a pencil before putting on lipstick, like coloring a picture.

I nod at the mirror, framing a girl I've only seen on TV. A model. A doll. Her eyes get bigger as I lean in closer.

"Wow."

She stares and I stare back at her. We blink together, our long lashes the big black wings of a crow we could fly away with. Amazing what some paint and powder can do. Erasing the sadness from my eyes, the paleness from my cheeks, the wrinkles from my lips. I'm a brand-new penny, a golden treasure. Momma's face appears in my mirror with me, her chin over my shoulder; still playing with my hair, so eager and happy.

"Just perfect . . . baby girl."

We smile and I can't help but to look for my smile in hers. I wonder if that's the problem. Too much of my daddy in me, not enough of her. Maybe if she had been able to see herself in me, she would have loved me a little more.

On the car ride back to the group home, I sit perfectly still, with my shoulders back like Momma always told me, staring at myself in the side-view mirror. For the first time, I can't wait to get back to the group home. I'm going to walk around every corner of the house so they can all get a good look at me. I want everyone, the whole world, to see I'm pretty.

I wish Ted could see me now. Wish I could look like this every day. But the only thing Momma bought me was the lipstick. The rest she bought for herself. At least I know what to do for my next date, thanks to Momma. She promised to take me shopping. Maybe I can buy a new dress, something blue. That is Ted's favorite color. Maybe Mr. Troy Worthington will go out of town again; then Momma and I can have another day like this one.

I know I shouldn't be getting my hopes up. That buzzing in my head keeps telling me none of this is real. But I can't help it. Maybe Momma could actually be my Momma for a while. Maybe she's better and things could change.

The sun is an orange burst, an explosion in the sky. The leaves on the trees are turning red like my lips, gold like my skin. Momma rolls down the window and the chilly fall breeze rushes in, but I'm warm and toasty.

"Today was fun, right, baby girl?"

I turn, strands of my hair blowing in my gluey lips. Today *was* fun. I haven't been with Momma in so long,

I forgot how magical she makes everything she touches. Turning something as simple as showing me how to apply mascara into a memory.

"We can have more fun days like this one," she continues. "All the time . . . if you want."

I do want. I want to be with Momma. She is like my best friend, my only friend. I never knew I could miss someone and hate them at the same time. But that's family, like Ted says.

"Hey, I was thinking. I'll go home and make you a pot of my chicken stew with dumplings. You used to love my chicken stew, remember?"

Chicken stew! That's my favorite! Momma always made her dumplings with extra rock salt, made them taste just right.

"You so skinny! They not feeding you good at all."

I'd kill for one of Momma's meals. I haven't had a decent home-cooked meal without any of the sides being made from a box or popped out of a can in forever. Seasonings didn't exist in baby jail.

"But . . . if you start bringing up old mess, they may not let you have fun days like this anymore. They may put you away again. You understand, right?"

And just like that, all the warming joy in my heart floats out the car window.

"You just got free; you don't want to start your new life with lies and mess. That won't do you no good."

143

I press the window button on the door. It doesn't move. The child-lock is on.

"You don't want to be put away again, do you, baby girl?"

I don't say nothing. I'm a block of ice, even with the fiery rage building inside me. I stare straight ahead, unmoving.

"Oh, now, don't sulk. I just want what's best for you, that's all! You know your momma always looks out for her baby girl."

We're closer to the group home now, where the trees are bare, leaves dead on the ground, soggy and black like her heart.

"Well, there you go again. Acting all crazy, like you can't hear. You know that's why they put you away the last time. 'Cause you don't want to talk. But I know you talk. I know you hear me."

She pulls up to the curb and I don't wait for the car to stop before popping the door open, leaving the lipstick behind.

"Mary? Mary!" Momma calls but I ignore her, stomping to the front door, my back straight as an ironing board.

"Well, fine then. Ungrateful! You always been ungrateful. And you can forget that chicken stew!"

The door almost smacks Winters in the face when I bust through, and I wish it had.

"Addison!"

He steps back, smiling, with an approving nod.

"Well, you look nice," he says.

I slam the door behind me. It shakes in its frame.

"Had a nice day?"

I don't say nothing. He drops his half smile and huffs.

"Humph . . . guess not," he mumbles.

We stare at each other, the flames inside me growing bigger. I can smell the smoke.

"I . . . uh . . . ," he starts again. "I talked to your momma the other day."

Don't kill him, Mary. Don't kill him.

"Mary, you okay?"

He actually looks concerned and I'm almost thrown off. But then I think about Momma.

"Are you?" I hiss in that deep voice again. A voice so unrecognizable, I almost look around to see where it came from.

His eyebrow cocks up, eyes squinting as if he's trying to see through me, an icy glass sculpture with fire inside. He huffs, watching me blow by him. New Girl is sitting at the top of the stairs, waiting.

"You look so pretty," she beams.

The smoke is choking me. I stomp past her to the bathroom, slamming the door.

"Mary? What's wrong?" she calls.

The faucet screeches and sputters out black water, then brown, then clear. I soak a washcloth to a boil, letting it burn my face as I scrub the day off me. Scrubbing harder to erase the memory. Punishing myself for being so stupid. When I'm done, I tie my hair up, change into my pajamas, and go straight to bed.

Ted finds me in the freezer again, trying to freeze the flames building within; what Momma called the devil inside me. The rage to kill. It's what everyone expects from me anyways.

"Babe, you can't catch cold," he says, pulling me out. "It's not good for the baby."

Baby? Which one? Which one am I going to kill this time? What will they blame me for this fucking time?

I'm fire, trapped in ice, ready to turn into wildfire and burn everything down around me.

Ted rubs my arms until the goose bumps fade and I step back, not trusting myself near him. He smiles, hands gently stroking my cheeks. How could he love me, even when I'm like this? Doesn't he know he could die in my blaze? How do I save him from myself but keep him for myself? Maybe I should take my pills again, so I'll remember not to hurt him.

Rubbing a hole in my temple, I resist the urge to cry again. This whole crying stuff must be because of Bean. It's stupid and embarrassing.

"Ted, I have to tell you something."

Transcript from the January 4th Interview
with Melissa Richardson,
Alyssa Richardson's Mother

Detective: Thank you, Mrs. Richardson, for agreeing to speak with us. I am so sorry for your loss.

Melissa: Thank you.

Detective: Now, any information you give us will really help build the case. We all want to find out what happened to Alyssa.

Melissa: Yes, okay.

Detective: Can you tell us what happened the night Alyssa died? Everything you can remember.

Melissa: Alyssa . . . had just turned three months. We'd been cooped up in the house and Greg thought it would be nice to go to his company Christmas party. I didn't really want to, but Dawn said she'd watch Alyssa for us. That made me feel a little better. The party was at this hotel in Times Square. There wasn't really good reception in there. I stepped out a couple of times to try and call to see how she was doing. No one picked up.

After the party, I called and Dawn said everything was fine. So we went to have a late night dinner with some of Greg's coworkers. I . . . we . . . we drove to Dawn's to go get Alyssa after. It was . . . my suggestion to bring Alyssa there, thinking it would be more convenient for Dawn. On the way, I called twice, but no one answered. I thought maybe they were sleeping, since it was so late. But when . . . when we got to the house, there were cops everywhere . . . and my baby had been dead for four hours. No one called me.

<muffled crying>

Detective: *Had you ever left Alyssa with Dawn before?*

Melissa: *No. It was the first time I had ever left Alyssa, period. But I knew Dawn. I . . . I never thought . . .*

Detective: *What happened when you first saw Alyssa?*

Melissa: *I . . . I knew something was wrong.*

Detective: *What made you think that?*

Melissa: *Because she looked like she'd been beaten . . . with a cane or stick or something. There were bruises . . . all over her. I know my baby. I know what she looked like when I brought her there . . . and it wasn't anything like that.*

Ted's eyes bug out. His mouth hangs open, words tumbling out slow.

"Yo, but . . . all this time? You've been sitting . . . here . . . all this time. And you . . . you never told anyone?"

I told Ted everything. About Alyssa. About Momma. About them trying to take Bean. I wrapped up the last six years of my life in less than ten minutes. He's the first person I've told the whole story to.

"Babe, you gotta tell someone!"

"Someone like who? No one will believe me."

"But you didn't fucking do it!"

"You know what they say, everyone in prison thinks they didn't do it."

"But you didn't though!"

He starts pacing in front of me, banging his fists together.

"Nah, nah! We . . . we got to do something. We . . . I mean I . . . you . . . maybe you need a lawyer or something."

I don't have the heart to tell him I already thought of that. Winters shut down the lawyer plan real quick.

"Yo, the cops. We gotta tell the police!"

I sigh. If I go to the police, they won't believe me. If I do nothing, they'll take Bean away. Ted can't adopt the baby, because he's in a group home just like me. Even if he tried, I'm sixteen, he's eighteen; they'd lock him up for statutory rape in a heartbeat. And then there is Momma.

Could I really send her to prison and live with myself? I guess this is what they're talking about when they say "damned if you do, damned if you don't."

Ted rubs his head, cursing under his breath.

"Lemme think about it. We ain't losing this baby. And if we do . . . well, then, aight. But I won't let you spend one more fucking minute in that place for something you didn't do!"

Dinner, then group therapy. As usual, I have nothing to say. It's hard to talk about your feelings when you have none. But when our session ends, Ms. Veronica corners me.

"Mary, can I talk to you for a moment?"

I'm in no mood for this woman. I'm mad tired, thirsty, and still hungry since Ms. Stein won't let me have seconds at dinner. "Just 'cause you got pregnant, don't mean you're gonna eat me out of house and home!"

But I really don't have a choice. I have to listen, otherwise they'll use any excuse they can find to throw me back in baby jail.

Ms. Veronica waits for all the girls to go upstairs.

"I have something for you."

She pulls out a thin red book from behind her and gives it to me. *Push* by someone named Sapphire. No last name?

"It's really good. I thought it may be something you could relate to."

"Ummm . . . thanks," I mumble. This is kind of nice of her. I mean, I'm happy to have something new to read, but I'm suspicious of anything Ms. Veronica thinks is good.

"Soooo . . . Mary. How are you?"

"Fine."

She cocks her head to the side.

"Really, Mary? You sure you're just 'fine'?"

I really don't know what to say, so I keep quiet.

"I heard you got some big news. You want to talk about it?"

What I want doesn't matter to her or anyone else, so I keep quiet.

"Mary, I've been going through your feelings book every week. You never mentioned you were pregnant or had a boyfriend. You know, you can talk to me about anything. That's why I'm here. To talk to you about your feelings, help you navigate what you are going through . . ."

I study the floor by her feet. A clump of hair hangs around her fancy flat shoes. In a houseful of women, there is nothing but hair everywhere. If we go a day without sweeping, it collects and tumbles around like the tumbleweeds I'd seen on those westerns Momma liked to watch when we did laundry. That was one of Momma's jobs, doing other people's laundry. Wash and fold for fifteen bucks a bag. People liked using her because of the way their clothes felt after she was done. Folded crisp, extra soft. Momma was good at cleaning everything. A cleanly house is a godly house. But there is no God in a group home.

"Mary? Mary?"

Ms. Veronica smiles.

"Hey, there. Where'd you go just now?"

I shake my head.

Ms. Veronica starts this long speech about sex and safety, STDs and AIDS and the meaning of love.

"So you see, Mary, you really want to make sure you love the person you're with. That that person is special to you. Because at the end of the day, your love creates life."

Her hands extend toward my stomach and I jump back, knocking over a chair, moving a good five steps away from her.

She was going to touch Bean! This stupid bitch was going to touch Bean!

"Oh! I'm sorry, Mary. I didn't mean to—"

She stops herself, standing there all nervous with her hands still hanging in the air. My hands ball into fists, heart pounding, trying to bust out.

"Have you . . . um . . . talked to Ms. Carmen, you know, about your options?"

Ms. Carmen made it clear I have two options: kill Bean or give Bean away.

"Given your circumstances, adoption might not be a bad idea. Just for now. Taking care of a baby is a huge responsibility. It may be best to give the baby away to a loving family that could provide . . ."

I don't want to hear any more about adoption. Ted and I *are* a loving family! We can provide. Ted's going to get a job, I'm going to college. Why can't they leave us alone! And what does she know about babies anyway? She don't even have one. I don't need her! I don't need anybody!

I walk away and Ms. Veronica doesn't chase after me. She knows better.

A hot shower, that is what I need to relax. I head straight for the bathroom. The water, as warm as it's going to be, washes over my changing body, soaking my hair and melting the day away. I exhale and think about Bean. I wonder if I have a boy, will he look just like Ted? Handsome, chocolate skin and bright eyes. Or a girl, will she be as beautiful as Alyssa? Alyssa was the most beautiful baby I'd ever seen.

Ms. Veronica is so stupid. What does she know about what's best for my baby? I'm what's best for MY baby! She must be working with Ms. Stein and Ms. Carmen, trying to get rid of me. Pretending to be my friend to get me to do what they all want. She's not on my side. No one in this house is on my side.

Now I really miss Herbert.

I change into my pajamas, comb out my wet hair, and brush my teeth. All and all, it took thirty minutes to get ready for bed. Enough time for them to ransack my room.

My mattress is off the top bunk and on the floor, the sheets and pillow gone. Clothes tossed in the hallway, panties hanging from the ceiling fan, and what remained of my SAT book looks like it has gone through a shredder. I stare into the empty room, my head throbbing. The material things I could give a damn about. What's most important is what was inside my mattress. I quickly flip it back over, feeling for the slit I had cut on the side. Empty. Someone stole my money. Four hundred dollars, my entire savings. Gone.

They turned a knob inside me. I hear the four clicks of the gas pop before the flame ignites. My heart is covered in peanut oil. I can smell it frying, burning to a crisp. My legs move like a robot's. I have no control over anything anymore. I'm gone. Someone else is here now.

The door to the other room is open. New Girl is alone, curled up in the corner of her bed, shaking like a wet dog in the cold. She's probably the only one in the house smart enough to be afraid of me right now.

"Who. Did. It."

She doesn't hesitate to snitch.

"It was Kelly. And Tara. I heard Kelly talking about the money. Tara ripped up your book."

I nod and walk back into my room, letting the facts sink into my blood while I clean up. I can't take on two of the biggest bullies in the house at the same time. No, I need to be smarter than them.

The girls are cackling in the living room with Ms. Stein, TV blaring. They'll act like I'm crazy if I go down there and make a scene. And Ms. Stein will take their side. She always takes their side.

First, I have to get the money back. I walk into Kelly's room, straight to her closet. New Girl watches, hugging her knees. The wad of money is stuffed in her coat pocket, like I knew it would be. Just like an idiot, she picks the worst hiding spot. Momma used to hide money in her coat pockets too and Ray would always take it.

Wait a minute . . . Momma!

Thinking of her insanity gives me an idea. But I have to act fast. I tiptoe downstairs and put on a pot of water, adding a capful of corn oil. I grab the bleach from under the counter and run to Kelly's room. When I'm done, I tiptoe back to my room, unplug the bedside lamp, and do what they'd never think I would do: go to bed.

The girls return to their rooms around eleven for lights-out, snickering when they see me sleeping, like they won one over on me or something. But they have no idea.

Ten minutes later, Kelly screams.

Tara jumps up, knowing whatever the scream is about has something to do with me. I leap off the bed with the lamp and come down on Tara's head like a hammer. Marisol, frozen in shock, watches Tara tumble to the floor like a sack of bricks. I run out the door before Kelly can make it to my room. The whole house is up now. Another fight with Kelly; who is her victim this time? Not me. Not tonight.

155

I race down the stairs, Kelly close behind me, reeking of the bleach I soaked her bed in. She's fast, way faster than Tara, but I have at least five paces ahead of her. Enough time to make it to the kitchen, grab the handle, and splash the pot of boiling water in her face. Every ounce of air once in her body pours out in a scream. It reminds me of Alyssa's momma, when she came to the house that night. Pain. That was what she was feeling, physical pain. Kelly sounds just like her now.

My hand hesitates toward the knife drawer.

It's okay to do it this time. She was gonna kill you. You're saving Bean!

The light pops on. Ms. Stein rushes in and drops to the floor by Kelly, her face a red beet. Ms. Reba, all confused by the commotion, walks toward me and I step back.

"Don't," I warn, and she stops short.

"Mary! Are you insane!" Ms. Reba screams over Kelly's wails.

"No. I'm pregnant. She was gonna kill me first!" Then I look at Ms. Stein. "And you let them beat me!"

Ms. Stein and Ms. Reba are in big trouble and they know it. Ms. Stein has to take Kelly to the emergency room; she has to report it this time, no getting around it. And they can't just pin this on me. Between my purple back and the rest of the house of girls who all have battle scars from either Tara or Kelly, I can scream self-defense easy.

And letting a pregnant underage girl get bullied in a group home, where they are supposed to be protecting us? Not to mention never filing a single incident report? They're screwed. And Ms. Stein knows it. You can see it in her eyes, even as she tries to treat Kelly, running her face under some cold water.

Thanks, Momma.

Momma, always hearing noises in the house that I never could, used to stay up all night with a pot of boiling water and a wooden bat, waiting for the boogieman that never came.

"What's the oil for, Momma?"

"So the water sticks and burns the shit out of him, baby girl."

I was always hoping she was talking about Ray.

Tara wakes up from her concussion to find Kelly's face, swollen and blistering. She takes one look at me and doesn't make a sound, just turns ash black, since she's too dark to turn pale.

"Damn," Ms. Stein mumbles. "Gotta take her to the hospital."

I sit in the living room while they try to come up with a plan.

"Should I call Winters?" I offer, holding back a smirk.

"NO!" Ms. Reba shouts at me. "We have it under control!"

The girls stand around, whispering to each other,

looking at me. New Girl doesn't smile, but looks relieved in some strange way.

Kelly's face is starting to bubble. Ms. Reba piles her into the minivan and Ms. Stein drives her to the hospital. She returns the next morning, without Kelly.

"Mary! Office. Now!"

Her office is a cramped room with tan metal filing cabinets, ugly green ripped leather chairs, and crooked framed pictures. The navy blue carpet is covered with dust, empty Girl Scout cookie boxes, Hostess cupcake wrappers, and donut crumbs.

"Well, this is some mess you made here," she says behind her huge wooden desk, papers and files covering every spare surface between us. "Got anything to say?"

"Yeah. When's Winters getting here?"

She swallows.

"He'll be here in a few hours."

"Good."

I cross my legs and she fusses around with her pencil. It smells like her in here, a fat woman who doesn't shower.

"So, uh, what are you going to say?" she asks.

"What I said last night. I'm pregnant and you let these girls attack me."

"Yeah . . . uhhhh . . . little dramatic, don't you think?"

"She was going to kill me."

We stare at each other for a long minute. I'm not backing down, not when it comes to Bean. I'll be damned if another baby gets hurt because of me.

"Okay, Mary, what do you want?"

"I want my own room and a new SAT book."

Ms. Stein scoffs.

"I can't give you your own room! What are you, crazy? There'll be anarchy! I need to put at least one person in there."

I think for a moment while she pulls out a new box of donuts.

"Then put the new girl in there."

She grumbles and stuffs a white donut in her mouth.

"Fine!"

"And . . . I need my birth certificate."

Ms. Stein has powdered sugar all over her black shirt. She tries to brush it off and it spreads, looking like shooting stars across her chest.

"What for?"

"I need an ID . . . they told me at school."

"Damn it, Mary! Why didn't you tell me that before? So damn stupid! You'll have to wait till Carmen brings it."

Ms. Carmen has it? What else does she have? Maybe she has everything about me. Maybe she knows who my father is?

"Does she have my file?" I ask.

Ms. Stein stops trying to clean herself and squints.

"What do you need your file for? What are you up to?"

I don't say anything. She laughs.

"Okay, Mary. Fine. You're just making it easier and easier."

I walk away, afraid of what she could mean.

In the darkest corner of the basement, the coldest place in the house, I am a shadow among shadows. The cold is a relief to my killer migraine and nausea. Everything hurts. Bean is stretching out, making itself comfortable, pushing on my back and bladder. I'm so hungry, but there is nothing to eat. Not even some of those fake slices of cheese Ms. Stein likes.

I finish the book Ms. Veronica gave me, throwing it so hard it slaps against the storm door on the opposite side of the basement. Is that how she sees me? Some nasty fat girl who can't read, getting raped by her daddy every night and cumming because of it? Does she think this is Ray's baby? No, she couldn't. She has to know by now Ray's dead, right? He died years ago, before Alyssa even. Dropped stone-cold dead on the sidewalk. If whatever it was inside him hadn't killed him, his head hitting the pavement would've finished the job. And Momma, my God, she is nothing like Precious's momma. She would never . . . just never! But everyone is evil in their own way I guess.

New Girl comes running downstairs. She is always moving so fast in here, like someone is chasing after her all the time. She spots me and stops short.

"You had them move me."

"Yeah."

"Why?"

I sigh and turn to her, rubbing my temples.

"'Cause, you just like me. And aren't you tired of getting your ass beat?"

She thinks about it then nods.

"Thank you."

"No problem."

"So, are you really pregnant?"

"I guess so."

"Are they gonna let you keep it? I mean, after everything that's happened?"

I cock my head, moving the pain to the other side.

"Would you believe me if I told you I didn't kill that baby?"

She shrugs one shoulder, mouth twitching.

"I don't know. I guess . . . it depends."

"On what?"

"On if you know what really happened to her."

Those big puppy eyes of hers flicker around my face and I almost want to tell her. Instead, I close my eyes and lean my head back. She waits, then jumps on the computer, typing like she's trying to break the keyboard.

"What are you doing?" I ask.

"I'm sending a note to my lawyer. About Tara and Kelly and Ms. Stein. He has to use this for my case."

"You have a lawyer?"

"Don't you?"

I don't even know anymore.

"Why do you need a lawyer?" I ask.

"Trying to get emancipated from my parents."

Emancipation means freedom. That's all I know.

"What do you mean?" I ask.

"It means you can be free from your parents."

That's crazy talk. You can never be free from your parents.

"You'll be like an adult," she says, typing away. "And then they can't make decisions for you anymore. It's a legal thing. You can do whatever you want and live alone."

Why have I never heard of this before?

"Can I do that?" I ask, unable to hold back my shock.

"I don't know. You gotta ask a lawyer. But first you gotta get exonerated."

Exonerate, that means to be free of blame. I've read about it before, but New Girl keeps on explaining like I'm stupid.

"It means they appeal your case so you're clear of all your charges. And it won't be on your record. It's a clean slate."

A clean slate?

"They can do that?"

"Didn't your lawyer try?"

I don't say nothing. My lawyer did so little before, I'm sure he did even less after.

"How come you know all this stuff?" I ask, feeling defensive that I know nothing.

"I've been doing a lot of research. For a while," she says, like it's no big deal. She clicks on a few more links. "Mary, come here! You got to read this."

My body locks up, the usual reaction to strange kindness, and I stare through her. Doesn't seem like she's up to something, seems okay, so maybe she really is trying to help. I join her at the computer while she explains what an appeal is, showing me a whole bunch of articles on people getting freed after being proven innocent. Then she shows me a website for this organization called the Absolution Project.

"They help people just like you," she says. "And they have a lawyer in New York! Your case is perfect for them. If you didn't do it, you should call."

She writes the number and address down on an old supermarket receipt. But I don't see how any of this is going to help me keep my baby. If Momma won't say what really happened, it's going to be a waste of time calling. I shrug and slide the number into my pocket.

"I have a boyfriend," Joi giggles. "His name is Markquann. He works at Macy's in the shoe section, so I get the dope discount. He goes to Brooklyn Law. He got his own place in Canarsie with one of them big black leather couches that's like an *L* and a big-ass flat screen. Like . . . the biggest you can get. He treats me like a queen y'all! He says he's gonna marry me."

There are several lies in this story that she is too stupid to recognize. But she's so happy. Even though I can't stand her, I'd hate to be the one to crush her hopes and dreams. Leave it to the rest of the house to do that.

"He got his own apartment? And he works at Macy's?" Kisha cackles. "Bitch, are you stupid? Niggas make seven dollars a hour there!"

"He's studying to be a lawyer too? Ha! You playing yourself," China adds.

Joi's grin starts to fade.

"Ladies, please," Ms. Veronica says. "Let Joi—"

"That nigga's not your boyfriend," Marisol says. "He just using you for pussy. You not the only bitch he fucking."

Joi rolls her eyes and waves her middle finger.

"Whatever, y'all are just jealous 'cause y'all ain't getting no dick in here."

Marisol laughs.

"Oh, I got a man and he fucks me right everyyyyyy night!" She moans, grinding on her chair before giving Kisha a high five. All the girls laugh, except China.

"Oh, word?" China huffs. "That's not what you were saying last night!"

The girls "ohhhhhhhhhh!" Marisol stabs China with her eyes.

"Fuck you, bitch! I ain't no fag," Marisol snaps. "You don't know my business! I got a man, okay! His picture in my room."

I let out a laugh, thinking of Marisol talking about Trey Songz, staring down at her from his place on the wall, singing her to sleep. But the look she gives makes me immediately regret ever making a sound.

"Aye, what the fuck you laughing at, psycho? Bitch, you have a man?"

"Yeah, Mary," Kisha says, "do you have a boyfriend?"

"Don't see how that bitch could have anything," Tara mumbles, eyes on the floor.

The air feels hot and muggy, like we're in an old iron. Maybe they'll stop. Maybe they'll . . .

"Well, clearly she was gettin' some somewhere," Joi laughs. "How else she get knocked up."

"Man, who would fuck her anyways?" Kisha asks.

"Maybe she got some of that good grandpa dick at the nursing home," China says.

The girls laugh and laugh. I don't say nothing. Neither does Ms. Veronica; real big help she is. They're getting close. Too close. Close enough to figure it out without trying. My eye twitches like a hiccup.

"Nah, maybe it was some young dude," Kisha says, holding her chin like she's thinking. "You know, some of them guy nurses be cute in them scrubs."

I try not to squirm, but my legs are ready to run. God,

why did I laugh? Why!

"So which one you let hit it, Mary?" China asks.

"I bet if we went, we'd see him," Joi says.

The room spins as my chest tightens.

Go. Run. Go tell Ted. Go tell . . .

"I wasn't allowed to have a boyfriend," New Girl blurts out. The room shifts attention, her voice like a car alarm. She looks in my direction and gives a small smile.

"I wasn't allowed to date or talk to boys at all. My mom wouldn't let me. She was . . . is . . . really overprotective."

"Is that why you tried to kill your mom?" Joi says with a smirk.

I turn so fast my neck snaps.

WHAT!

"Oh shit, psycho didn't know," Joi laughs. "New Girl tried to kill her moms."

New Girl swallows and turns gray. She never told me. And I just let her move in with me. How could I be so stupid!

"I didn't try to kill my mom," she says, flat as a board. She doesn't sound convincing. Even Ms. Veronica raises an eyebrow.

"Pshhh . . . yeah, right," China says.

"So wait, she tried to off her moms?" Kisha asks. "How?"

"She pushed her down the stairs!" Joi says.

The room gasps.

"Yeah," Joi snickers. "Her moms was coming up the stairs and she push her back down when she got to the top. And they were some big stairs!"

New Girl's eyes flood with tears, looking in every direction the story is coming from like a dog following a ball.

"Oh, word?" Tara says.

"Yeah, and you know what else. Her dad was allergic to peanuts. So New Girl made some soup and put mad peanuts in it, or something like that. He had to go to the hospital too; he almost died. She did it mad times till they figured it out."

"Damn, that's fucked up," Marisol says, and turns to her. "Yo, what they do to you?"

"I didn't push her down the stairs," New Girl shouts. "It was an accident!"

I know all about accidents.

I didn't mean to throw her . . .

"Her moms still in a coma," Joi continues as if New Girl wasn't even in the room. "Been that way for a year. That's why she's here."

"Okay, everyone, let's calm down," Ms. Veronica says, trying to take back control of her meeting. China waves her off like she is a gnat. New Girl has the shakes. She sniffles before letting out a weak whimper.

"It was an accident," New Girls cries.

"If it was an accident, then why you in here?" Kisha says, laughing.

"'Cause it wasn't no accident," China says. "Ain't no one in here 'cause of some accident."

Ain't that the truth.

The moon pours through the window like milk into a dirty glass. First night in our new room and neither one of us can sleep. I move half an inch and the mattress springs creak beneath me. At least it's not a bunk bed, just two simple twin beds on opposite sides of the room. One closet, one desk, a table lamp, and a wooden chair. The best part about our room is also the worst part. A big window, with ugly thick black bars blocking our view of the world. Reminds me of baby jail. Actually, everything about this house reminds me of baby jail.

I counted the bars once, the mesh metal against the small window in my cell. Four hundred and sixty-six little squares. Forty-six cement blocks made my room with ninety-two lines, seventy-four cracks in the floor, twelve diagonal lines in the glass on the door. I counted everything . . . over and over again.

"Are you awake?" New Girl whispers.

"Yeah."

"Can't sleep?"

"Guess not."

"Mary . . . we're friends, right?"

Friends? I don't even know what that means. I haven't had one of those since Alyssa. I didn't have friends in baby jail. And what makes us friends? Even though she is the only person I talk to, other than Ted, can we really call each other friends? I mean, we're way more alike than different so I guess there is no other word for it.

"Yeah, I guess so."

I look over and see New Girl snuggling tighter to her pillow, smiling.

chapter seven

Notes from Dr. Alex M. Spektor,
Chief Psychiatrist at Bellevue Hospital, NY

Could she have been misdiagnosed with ADHD? It is possible. One of her teachers mentioned she fell asleep frequently during story time. Another report stated that when Mary was first taken into custody, she slept for almost seventeen hours straight. Lack of sleep is often confused with ADHD. But to prescribe a child Ritalin and Catapres, a medication that treats aggression, when Mary showed no signs of such behavior? It was erroneous, irrational, and excessive. Further, if she were on the medication and dosage as prescribed, she would not have had the strength to carry out the crime. The combination would have made her highly lethargic. One could almost say

170

the prescribed medication was a form of pacification. But, from what?

"Yuh went up forty points in math."

Ms. Claire hands me my latest scores by the church basement steps after class ends. The scores are proof that practice makes perfect, just like she said it would. This is my third time coming here. She hosts the workshop in some church off Flatbush, near all the West Indian people, the "coconut heads" Momma used to call them. She lets me come for free. It smells like a thousand of Momma's old Bibles, and everything inside is red. Red carpets, red windows, red cushions on the folding chairs. Funny, I haven't been to a church in years, but here I am, still coming to learn.

"Here, take a look at dis list. It's 250 of di hardest SAT words. Dis different than what I gave the other students. Yuh know those words already. I want yuh to learn these."

I take the list and read the first word. *Abjure*: to reject, renounce.

"Yuh don't haf to tell me about yuh life if yuh don't want but, are yuh in school at'all?"

"Yes. Vocational."

"What they teaching yuh?"

"How to do hair."

She snorts.

"Chuh! Means yuh not reading properly. Yuh need to

start reading more."

"I do read."

She raises an eyebrow.

"What's di last book yuh read?"

"*Push*," I admit, disgusted with myself.

"Precious? Lawd Jesus, no! Go to the library and pick out some books for yuhself. And yuh need to start reading a newspaper every day. Circle the words yuh dun know. Okay?"

Can I go to the library? No, probably not. They probably don't let convicts have library cards.

"Okay, meh see yuh in two weeks," she says. I nod and start to walk out, but she grabs my arm.

"Eh eh, where yuh think yuh going with no coat! Yuh leave it downstairs?"

I shake my head.

"Well . . . where's yuh coat, gyal?"

That's a good question. Because the one coat I had disappeared in the house a couple of days ago. I shrug, staring down at my feet. She sucks her teeth and pulls the green scarf off her neck.

"Here. Keep your neck warm at least before yuh catch cold. Meh betta see yuh wit proper clothes next time."

It's soft and smells like her perfume, like oranges and flowers. I wrap it around my neck twice.

"Thank you," I mumble.

She glances at my stomach like she wants to say

something, then changes her mind.

"Well, lata then. Be safe."

That is real hard to do nowadays.

"Mary! Come help us take groceries out the car!"

Ms. Reba has the front door open with an assembly line of bags from the car, straight into the kitchen.

"What's all this can stuff for?" Marisol asks, smacking and popping her gum.

"Storm's coming. Stores were packed, but I got what I could."

"This storm ain't gonna be nothing," China says, unloading cases of water.

"Mary! Would you stop daydreaming and bring this inside," Ms. Reba snaps.

Feet swollen and back aching, I carry a few bags full of sardines and lima beans into the kitchen. I'm tired all the time now. Bean is a weight on all my veins. When I come back out, Ms. Carmen pulls up with Kelly in the passenger seat. She steps out of the car, and I look away quick to keep my jaw off the ground. No one else does the same. They all stop and stare.

Kelly's face is a lumpy red tomato, shiny and slick with some type of gel. She is a melting wax candle covered in plastic, hands and arms wrapped in white bandages.

"Oh shit," Kisha mumbles.

Joi runs over to Kelly, welcoming her home. Kelly is all

polite-like, as if she is a solider returning home from war, deserving medals and standing ovations. She tried to kill me! She doesn't deserve a medal or sympathy.

Kelly walks toward the door in silence, the wind tossing her blond hair around. New Girl trips over herself, trying to get out of her path, like Kelly is a brewing storm. She steps inside, but not before taking one good long look at me, through her puffy eyes and reddened cheeks. The glance lasts only a short second, but makes it perfectly clear.

Kelly is going to kill me.

Once we finish unpacking the car, New Girl and I run to our room, both thinking the same thing: survival.

I slam the door shut and we push the dresser in front of it.

"What if she gets in here at night?" New Girl whimpers.

Not "if," more like "when." I move the table lamp closer to her.

"If she comes in, she'll be coming for me. When her back is turned, just hit her over the head with this and run."

New Girl swallows; her face goes rigid, like she is trying to imagine herself being capable of such violence.

"What about you?"

My heart beats faster. I lift the mattress and yank a piece of wood off the bed frame. It slips splinters in my fingertips, but I ignore the pain and prop the stick under the right side of my bed, within reach. I'd seen this once in baby jail. A girl attacked her roommate with a broken bedpost. They switched all our beds to metal frames two weeks later. I keep my knife hidden under my pillow. Don't want New Girl knowing about it just yet.

All that and I still feel like a sitting duck. Nowhere to run or hide. The window? There's bars on it, but maybe we could break the glass and scream for help. But would anyone come?

"Why didn't they keep her or move her someplace else?"

I don't care why, I just wish they did. Ms. Stein must have brushed it off as some accident so she wouldn't get in trouble. That's the only way she'd be able to come back here. Bean makes its presence known by making it harder to breathe. I stare at the dresser propped up in front of the door, its weak wood not enough to save us. If Kelly comes for me, she'll be coming for Bean too.

I've got to get Bean out of here.

The nursing home is alive and active, a complete oxymoron. That's a word I learned in Ms. Claire's class. The nurses and orderlies run in and out of rooms, prepping patients for evacuation. Ted is where I thought he would be. In the kitchen, looting through the canned goods. I stop and smile at him in the doorway.

175

"These things are mad big," he says, smiling as he picks up a can of tomato sauce. It's the size of a basketball. He tosses it lightly in the air, catching it one-handed. "I can sell this shit. I need all the money I can get."

Ted puts the can in his bag and leans his head against the wall, eyes closed with this pained expression.

"What's wrong?" I ask.

He winces, opening one eye to peak at me. He doesn't want to tell me, but does anyway.

"I gotta leave the house," he says.

My heart sinks, the weight of those words like stones.

"What? Why! I thought they said you could stay after you turned eighteen."

"That was only 'cause they liked me. But social services came in and said they needed the bed."

Ted is eighteen, death age for kids like us. He is out of the system, which means they don't have to house him anymore. He's on his own.

"Where you gonna go?"

Ted shakes his head. "I don't know. I'll . . . figure something out."

He laughs a little, his hands shaking.

"You know the fucked up part. PO told me I still gotta check in every day, 'cause I'm still on house arrest. How I'm gonna be on house arrest and ain't got no fucking house to live at! Said they gonna talk to my moms . . . that bitch don't fucking want me either!"

He pauses, then throws a can across the room. It crashes into some pots on the metal counter.

"Some fucking bullshit! They kick me out on the street with no fucking job, but if I do some shit to put a little bread in my pocket, they gonna fucking lock me up again! What the fuck they expect me to do! And then there's you . . . yo, you realize if you were white, you wouldn't even be in this shit? They would've said you were one of those crazy white kids, like the ones who shoot up schools and shit, and sent your ass back home! But now, I can't do nothing to save you!"

He throws another can at the stove, the crash ear piercing.

"FUCK!"

There is so much pain behind his scream, so much frustration. He steps a few feet away from me, his back turned, breathing heavy. He doesn't want me to see him cry. I stand there, not knowing what else to say other than what I came to say.

"We should do it. Tonight."

"Do what?" he mumbles.

"Run away."

He sniffs and whips around.

"You kidding? In this storm?"

"It's not gonna be a big storm, maybe just some rain."

"They shutting down the trains and buses in two hours."

"So we'll walk."

He shakes his head, like he can see right through my front. "What's wrong, Mary? Did something happen?"

I want to tell him about Kelly. About the look she gave me. About how even though I'm pregnant, nothing will stop her from killing me. But the less he knows, the better. He has enough to worry about.

"It's perfect," I say with a straight face. "No one will notice we're gone."

Ted nods, doubt in his eyes. He rubs my arms then holds me.

"Aight. Whatever you want. I'm down."

The sky is a swirl of black and gray, the color of smoke. The wind slaps my face as I walk over twenty blocks back to the group home. The bus driver stopped mid-route, talking about how the wind was going to blow the bus over.

By the time I'm inside, the sun is long gone. Then the rain starts, on and off and on again like a summer shower. I think about Momma, about the time she said she was in a tornado.

"It was the scariest moment of my life! I thought I was gonna whip into the air and never come back down. It sounds just like people say, like a choo-choo train coming!"

The wind whipping around the house sounds no different. It shakes all the windows and doors, whistling through the cracks, begging us to come out and play. New Girl and I hide in our room, away from Hurricane Kelly. Kelly has spoken no more than two words to anyone since she walked in the door. Her silence is louder than the wind.

New Girl jumps at every howl and clatter. She leaps from her bed and sits in the chair propped up against the dresser.

"We should stay away from the windows. In case they break and shatter in our faces."

I nod, moving farther down my bed, imagining the shards flying into our eyes, blinding us. My leg brushes against the small bag I packed for my escape. A toothbrush, deodorant, an extra pair of jeans, two shirts, my hoodie, and five pairs of underwear. Momma always said don't ever let people catch you with dirty drawers. I want to take my SAT book, but it would be too heavy to carry. Who knows how far we'll have to walk.

The glass trembles violently in its frame. This is bad. And I'm supposed to meet Ted at eleven o'clock. It's 9:15 and it sounds like the end of the world outside. The thought of Ted walking out there . . . I'd kill myself if anything happened to him because of me. Lightning sparks, flashing . . . camera bulbs, like in front of the courthouse. Why so many people? Where's Momma?

"What did you say?" New Girl asks.

I don't know. What did I say?

My tongue rolls to the back of my throat and I shake my head.

New Girl trembles. "You remember Katrina, right?"

I remember. Momma and I watched it on CNN. There were reports of COs shooting prisoners and using their dead bodies to float on. If that happens here, I'll be the first raft they'll pick.

Lights flicker and the glass shakes again. New Girl clutches the red flashlight Ms. Reba gave her.

"If something happens, you won't leave me," she blurts out. "Right?"

With a heavy heart, I glance down at my backpack and sigh. "Where am I going to go?"

The corner of her mouth slips into a small smirk. "Let's go to the basement. I want to see what's happening out there."

We tiptoe downstairs, passing the TV room, where the rest of the girls watch some movie with Ms. Stein and Ms. Reba. Kelly peers over her shoulder, locking eyes on us. New Girl grabs my hand and we run.

The basement is a freezer, but at least the wind isn't as crazy. Upstairs, it sounds like the Apocalypse, the end of the world, like in the Bible.

New Girl boots up the computer and I sit next to her. A little gray mouse runs by our feet. She scrolls through pictures people have been posting on websites. Red Hook, under water; Rockaway Beach, under water; lights out in half the city; cars floating down Fourteenth Street to underwater parking lots.

"Didn't they see the water coming?" I ask. "Why didn't they move their cars?"

"It comes fast," she says.

"Can't be that fast."

THUMP! New Girl shrieks. What was that! Kelly? No, something bumped into the storm door. Relieved, I exhale but New Girl fidgets.

"Mary, you can't hide forever. You have to do something. You have to tell someone what really happened."

Muscles tighten around my neck and I shake my head.

"I can't. They won't . . . understand."

"You can't do this alone. You need a grown-up that the other grown-ups will listen to. The lawyers at the Absolution Project . . . they can help you."

What if they don't believe me? What if they do? Can they save me and Bean? And Momma, what will happen to her?

Another THUMP hits the door that makes us both jump.

"It sounds bad out there," I whisper, thinking of Ted.

She sighs. "Well, at least we still have power."

As if on cue, the lights flicker and shut off. Upstairs, the girls' screams fill the darkness.

"Reba, what the hell!" Ms. Stein hollers. "Get that generator working!"

New Girl's hands tremble around the flashlight. The dark never bothered me. I always found it peaceful.

181

Ms. Reba runs down the stairs with her heavy feet, a flashlight strapped to her head like a miner. Between that and her orange safety vest, she looks ridiculous.

"Hey! What are you two doing down here?" she asks, rushing to the storm door. She unlocks the door and the wind throws it open, clocking her in the face. Icy water rushes in, wrapping around my ankles. New Girl screams. Ms. Reba curses and tries to close the door. In the quick second her flashlight shines outside, I catch a glimpse of the backyard. I hope I'm seeing things, because there is a lake out there that wasn't there this morning.

A waterfall pours in, fast and freezing. Ms. Reba pushes chairs and branches out of the way and finally shoves the door closed, but the water is still rising.

"What's going on down there?" Ms. Stein hollers from upstairs.

"The basement is flooding," Ms. Reba says, setting a light flash up toward the ceiling.

"What!" The girls react but no one dares to come downstairs.

"Sarah, go upstairs and get some pots and buckets. Mary, start moving stuff to the stairs. We need some sandbags. Everyone, it's all hands on deck!"

"The computers, Mary," New Girl whispers to me, pointing the flashlight toward the corner. She's right, if they get wet, Ms. Stein will never replace them. I nod and splash toward them as she runs upstairs behind Ms. Reba.

The power is off so it's safe to unplug them. I wrap the cords around the monitors and lift. Damn, it's heavy. Maybe I'll start with the keyboard and mouse . . .

Then, something yanks my ponytail and I fall backward so fast I don't have time to scream. I'm underwater! I can't breathe! I can't tell which way is up or down. My head pokes out just long enough to see what's holding me.

Kelly.

With a nasty grin, she shoves my head back under. Water burns up my nose as I scream, struggling against her weight, thrashing and choking, reaching for anything.

Kelly is so strong. Probably won't even break a nail as she kills me. I kick the floor, trying to get my balance until I feel her dragging me, more dirty water clogging my mouth. She launches me and THUMP! My head hits the door and I fall back into the water with a flop. I can't see . . . water in my eyes . . . my head . . . I'm dizzy.

Get up! Get up! Run!

I scramble to my feet, gasping and coughing for air as she punches me dead in the face. The world is spinning . . . black spots . . . buzzing. She pins me against the door and I try to kick her . . . until I feel something sharp pressing against my stomach and freeze. The blade kisses my skin.

"Say anything," she whispers. "And I'll cut it out of you."

Bean! Bean! I'm so sorry, Bean!

"Please," I choke, trembling. "Don't."

Kelly grasps the back of my neck with her cold hand, forcing me to look at her, to stare deep into her eyes. The eyes of a real killer. Then the knife is gone. She shoves me one last time before walking away, as if nothing ever happened and the darkness becomes darker.

chapter eight

Notes from Dr. Jin-Yee Deng,
Psychiatrist at Bellevue Hospital, NY

Over the eight months she stayed at our facility, Mary never said a word. Even when her mother came to visit, she remained mute and detached. Then, in July, on a regular Wednesday morning, Mary began talking to colleagues and nurses. She was lighthearted, almost playful. It was a break from her psychosis. Unsure if we would witness this type of activity again, we spoke in depth. Over the course of four hours, we learned more than we had in eight months. Maybe more than we'll ever learn again.

A week after the storm, with the blade pointed at Bean still fresh in my mind, Cora Fisher takes my call and schedules an appointment on a Saturday without hesitation.

The office for the Absolution Project is in Manhattan, which is a big deal. Whenever we went to the city when I was a kid, Momma would starch and press our Sunday best, scrub behind my ears, and pick the dirt from under my nails until they bled. She'd tie special ribbons in my hair and slick my face, elbows, and knees down with Vaseline.

"Don't want nobody thinking we live in no ghetto."

So I couldn't help myself. I scrubbed under my nails, wrapped my hair in a bun, drowned my face with lotion, and put on the dress that didn't fit me with my best pair of jeans underneath. I washed my laces in the sink last night with dish soap. They're still damp as I slip them through my sneakers.

I take New Girl with me since she seems to know all this legal stuff. She lets me borrow her long black sweater to go over my dress. At checkout, we ask if we can go into the city to help out at the food donation center. Ms. Reba lets us go. We take the train to midtown, passing the big Macy's that takes up an entire city block. The sidewalks sparkle in the sun like diamonds baked into the ground. Even though we told Ms. Reba, I'm a little worried about my anklet. We're all the way in the city; it has to be more than three miles. I figure the quicker we get to the meeting, the faster we can get back to Brooklyn before the marshals come searching for us. I pull New Girl along and walk faster.

Security has our names at the front desk of a tall glass office building. We take the elevator to the twenty-eighth floor, our ears popping all the way up. New Girl knocks on Suite 2801, nervousness pinching me. A woman swings the door open, her smile dropping at the sight of the black eye Kelly left on me.

"Hi, there," she says, stunned, and I recognize her voice from the call. "Come on in."

My stomach drops back to the lobby. This is a mistake. Ms. Cora doesn't look like a lawyer. She looks too young, like eighteen, dressed in loose jeans and a red sweater. And she is Indian, like the ones Momma says take all the jobs overseas. I don't want another bad lawyer, though I never picked the first one. New Girl nudges my arm and walks in. I play it cool and follow.

"I'm glad you could make it," she says. "Right this way."

The office is very small and somewhat tidy with lots of polished cherrywood furniture and fake plants. There is a bookshelf with thick textbooks that look like encyclopedias. Just like the ones I used to read at Alyssa's house. She leads us into a small conference room where a young white guy with thin black glasses is setting down a plate of cookies next to bottles of water.

"This is Terry, my assistant. Terry, say hi to the pretty ladies."

"Pleasure meeting you," he says, extending his hand. I don't take it.

We take our seats, quietly staring at each other, not knowing where to begin. I really want one of those cookies. They look delicious and I'm starving, but I don't want to look greedy. She glances at me, then at the cookies, pushing the plate in my direction.

"Here, please have one. Have more than one. They're for you."

I hesitate, then take two. New Girl takes four.

"Water," Terry offers. I take a bottle. Fiji; that's an island. Wonder if the water is really from there.

"Well, first off, let me start by saying, I was glued to . . . just fascinated by your case from day one, when I first started law school in fact," Ms. Cora says. "I think you had just turned nine. Oh, that means you had a birthday recently, right?"

She knows my birthday. I don't even think Momma knows my birthday.

"Well, from the very start, I believed they mishandled your case, entirely," she continues. "And the outright biased media coverage that persecuted you, a child, before you ever stepped into a courtroom . . . it was just unethical.

"Now, I don't know all the specifics but I feel your testimony—your true adult impression of the night's events—could drastically change the outcome. But we must first have enough reasonable evidence to persuade the judge to consider an appeal. And that's the hard part, getting a judge to consider reopening a case on a deceased infant."

"Alyssa," I say.

I hate when people refer to Alyssa as just a dead baby. She had a name.

"Alyssa. Right." She smiles. Terry fidgets in his chair.

"Then after all that, I can be . . . emancipated. Right?"

"Well, one step at a time," Ms. Cora says.

I sit back, sipping more water. Am I really about to do this? Am I really about to open up this can of worms and boxed-up secrets?

Ms. Cora smiles at me. "Mary, what's most important to you right now?"

I rub my stomach, knowing what's at the top of my list.

"Keeping my baby."

"Okay, then that's what we'll fight for," Ms. Cora says, knocking the table with her knuckle.

"But . . . I don't have any money."

"Let me worry about that for now." She smiles, warm and genuine, but the hairs on my arms spike up.

No one is this nice for no reason. It's time to go! This is a trap. I mean, it doesn't seem like she is trying to trick me, but I've been tricked before and I can't make another mistake, not with Bean. But go where? Maybe New Girl's right, I can't go against the grown-ups alone. Maybe this lady really can help me.

"Okay . . . what do I need to do?" I ask.

"Well, first, I'd like you to tell me, from start to finish, what really happened that night."

I bite my tongue hard, swallowing the taste of blood. Does she mean, like, what REALLY happened? Why? I mean, I don't know these people.

"Mary, you can trust us," Ms. Cora says. "We're here to help."

She reaches across the table and tries to hold my hand. I snatch it back. Terry and she share a nervous glance. New Girl nudges my arm and nods at me.

"Do it, Mary," she says.

My throat tightens, staring at these strangers. How could I tell them what really happened and have them not hate me?

"You'll think . . . I'm a horrible person."

Ms. Cora nods.

"Mary, trust me," she says. "The only way to change your circumstances is to change what you've been doing up to now. It's scary, I know, but there's no judgment. I'm here to help you, but the only way I can is if you tell me the truth."

That sounds a lot like what Ms. Claire told me.

Change is scary. But can I trust her?

Guess there's only one way to find out.

"Okay," I sigh. "But don't say I didn't warn you."

Notes from Dr. Jin-Yee Deng,
Psychiatrist at Bellevue Hospital, NY

When asked about the victim, Alyssa, Mary's face would simply go blank. She seemed to have no recollection of the events that took place that night. The last thing she remembered was going to sleep. After that, she said her next recollection was standing in her living room, covered in dirt.

When I'm done, the entire room stares—wide-eyed, mouths gaping. New Girl is pale as a ghost and Terry looks green. Ms. Cora is the first to attempt to talk.

"I have to . . . I just . . . I mean. Holy shit!"

"We're going to get right to work on this," Ms. Cora says, leading us to the front door.

"Okay," I mumble, feeling exhausted from telling my story.

"Today's our day off; that's why we're a little dressed down, but we'll be working through the weekend. I know the group home rules. Anything comes up during the week, we'll visit you there. And if you need anything at all, call me right away."

"Here, let me get you a card," Terry says, running back to his desk. It's cluttered with mad papers and folders. He lifts some files and I see Alyssa, her picture on the cover of some book. I stop breathing, making my way to where he's standing. Sliding the book from under the pile, the room freezes around me.

Alyssa. I haven't seen her in so long I thought I forgot what she looked like. But she is exactly how I remembered; soft curly brown hair, tiny nose, the littlest fingers and the biggest blue eyes. She is dressed in her red jumper with the white bib that says, *I Love My Mommy*. I remember when she took this picture. I was standing nearby, being a good helper, holding her bottle like her mommy asked me to.

I touch the picture, rubbing a thumb down her cheek, wishing she was real. You ever kiss a baby's cheek before? It's so soft, you can snuggle to it for days. Tears prick at my eyes, a sob building. I clutch the book to my chest and close my eyes, trying to feel her warmth again. Alyssa. My Alyssa.

When I open my eyes, Terry is staring. The title of the book, *What Happened to Alyssa?*, is in big bold white letters above her forehead. There are more books on his desk, one with my name on it: *When Children Murder: The Mary B. Addison Trial.*

"It's a book about me?"

Terry glances over at Ms. Cora, who steps closer, almost protectively. He clears his throat.

"Yeah . . . there're a lot of books about you," he mumbles.

The titles of the books stacked on his desk merge together into one. Mary . . . Alyssa . . . Children . . .

Murder . . . Trial . . . Alyssa. These books about me, it means the whole world knows what I did. Or thinks they know.

"But . . . how? How could they write anything about me without . . . or like . . . you know, asking."

"That's a very good observation, Mary," Ms. Cora says as she and Terry organize his desk, hiding the other books. Something tells me they didn't want me to see this. But why?

"And trust me, when all this is over, we'll be able to file several suits for slander and defamation of character," she says.

"And then what happens?"

"Then you'll get money, Mary," New Girl says, cheerful. "You may never have to work for the rest of your life!"

We all turn to New Girl, standing by the door with a delirious smile. Ms. Cora doesn't seem too happy about that answer, but she doesn't disagree.

"Well, something like that," Ms. Cora says.

Terry holds his hand out. I look, but clutch the two books to my chest. I'm not ready to let her go again.

"Can I borrow these?"

Terry's eyes widen and he looks over at Ms. Cora.

"Uhhhh . . ."

Ms. Cora sighs then smiles. "Sure, Mary. If you'd like."

Interview with Anonymous #2, Inmate at
Bedford Hills Correctional Facility

Everybody seen the news, everybody knew about Mary and what she'd done. I think she was like fourteen or something when they finally let her out the hole. You ever seen one of them war prisoners, them Middle Easterners kept locked in the dark for years?! That's what she looked like, all skin and bones, pale as a newborn who never seen the sun before. They threw her in the pit with us and she was like Kunta Kinte, wide-eyed, don't speak a lick of English and scared of her own damn shadow. Every now and then they throw some youngins in with us. The ones who too bad to be in juvie or they get transferred out since them girls can't stay in there past seventeen. But Mary . . . she was just a kid.

"Didn't I tell you, Mary? They're going to fix everything. And they're going to make you rich!"

I chuckle as New Girl skips along outside, beaming.

"Then, once I get emancipated, we could find an apartment together! Maybe we could live in the city!" She stares at the sparkly ground. "Wouldn't that be so much fun?"

Guess it would be kind of fun, to be on our own, living in the city, like real grown-ups. Her, Bean . . . and Ted.

"I'm gonna go somewhere," I say as soon as we're at the subway.

She frowns, eyes blinking fast. "Where?"

"Somewhere."

"Can't I go with you?" she begs, clutching my arm and I wiggle away.

"No . . . I'll just see you back at the house."

New Girl jerks a little, as if she was going to stop me, but instead she heads down to the subway. I wait, then try to call Ted. Twice. No answer. Last time we talked was the day after the storm. But now, I have to see him and tell him about the meeting, about the books, and the money. We're going to be okay, he doesn't have to worry anymore!

It's a long ride to the boys' group home, the last stop on the train and a bus. But I'm too excited to notice. Ms. Cora is going to fix everything. We'll be able to keep Bean. And I'll have money, lots of it. Maybe we can get a babysitter and both go to school.

The bus lets me off a block from the house. You can just tell it's a group home; a run-down medical building in the middle of a neighborhood, just like mine except much bigger. The door is battered, like it's been broken down a few times. Ted said he lived with ten other boys. That seems like too many . . . and dangerous. I think of that story, his story, about the girl being raped, and stop walking, my back muscles tightening. A curtain pulls back; someone is watching me from the second floor. I try calling again. No answer. Something doesn't feel right. Maybe this isn't such a good idea.

Another bus pulls up and a boy jumps out. He looks

about my age, tan skin, fitted hat with a bubble jacket. He stays at the group home, you can see it in his eyes. We all have that same look.

"Hey," I say when he passes.

"Yeah?"

I point. "You live in that house?"

He takes a step back and eyes me.

"Why?"

"Umm . . . do you know Ted?"

The boy groans and rolls his eyes. "Not again," he mumbles. "You one of his girls?"

One of his girls?

"Look, y'all can't keep coming around here. That's why he got kicked out in the first fucking place. Didn't he tell y'all that? He got a phone, hit him there!"

A gun fires from somewhere, blowing a hole right through my chest as big as a soccer ball. The draft breezing through it makes me shiver. I can die right now and not even care.

"You must be new," he snickers.

"I'm his cousin."

I don't know why I said that, but it seems like a good lie. He frowns.

"Oh. Well, he be at the Tilden Houses with some chick named Leticia sometimes. You can probably find him there."

Tilden is in Brownsville, one of the worst projects in

Brooklyn. That's what Ted told me anyway. Said it was really dangerous. Said all kinds of gangs are there, raping girls and robbing old ladies, shoot-outs and drive-bys in broad daylight. So why would he be there?

"Which way?" I ask.

"About ten blocks that way."

Continued Interview with Anonymous #2, Inmate at Bedford Hills Correctional Facility

I tried to help her when I could. You know, show her the ropes, tell her what's what. Who to stay away from and what to buy if she had money on the books, that kind of stuff. She never had much though. Poor child couldn't even buy soap one month. Her momma come in here looking like the Queen of Sheba, but couldn't spare a dime for that little girl.

You can see the buildings from two blocks away, towering in the sky like brown logs with beige stripes painted down the sides, sun fading fast behind them. *Crips up* is spray painted on a wall across the street like a stop sign. Fear scratches at my skin, but I keep walking through the parking lot, up the gated pathway toward the bright blue front door. People are staring, watching through their tiny windows. Feels just like the first time I walked into baby jail, like I'm out of place and don't belong.

The cold wind kicks up leaves and trash around me.

Streetlights come on in small orange bursts. It's getting late. I shouldn't be caught out here at night. But Ted, where is he and what did that boy mean by "girls"?

A lady and her little girl walk out the blue door. The woman gives me a stern once-over, then holds the door open. I slide inside and watch them, bundled up in their wool coats, tights, and church shoes. Reminds me of Momma and me, heading to evening service. The thought of Momma makes my stomach tighten. She'd kill me if she found me hanging around some projects.

My legs are weak from the long walk, Bean weighing me down, and I rest against the wall of mailboxes. The lobby smells like old beer cans, like the ones Ray used to drink. There is music playing from somewhere, echoing in the halls, shaking the floor with a violent beat. Someone's having a party. Is that where Ted is? Does he listen to that kind of music? I don't know. It's like I know nothing about him now. This is stupid! I have no idea where I'm going. There's a million apartments; how am I supposed to find Ted in here? But I've come too far to turn around now.

There is an elevator next to a stairwell in the far corner and I press the button. I should start from the top floor and work my way down. Maybe I can . . .

"Don't get in that elevator," a voice snaps behind me. I jump and spin around. A girl walks in, the door slamming shut behind her like a sledgehammer.

"Unless you wanna get stuck in there," she says, smirking.

Either her jeans are too tight or she was too thick to fit in them. She has on makeup like the ladies at the MAC counter, dark skin with a long ponytail that touches her big butt. She smacks on her gum, fixing her giant earrings, giving me a once-over as I squirm away. I don't trust anyone after baby jail, especially other girls. She laughs and disappears down the hall. The elevator closes, screeching like nails on a chalkboard, as I hear her knock on a door.

"It's me!" she says.

A muffled voice answers. "Me who?"

"Leticia, open the door, stop playing."

Leticia!

CLICK CLICK. CLICK. The sound of bolts unlocking echoes and I run in her direction, flying around a corner, almost slamming right into her. She jumps back.

"Yo! What the fuck?"

Leticia opens the door at that very moment, looking just like Marisol. Long hair, lots of makeup, big breasts. She stands there, a halo of smoke around her, smelling sweet like the weed the COs in my cellblock used to smoke, fried chicken popping in the kitchen behind her. She looks at me, then at Big Booty.

"Who's this?" Leticia asks.

"I don't know!" Big Booty says, throwing her hands up. "The crazy bitch just ran over here."

"Leticia?" I blurt out and her eyes narrow.

"Who the fuck are you?" Leticia barks at me.

"Yo, what the fuck is going on?"

All the air sucks out of me the moment I hear his voice. I change my mind. I don't want to know what he is doing here. I don't want to know anything at all.

"What y'all hanging at the door for," he says.

He swings the door open wider, slapping Leticia's ass in the same motion with a smirk. But as soon as he sees me . . .

"MARY!"

Ted. Shirtless with jeans, standing behind another girl. Another me. The sight a punch to the chest and I cough up a gasp.

"Mary . . . what are you doing here?" he asks.

My tongue turns to sandpaper. Leticia and Big Booty share a confused glance.

"Uhhh . . . Teddy, who's this?" Leticia snaps.

Ted reaches for me and I back into a wall. As if one touch would burn all the skin off me. I'm dead anyways. Dead to him. Tears come up in a hiccup and I take off running.

"Mary!"

He catches me by the lobby door, pulling me back in. I slap, push, and kick, trying to fight, but he is everywhere. The hands and arms that I once loved holding me are now hurting me. It's like fighting the orderlies in the crazy house, the COs in baby jail. They won't let me leave.

"Mary, please! Stop!"

Leticia and Big Booty are with us now, watching.

"Teddy, what the fuck you doing?" Leticia asks. "Who is this bitch?"

Ted pins me to his chest, my back to him.

"Baby, please, let me explain," he whispers in my ear.

No, I don't want to know! I hate him! I hate him! I . . . turn and bite his arm as hard as I can.

"Ahhhhh!"

Free, I run out the door and into the night air. My legs feel heavy in the cold. I make it down the pathway before he catches me again, wrapping his bare arms around me like a straitjacket.

"Yo, calm down! Stop it!"

"Help!" I scream but it comes out gurgled.

"Chill! I'm not letting you go home alone like this!"

As if on cue, a cop car pulls up and we quickly step away from each other. We both have priors, neither one of us wants the attention. He claps a hand over the bite on his arm, now oozing with blood, and I walk away like he didn't just shatter my entire world.

Frozen stiff, I walk into the house three minutes before curfew. Everything hurts, from my head to my toes and every body part inside. Ms. Stein comes limping from the TV room and I wipe the snot and tears off my face.

"Good. You're home. You can wash the dishes and

scrub those damn pots. No food left, should've been on time for dinner. And here, what you were looking for."

She shoves a folded piece of paper in my hands and limps off.

I unravel it with a gasp of relief. My birth certificate, from the New York City Department of Health. I study it hard, the excitement swallowing the cold. I'm not sure what I'm looking for, exactly. Maybe just proof that I belonged to someone other than Momma.

Name: Mary Beth Addison
Date of Birth: October 13
Sex: Female
Mother's Name: Dawn Marie Cooper-Addison
Father's Name: N/A

Wait, "Father's Name: N/A"?

I read it over ten times, making sure I'm not seeing things again, before sliding onto the floor, my body giving up. A fat cockroach crawls by my hand, its wings and legs as long as toothpicks. I want to smash it, but that would make me a killer.

How could he, the other half of what makes me *me*, be non-applicable, like he doesn't exist at all? Or does it mean not available?

No, he was at the hospital, I'm sure of it. He had to have seen me come into the world, he wouldn't have missed it.

He is real, he has a name, he loves me, he wanted me. He wanted to be there.

Unless Momma told him not to come.

Notes from Dr. Jin-Yee Deng, Psychiatrist at Bellevue Hospital, NY

During our four-hour conversation, Mary was very adamant that her father was going to come and collect her sometime in the near future. She described him in great detail, though admittedly, had never met him. It was clear that she was under the misguided impression her father was still alive, and that her mother never told her otherwise.

"Want to talk about it?" New Girl asks from the other side of the room, watching me like a quiet and thoughtful dog.

"Not really," I mumble.

"You haven't said a word since you got back," she says. "Boy stuff?"

"Everything."

She shrugs and changes for bed.

I can still taste Ted's arm in my mouth, salty with sweat and blood. Salty from Leticia. If I was really angry, I would've taken a piece of his arm with me. But I'm only the weakest part of angry; I'm hurt. Hurt makes you want to lay in the middle of the street, dead on the ground, muscles gone limp. It's an SAT word I think: *lethargic*.

"Sarah?" Her real name feels a little weird to say.

She looks over, tense and uncertain.

"Yeah?"

I clutch the book with my picture on the cover so hard that the paper cuts leave speckles of blood on the pages like raindrops.

"They think I'm a monster."

Excerpt from <u>When Children Murder: The Mary B. Addison Trial</u> by Jordan Millon (pg. 181)

When you speak about Mary, you need to understand the definition of a psychopath and how it applies to her. Psychopaths are completely detached from their emotions. They feel no remorse or guilt from their actions, no concern with the ideologies of right and wrong. They do not see victims, they only see the means to an end. This is what makes psychopaths most dangerous.

No matter what witnesses may say, Mary's dissociation from her victim, a three-month-old baby, is a sign of her true self. If circumstances were different, if she had merely dropped the infant by accident, a lighter diagnosis could be made. But Mary inexplicably and without warning beat a baby to death and has yet to shed one tear for it. She stood by while paramedics tried to revive the child. One report mentions she was smiling. Smiling? You have to ask yourself, what kind of child would do such a thing? I'll tell you what type, an evil one.

chapter nine

When I turned old enough to be unrecognizable, I got my first period. I was in the library, chained to a metal seat with an encyclopedia, reading about Neptune and neurons when the pain first started. Cramps beating against my stomach with bats wrapped in barbed wire. I prayed whatever it was would kill me. But it kept going, for hours, until a CO came to bring me to my cell, and found me sitting in a pool of my own blood. *This is the end,* I'd thought, hoping I would bleed to death. I was ready to die, ready to see Alyssa again. Instead, they brought me to the nurse's office and gave me a pack of itchy cotton pads. Nothing is more painful than believing you're close to glory, only to find out you're still in hell. It was the only time I'd ever thought about killing myself.

Until today.

"Mary! Are you deaf or something? Don't you hear me calling you!"

Ms. Stein hovers over my bed, spit flying out her fat mouth as she screams in my face.

"I think she's sick," New Girl says softly.

"She ain't sick. Mary! Get out this damn bed, what are you doing!"

I roll over and face the wall. She keeps on yelling, even pulls the sheets.

"Mary! You got to get to school. You're gonna be late! Get the hell out this bed!"

She pokes my arm one, two, three times before I sit up and look at her. Her eyes widen like I was a dinosaur, ready to rip her to pieces. Because I really am ready to kill her if she touches me again. She backs away from my bed, bumping into New Girl's.

"Fi . . . fine, Mary," Ms. Stein says, while New Girl creeps away. "You sick? Alright. You can stay home, but just today."

I stay in bed for four days straight, sleeping. Every time I wake up, I'm tired again. New Girl sneaks me food from dinner, wrapped in napkins. I find it on my bedside table in the middle of the night, pick at it a little, leaving most of it behind for the mice.

On therapy day, Ms. Veronica comes up and tries to talk to me. She snaps her fingers in my face and I ignore her. She and Ms. Stein go in the hallway to talk.

"I think she may be seriously depressed," Ms. Veronica says, all worried. "What happened?"

"Nothing! She came home one day and was like this," Ms. Stein shouts, aggravated. "Had to call the nursing home and tell them she's sick. They've been looking for her."

Ted's been looking for me.

"We may need to have her evaluated," Ms. Veronica says.

All they do is evaluate me. They've been evaluating me since the day Alyssa died.

"You, uh, think she's having another episode or something?" Ms. Stein asks.

"I don't know. I'm just making a suggestion."

Episode? What is she talking about? I'm not Momma!

"Well, she has been talking to herself a lot more lately," Ms. Stein says. "Not to any of us though."

No way! I stopped doing that years ago. Didn't I?

I don't move. I just lay like a dead worm, listening to their lies.

"You think, maybe, it was too soon to let her out?" Ms. Stein asks, pretending to be all worried. She ain't worried. She's lying, trying to get rid of me any way she can.

"Has she been taking her medication?" Ms. Veronica asks.

"I don't think so. Last time I checked, they were all pretty full."

"This is so strange," Ms. Veronica says. "She writes so much in her journals. She's filled up four books already. I thought she was making progress."

I turn over and fall back to sleep.

On day six, Ms. Stein busts into my room like she ain't going to take no for an answer.

"Mary! There's some lady on the phone. Says she's your lawyer and if she don't talk to you, she's going to call the police. What's this about? What you doing with a lawyer?"

I roll out of bed and the room spins. My stomach is bigger, like it grew overnight, and I almost topple over. I smell like a bum on the subway.

"Mary! I'm tired of this shit! You better tell me what's going on. What you got a lawyer for?"

For the first time in days, I answer one of her questions. I shrug.

She follows me down to her office where she left the phone.

"Yes," I say, my voice hoarse and scratchy.

"MARY! Jesus, I thought something happened to you," Ms. Cora says. "Are you okay?"

"Yes."

"Why do you sound like that? Is that lady in the room with you?"

Ms. Stein is standing behind me, breathing funny from her walk up and down the stairs.

"Yes."

208

"Ugh, I knew she was going to be a pain in the ass. I've been calling the last three days. Anyways, no need to talk, just listen. We're ready to file a motion, I just wanted you to be aware. Can you come by my office on Wednesday? I want to go over some more details with you before we do."

"Okay."

"Mary, are you alright? Are they mistreating you? You can tell me. Just say yes or no and I can get you out of there."

Is it that easy to get me out of hell? And go where? No Ted, no Daddy, no Momma . . . I might as well stay. Life is the same, inside and out of here. I glance at Ms. Stein, standing by the door, anxious and angry.

"No."

Ms. Cora is silent for a bit.

"Okay, if you say so. But if that woman gets in my way again, she'll be mopping floors at Rikers after I'm done with her."

Whoa, wasn't expecting that. I'm almost relieved she has such fire in her. She'll need it to win.

"So Wednesday, yes?" she says.

"Yes."

"Good. See you then."

On Monday, I take my first shower in a week, eat two bowls of cereal, and go to school. After class, I head to Greenview. Ted must have been watching from a window somewhere because he runs through the lobby to meet me.

"Mary!"

He stops short, hitting an invisible wall when I give him the same look I gave Ms. Stein. The response is the same: fear. I'm getting pretty good at this. I brush past him and he follows.

"Mary, please, baby, can we talk? Can we go somewhere and talk? I just need to . . . I can explain. Please?"

Ted is a ghost. I hear his voice but I don't see him. Maybe he died. Maybe he'll move on.

"Baby, talk to me! You know I've been mad worried about you," he says, desperate. "You turned your phone off?"

In the kitchen, I grab an empty plate. I'm so hungry I could eat an entire floor's worth of food and it still wouldn't be enough. I've been starving Bean. Our Bean.

Ted follows while I load up my plate with mashed potatoes, string beans, and four slices of dry meat loaf. I take my plate to the locker room and sit on the bench. He stands near me, rubbing his head nervously.

"I can't believe you came there," he says. "You know how dangerous that place is?"

The food has no flavor. I know it's on purpose because the old people can't have too much salt or butter, but it tastes like air.

"Niggas be robbing and raping girls like you. How'd you even know where I was at?"

There is an old crinkled newspaper on the floor by Ted's feet. I scoop it up and skim the first page.

"How's the baby? How's Bean? I see he's growing . . ."

Ted reaches for my stomach and I drop the fork, holding the knife at his neck, right at his Adam's apple. He backs up.

"Yo, Mary, chill!"

When he is a good five steps away from me, arms held up like I have a gun, I go back to my paper. The first word I don't recognize is *tacit*. I grab a pencil out of my smock and circle it.

There was only one CO in baby jail that liked to open my cell. This tall fat white man with a red beard, I never knew his name. He'd come in, put my dinner on the floor, jerk off with a grunt, then leave. I'd lay there, letting the remnants of him dry on my skin before wiping it off with the bedsheet. It would be days before they'd let me take a real shower to wash myself clean. It really was no different than what Ray used to do to me, so I didn't complain about it. It was what I deserved. I killed a baby.

Allegedly.

I think of him as a cool breeze joins me in the shower. It runs through the curtains, tickling up my legs, like his chilly hairy hands undressing me, touching my new body, developing right before his eyes. The whole house is drafty, but not like this. I step out of the shower and the bathroom door is a wide-open invitation. I stand there, dripping wet, a puddle of water surrounding me.

I never leave the door unlocked. Ever.

Another breeze glides in. Shakily, I test the doorknob. It's not broken, but there is a keyhole I never noticed before. Someone must have a key to the bathroom. But why would they open it?

I look up and China is in her room across the hall, staring down from her bunk bed. Staring at me naked. Was she watching me take a shower this whole time?

Am I dreaming?

I wrap myself in a towel and run down the hall. New Girl isn't in the room. Her side is perfect as always. But my side . . . it looks like there's been a blizzard. My bed is covered in a blanket of snow-white feathers and cotton. I pick up a piece and hold it to my face. It smells like my hair gel. My pillow . . . it's been ripped to confetti.

Kelly. It had to be.

New Girl walks in with her laundry, while I clutch my towel to my chest, wet hair dripping down my shoulders. She pauses, glancing at the mess, but says nothing and folds her clothes like normal.

"Reba's cat peed in my laundry basket again. Washed my clothes twice and I still can't get the damn smell out."

Is she stupid; how can she just ignore this? What's wrong with her? I'm so pissed but scared at the same time that I don't know even what to say.

"I tried to call my dad again," she says, while slipping on her pajamas. "But no one answered."

Or maybe she is just numb to this kind of stuff now. Maybe this house has finally crushed all the goodness out of her, to the point that she doesn't even care anymore. I dry off, put on my pajamas, and start cleaning.

"He's mad at you," I mumble.

"I don't get why. It was an accident."

"And the peanuts?"

New Girl's cheeks turn red, staring at the floor.

"He ate those nuts by accident and blamed me for it. He's not good about his diet at all. Mom always said he ate too much junk food. I love my dad. I'd never hurt him."

I want to ask what it was like, having a dad. A real dad. But I'm too embarrassed. I don't want her asking who or where mine is since I have no clue. Momma knows. I know she knows, she just won't tell me.

"Why do they think you were trying to kill them?"

New Girl shrugs.

"You know how crazy parents are."

She's right. I do.

"My mom has cancer and my dad . . . he was just tired all the time from working two jobs. I was only trying to help out and make him dinner, but I wasn't allowed to touch the stove. That's why they got mad. And I left the gas on, by accident."

She wasn't allowed to touch a stove? Momma had me at

the stove since I was three.

"They were so smothering. Wouldn't let me watch TV, drink soda, have a cell phone or Facebook page, or . . . anything. They didn't even let me go to school, said it was too dangerous. I have more freedom here."

I guess that is hard, having COs as parents. Still, I don't see the big deal.

"What's wrong with your mother?" she says, folding back her bedsheets.

"How do you know something's wrong with her?"

"You talk about her."

"No I don't."

"Yes you do. In your sleep, sometimes."

I'm having nightmares again? When did that start?

"Does she drink or something?" she asks.

"Why would you say that?"

"I don't know. A lot of the girls . . . their parents got problems like that."

I stare at her hard. Momma is not like other parents. She doesn't do drugs and she only drank because of Ray. That's not her fault.

"She's not a drunk," I snap. "She just . . . forgets to take her pills sometimes. What's wrong with your parents?"

New Girl sighs and turns off the light.

"They're perfect and I'm not."

Notes from Dr. Jin-Yee Deng,
Psychiatrist at Bellevue Hospital, NY

Through records, we confirmed Mary's father had, in fact, passed away before she had been born. Her mother confirmed Mary knew this, but had never seen a photograph or video of him.

When reminded of her father's demise, Mary's reaction was that of disbelief and amusement, stating, "My real daddy is gonna come get me. You'll see."

Momma looks mad when I walk into the visitors' room. And she's a week early, which is unlike her. I keep my distance and don't stand too far from the door.

"What you up to, child! What's gotten into you?" she spits, hands on her hips matching the sass in her voice. "Ain't I told you don't be bringing up no old mess!"

Today's church suit isn't like the others. It's dark gray with black shoes and one of those black hats with the birdcage. She looks like she belongs in a funeral home.

"They told me you got some type of lawyer! What for?" she asks.

We stand there staring at each other.

"Answer me, young lady! What you get this lawyer for and why didn't they ask me? You can't just . . . run off and do whatever you want. You can't just go making your own decisions! You just a child!"

Maybe I'm still asleep and this is all a dream. Maybe Momma hasn't been taking her pills and is seeing things again. Or maybe she got the Alzheimer's and belongs on the fifth floor. That has to be it. That's the only explanation for her complete blindness. I stopped being a child six years ago.

"Momma. I'm PREGNANT."

I say it nice and slow so she gets it, but she looks at me as if I said the stupidest thing ever. Same look she gave me when I tried to tell her about Ray coming into my room at night.

"Well. Since you so grown, since you don't need your momma no more, fine then! Just fine!"

She grumbles while slipping on her coat.

"I ain't have to take this shit no way."

All I can do is stand there like a dummy, speechless and amazed. I can't believe she has the nerve to be mad at me! She flips her scarf over her shoulder and stops to glare at me.

"Blessed is the man who remains steadfast under trial," she preaches, her finger waving. "For when he stood the test he will receive the crown of life, which God has promised to those who love him!"

And then she storms out, so mad she could spit flames, with her record-breaking short visit.

chapter ten

New Girl's still sleep, along with the rest of the house; the only time it's ever quiet in here. The sky is fading from black to a dark sea blue so it's at least six in the morning. I should know because this is the eighth day I've watched the sun rise. The eighth day I've gone without sleeping. The eighth day, at this exact time, my body tells me two things: I need to pee and I need some water.

After I finish up in the bathroom, I tiptoe downstairs, doing everything not to disturb the peace the early morning brings, anything not to wake the rest of the monsters. But a low voice echoing from the living room stops me at the first landing and that sinking feeling of dread curls up next to Bean.

"Hi, Daddy! Hello? Hello, Dad? It's me, Kelly."

I knew Kelly had a daddy, but it's still weird to hear her

talk to him. It makes him real and she seems too evil to have such a gift.

"Yeah, I know it's really early but there isn't another time to talk. These girls are always following me around in here. They're always in my stuff, Daddy."

Her voice is so innocent-like, not fitting her at all. I move down a few more steps, hugging the wall, and spot her curled up in Ms. Stein's chair with the house phone we're not supposed to use without permission.

"Daddy, I really think . . . Oh! Nothing, really. I'm just calling to make sure you're coming on Sunday for visitation. I need to go to . . . what? Why didn't you tell me? Well, when will you be back? Four weeks! But what about New Year's? No, you said you'd come and you'd bring Ginger. . . . Well, maybe you can talk to Ms. Stein and see if . . . ugh, yeah I know, Dad. But we don't have to tell Mr. . . . what? Yes, DAD, I'm taking them. No, you don't have to call her! I'm taking them, every morning, like I said I would."

Pills! She taking pills? What kind? Are they like Momma's?

"But can you just . . . just how long do I have to stay here?" she begs. "You said it would only be a little while. Yes, Daddy, you don't have to . . . okay . . . okay, fine! Okay? Well, can you at least come see me before you go?"

I lean a little farther but my foot slips down one step with a loud thump. Shit! I stumble back, trying to keep quiet but it's too late. Kelly notices and quickly slams the phone down. Caught, no use pretending. We stare at each other, her eyes narrow slits filled with rage, her hand still gripping the receiver. My eavesdropping just gave her another reason to kill me. I'm too scared to move, too heavy to run. Trapped again.

If I just let her kill me, it'll all be over. But Bean . . .

Just as she stands up, ready to attack, Ms. Reba comes out of her bedroom in her night sweats. She yawns, before noticing the both of us.

"What are you two up to?" she barks.

Kelly doesn't break her stare. She cracks her knuckles against her hips then shrugs at Ms. Reba.

"Nothing. Just making breakfast," she says, her voice back to normal, and heads for the kitchen. Ms. Reba raises an eyebrow at me and I head back upstairs. Saved, but only for the moment.

It took Ms. Cora two days to convince me to go. Two whole days. Trust me, it will be fine, she kept on saying. I told her she's crazy and refused but gave in on the third day. We drove to the precinct the next morning.

"Now remember, you're going to tell the whole story, just like you told me. Don't leave anything out. Every detail is important. The detective is doing a huge favor talking to us first before we make our statement to the DA. And don't forget the part about the . . . Mary?"

As soon as I see the building, my feet stop working. Sounds drown out until I can hear nothing but teeth tap-dancing in my mouth. This building . . . all these windows . . . they're watching, waiting . . . to take me.

"Mary? Come on."

Ms. Cora pulls my arm. I shake her off and clutch to a nearby bus sign, but my legs still want to run.

"What are you doing?" she asks.

The shakes start, bad. I can't go in there. I can't! It's the last place before this whole nightmare started, the doorway between the then and the now. If we never went in there, if Momma never . . .

"They're going to give me a cheeseburger and take me away again!"

Ms. Cora stops pulling me and straightens, her eyes softening.

"Mary, I'm sorry, but what they did to you was wrong. They questioned you without an attorney present and your mother gave them permission to do so. It was a setup. But this time, I'll be there. I promise, they won't pull that bullshit while I'm there. I won't let them take you. No burgers. Now, let go of this dirty thing!"

They put me in the same room they did before and I think the same thing as I did back then: the floor is so nasty. Momma would be disgusted. The door opens and a memory walks in.

"Hello, Mary. Do you remember me?"

Mr. Jose hasn't aged one day. Still has dark black hair with a little bit of gray in his beard. Tall, lean, and tan with a thick accent like Marisol.

My chest tightens as he closes the door. He has a file in his hand, a real thick one, and a little recorder. He sits across from us, just like last time.

"Nice to see you again," he says, smiling, like he cares.

You're no Benson. You don't care, you suck at your job.

"Can I get you anything? Water? Maybe a—"

Ms. Cora grabs my hand as I rocket up from the chair, stopping me.

"It's okay! It's okay! No burgers, remember? We talked about this."

Mr. Jose glances between Ms. Cora and me a couple of times. He puts his hands on his thighs, closer to his gun. I think about the knife in my bag and change my mind.

"Sit down," she says, not as patient as before.

A whole twenty seconds pass before I sit, but push my chair closer to the door. Ms. Cora smirks, shaking her head.

"Can I just say, strictly off the record," she says to Mr. Jose. "When I called, you didn't seem surprised to hear from me at all."

He smiles and I move my bag between my legs.

"You know, sometimes you just have a hunch about things. And this case . . . I always had a gut feeling there

221

was a big piece of the puzzle missing."

Gut feeling?

"You mean evidence?" Ms. Cora asks.

He grins.

"No, there was plenty of evidence. But . . . nothing seemed to add up. Their stories never matched the evidence found. I said that plenty of times, but people told me to leave it alone. Same people won't like that I'm talking to you now."

"Well, people tend not to think clearly when a black girl is suspected of killing a little white girl," Ms. Cora says, crossing her arms.

"No, people tend not to think clearly when a baby is murdered. Period. At the end of the day, what's important is finding out what really happened to that little girl, bringing the person responsible to justice."

Ms. Cora nods in agreement and Mr. Jose looks at me.

"So, are you ready to talk?" he asks.

My gut flips as I count the grays in his beard. Maybe he is a little like Benson. Still, I don't trust him. He was the one who put me away. Gave me my cheeseburger and took me to the crazy house. Only said yes to the cheeseburger because I'd never had one before. That's what I get, trying to be sneaky without Momma knowing. Should've said no.

"Mary, you don't have to be afraid anymore," he says. "Whatever it is, I'm here to listen. Just give me a chance to set the record straight."

I look at Ms. Cora, who smiles and touches my back.

"Go on. It's okay. I'm here with you."

Ms. Cora says she won't let them take me this time. Maybe Ms. Cora is like Elliot Stabler, Benson's partner. She reads through the bullshit. I believe her. I trust her.

So I close my eyes and tell him the real story.

Transcript from the November 23rd Interview with Mary B. Addison, Age 16

Detective: For the record, can you please state your name and age.

Mary: Uh . . . my name is Mary Beth Addison. I'm sixteen years old.

Detective: Alright, Mary. Now, just tell me everything that happened. From the very beginning.

Mary: Okay. Ummm . . . Alyssa was crying from the moment her momma dropped her off. Momma kept trying to rock her to sleep. She didn't like the way she was being rocked, I don't think. She cried louder and louder. I took her and rocked her and she fell right asleep. Momma said, "Fine, she should sleep with you then." Then Momma set the crib up in my room.

We were asleep when Alyssa started crying again. Momma came into my room cursing. She was having "a day." I asked if she was taking her pills; she slapped me. Then told me to get them for her. I went and got her pills. She said, "Stupid, I told you to bring your pills! I need to calm this baby down." Alyssa was crying really loud. I got my pills and gave them to her. Then she told me to warm up a bottle. I went into the kitchen and put the bottle in the microwave. I was gone for thirty-five seconds, because that's how long Mrs. Richardson always told me to heat the bottle for. When I went back in the room, Momma was stuffing something in Alyssa's mouth. I thought it was the witch stuff that Mrs. Richardson uses, but it was the pills. Then Momma tried to shove the bottle down Alyssa's throat. She started choking. Momma grabbed her hard and tried to save her, hitting her back. But she was hitting her too hard. She stopped crying and wasn't breathing. I ran and tried to call 911, because that's what you do in an emergency, we learned that in school. But Momma slapped the phone out of my hand.

She told me stop because if they come and find Alyssa dead, she'll go to jail. She said we had to bring Alyssa back. She told me to bring her Bible and her cross. I kept saying that we can't, but then she was hitting me and I started crying. She went in my room with Alyssa and locked the door. I heard noises. Like she was hitting something. I kept banging on the door but she wouldn't let me in. Then I broke in the room.

Momma was swinging her, by her feet, and singing, chanting.
I tried to grab Alyssa but she flew out of my hands and hit the
wall . . . I didn't mean to throw her. I was trying to save her!
I didn't mean to . . . I'm sorry.

Detective: It's okay, Mary. It's okay. Take your time. Do
you need a break?

Mary: No. No, I'm okay. Then Momma . . . shoved me
out the room again. The phone was ringing and ringing, but
I was too scared to answer it because I dropped Alyssa and I
knew that was bad.

Detective: Then what happened?

Mary: I don't know how long it was, but Momma came
out. She sat me on the sofa and said she couldn't save her
and that she was dead. I was crying and Momma held me.
Then she said, "How much do you love your momma,
baby girl? You wouldn't want nothing to happen to your
momma, right?" Then she told me all the stuff that would
happen to her, how they would beat her up in prison and
maybe even give her the death penalty and that I would be
in foster care, getting raped by men. But, she said they go
easy on kids and that I wouldn't even go to jail. That I
would be free real soon and we would move away, start over,

and she would buy me a puppy. She said, "So if anyone ask, tell them you did it, baby girl, you tried to save her. They won't punish you too bad. You won't get a beating. And you'll be saving your momma." She made me promise, swear on her Bible.

Then she gave me a blanket with all this stuff inside and told me to bury it in the backyard. "Bury it deep or we be dead meat," she said. I was so scared, I didn't want to get into trouble, so I ran outside and started digging with my hands. It was so cold out, felt like I was digging forever. It had been raining all day. My nails . . . there was so much dirt under them, mud all over me. And lights . . . these little flashing lights. Our neighbor had his Christmas lights on. Momma came outside and told me I was in the wrong spot. "Not this tree, the other tree!" So I ran over by another tree and started again.

Then there was this big light, like a flashlight. Mr. Middlebury turned on the lights in his backyard. He was yelling at me; I didn't know what he was saying. I didn't know what to do, so I ran to tell Momma. When I ran inside, the police walked in. I thought Mr. Middlebury called them.

Then I heard Momma tell them, "I don't know what happened. She was alone in the room with her."

Detective: Why didn't you say anything when the police got there?

Mary: Momma told me not to. And she was watching . . . I'd get a beating if I did, because she made me swear on the Bible. Swear to God.

Detective: Do you know what kind of pills your mother was taking at the time?

Mary: Not really, they had long names.

Detective: And . . . this cross you mentioned, what did it look like?

Mary: It was small, and gold, used to be on a chain. It had these different color crystals on it.

Detective: What colors were the crystals? Can you remember?

Mary: Umm . . . like blue and yellow and red. Definitely red.

Detective: Did your mom wear the cross a lot?

Mary: All the time. It was her mother's. She never took it off.

• • •

"You did good in there," Ms. Cora says on the car ride back to the group home. "I'm really proud of you."

I don't say nothing. I can't stop thinking about what just happened. That was exhausting, pouring the entire truth out after holding it in for so long, like holding your pee forever and finally letting it go. I'm drained, light-headed, and a little nervous. At least Mr. Jose asked all the right questions this time. He has been close to the truth all along.

"So what are you doing for Thanksgiving?" she asks.

Damn, that's coming up, I forgot all about it. I was supposed to spend it with Ted. We were going to go to the parade and Boston Market. Not anymore.

"I'll be at the group home."

"Well, why don't you spend it with me and my family?"

"No thanks."

She frowns, stealing a glance, and I wonder what she is thinking.

"Okay, I won't pressure you," she says. "But, if you have no plans for Christmas, then you should come. That's when we have our big party."

I don't want to think about Christmas yet. Christmas reminds me of Alyssa. And I don't want to think about Alyssa any more than I already do.

Momma is cooking.

She's probably stuffing the turkey right now. Already

cleaned the greens, shredded the cheese, and boiled the sweet potatoes. Did she make her sour cream pound cake? Or her cranberry sauce with the orange peels? She probably won't glaze the ham until later. It's early and she still has the rice and peas to take care of.

"Mary! Quit daydreaming and put the water on!"

Ms. Stein is directing Thanksgiving dinner from her seat in front of the TV, watching the Thanksgiving parade. The kitchen counter is covered in cans and boxes, the makings of our dinner: Glory's collard greens, string beans, corn, three boxes of Kraft macaroni and cheese, two boxes Stove Top Stuffing, one can of cranberry sauce, and one box of Entenmann's pound cake.

Marisol and Kelly went to their families' houses for the day, which leaves Tara, Kisha, China, Joi, and I left to cook. New Girl walks down the stairs, all dressed up, her hair washed and blow-dried straight. She looks pretty, not sick and mousy as usual.

"My dad is picking me up today," she said earlier in our room, busy deciding what she was going to wear. "We're going to my aunt's house in New Jersey. I'll be back after nine, but he said he would talk to Ms. Stein about curfew."

She puts on her peacoat and sits on the bench by the door, smiling. I've never seen her this happy before. She can't wait to see her dad. I would be the same way if I knew who he was.

Ms. Reba shoves the turkey in the oven. She seasoned

it with butter, salt, a little pepper, and nothing else that would make it taste good. She also threw the turkey neck and giblets in the trash. Momma would've had a heart attack if she saw that.

"You ain't spending today with your moms?" China asks.

I shake my head.

"Why?"

That's a good question.

I put on the water for the macaroni and cheese. China shrugs and starts to open up a can of green beans while Tara struggles to read the Stove Top Stuffing instructions.

I guess this is better than spending Thanksgiving in baby jail. The food will taste the same but with better conditions. The COs hated working on any holiday and were extra mean. I spent most holidays on lockdown, the day passing like any other.

"After that's done, set the table! And don't forget the cups. And put them rolls in the oven when the turkey's done," Ms. Stein says.

The turkey will take at least four hours, so I have some time to kill. I sneak upstairs and check my phone. Two voice mails from Ted, begging me to call. The last message is from Ms. Cora.

"Hi, Mary! I was going to call the house but, well, you know. Anyways, I have good news. We filed the post-conviction motions yesterday. They'll review and we should have a hearing by the beginning of the year. I'll call you next week so we can start to prepare. Anyways, enough of that legal talk. Hope you're having a happy Thanksgiving."

A hearing? A trial? Wow, this is really happening.

I grab yesterday's newspaper and dictionary and lay down, circling a new word: *perfidious*. It means unfaithful and disloyal, like Ted.

Momma . . . maybe I should talk to her again, make her see . . .

Bean makes me so tired it's hard to keep my eyes open.

"Goddamn it, Mary! I told you to set the table!"

My eyes fly open and the sun is setting. So much for a quick nap.

I rush downstairs, the house smelling of turkey. New Girl is exactly where I left her, leg tapping like she has some type of nervous tic. She looks up at me, her eyes big and watery.

"He . . . he's just running a little late," she says, her voice cracking under her fake smile. "Traffic. Lots of traffic. He'll be here any minute."

It's been five hours.

I don't say nothing. Instead, I go to the kitchen and find the turkey out of the oven. Beige in color, dry as a paper bag. Not even some of that generic gravy could help this bird taste better. Joi pops the cranberry sauce out onto a paper plate.

Tara turns the Stove Top Stuffing into mushy slop, similar to what we used to eat in baby jail. China does her part by at least adding some seasoning and butter to the green beans, corn, and greens while Kisha mixes the Kool-Aid. I push the dinner rolls into the oven and start setting the table. Ms. Stein bought Thanksgiving-themed paper plates and a matching tablecloth.

New Girl stares off into nothing. Her pale face is sweating from sitting in that hot peacoat for so long. China walks in and sets the sides on the table. She glances at New Girl.

"I don't think her peoples is coming to get her," she whispers, uncovering the dishes. "She should probably just give up."

Our eyes meet, both knowing it ain't that simple to give up on people you love that don't love you the same.

"Dinner is ready!" Ms. Reba announces, bringing the dry turkey to the table. Tara brings in her stuffing, knowing damn well she should throw it in the trash.

Ms. Stein hobbles into the dining room. She looks over at New Girl, but doesn't say anything. China is the only one kind enough.

"Aye, New Girl. Why don't you come over here and eat with us while you wait for your peoples."

New Girl shakes her head a few times.

"No . . . no. My dad will be here any minute. I don't want to . . . spoil my dinner."

Ms. Reba and Ms. Stein glance at each other, sharing a guilty look.

"Poor child," Ms. Stein mumbles as she sits at the head of the table. Tara sits down next to her, greedy as ever.

"Who gonna say grace?" Kisha says.

"Grace?" Ms. Stein grumbles, while Ms. Reba sharpens the knife.

"Yeah," China says, looking at me. "We got a lot to be grateful for."

She's right. God didn't abandon me. I'm alive. I'm out of baby jail and got a lawyer that's gonna help me keep Bean and set the record straight. I'm gonna go to college. And Ted . . . well . . . I don't know. I rub my stomach and glance at New Girl, who's struggling to hold back her tears.

She pretends she doesn't see me coming, remaining frozen while I sit next to her.

"I know what you're thinking," she whispers, her head hanging low. "I'm stupid, right? To just sit here . . . but he wouldn't . . . he just wouldn't. He's just . . . running late. There's a lot of traffic today, with the parade going on."

I put my hand on New Girl's knee and don't say what we're both thinking. Because I've been there before, I know what she's feeling. Parents aren't supposed to disappoint their kids like this. It's the cruelest type of punishment. I tap her knee and stand. She nods, takes off her coat, and follows me to the table.

"Just for a little while. I can't have too much. Don't want to ruin my dinner."

Ms. Veronica is late. Again.

But Ms. Stein don't care; she has us all sitting in our circle in the basement, waiting. No supervision, no one to stop all of them from ganging up on me at any moment. I sit closer to the storm door, farthest from Kelly.

"Damn yo . . . this is so fucking stupid," Joi whines. "Where is this bitch? I have to call Markquann before lights-out. He was supposed to take me shopping today and I haven't heard from him. I'm worried about my boo."

Marisol chuckles. "You still think you dating that nigga? *Estúpido.*"

Joi rolls her eyes.

"Whatever bitch, mind yo' business."

"I'm so sick of this shit, man. I don't need no doctor like you bitches. I'm straight," Marisol says, flipping back her hair. Kelly chuckles and crosses her arms.

"Straight in what way?"

Marisol shoots her a glance that would've started a fight any other day but China jumps in.

"Nah yo, I can fill in for her. I'm good at this, getting shorties to talk about their feelings and shit," China says and cracks her knuckles. "So Tara, tell me, what are you feeling right now?"

"Hungry," Tara says and the group snickers.

"Interesting. Let's try something else. What you wanna be when you get out of here?"

Tara shrugs. "I don't know."

"Don't you turn eighteen, like, soon?" Joi asks.

Tara nods. "Four months."

The room sighs. She really doesn't have to say anything more; everyone knows what that means. I think about Ted and rub my stomach.

"Yo, you should join the army or something," China offers. "You mad strong, they'd like you."

"Why would I wanna fight for some white man's war?"

The group laughs. Tara giggles, sounding normal, cheerful, despite what she's up against. I wouldn't be laughing.

"That's what my daddy used to say," Tara says. "My daddy was like, mad smart. When my moms didn't want me no more, he took care of me. I was the only one of the kids that got to live with him, that's how much he loved me. He used to say never fight for the white man, 'cause the white man don't care nothing about black people. He died when I was thirteen, white man's AIDS got him. I got sent to the white man's foster care, the white man's school, the white man's prison, and now I'm in the white man's basement talking to y'all."

The group cackles as loud shuffling echoes above us. Ms. Veronica comes booming down the stairs, almost tripping at the bottom.

"Girls, I'm so so so sorry!"

"Ms. Veronica, you late. Again!" Joi shouts, foot stomping.

"I know, I know, but traffic . . . traffic was just terrible. Whew! Okay, okay, so where should we start? Oh no, wait, let's take out our feeling notebooks first. Right?"

"Nah, Ms. V, I'm the therapist today," China says.

Ms. Veronica flusters then nods.

"Um, okay! You know, role reversal could be good for us here."

China grins and leans back in her chair, pretending to take notes.

"So Ms. V, what you wanna be when you get out of here?"

"She already out of here, dumb ass," Joi groans. "She ain't ever even been in here!"

"Man, you don't know her life! But fine! I'll change the question. Ms. V, you made it out the hood. Congratulations! Now, why you do what you do?"

Ms. Veronica fidgets, but holds a fake smile.

"Well, people say I'm a good listener. I can really get people to open up."

Kelly chuckles. "Is that what you think you're doing here? Getting us to 'open up'? I hate to break it to you, but you're doing a real shitty job."

Ms. Veronica takes a deep breath.

"Well, I'm sorry to hear you say that, Kelly," she says, her voice shaky but determined. "But I am trying my best to . . . give you the emotional tools . . . to help you succeed."

"How? By making us write in these stupid books?"

Kelly tosses her book in the middle of the circle. Ms. Veronica's face stiffens.

"You know, even though I haven't been exactly in your situations, I can still relate," she says, growing defensive. "I . . . I lost my first boyfriend, my first love. And I was in a dark place for a long time. Even had to move back home with my parents. But I dug my way out of my depression, went back to school, and found a career that I love. So you see, ladies, I'm here, almost to be an inspiration. That you, too, can overcome anything."

An entire minute goes by and no one says nothing. Finally, Kelly busts out laughing.

"What is so funny?" Ms. Veronica demands, clearly offended.

"Yo, Ms. V," China says slowly. "No disrespect, but are you really trying to tell me you having a dead boyfriend is like being in a group home?"

Ms. Veronica's face turns red. She starts to say something but stops herself.

"You know it must be real nice being able to come and go whenever you please, even to go to school," Kisha says sharply. "Not having no record and getting a job wherever you want."

"And it must be real nice having a home to move back

to," Joi snaps. "With real parents taking care of you. You lost your boyfriend? Looks like you were able to replace him real quick. I lost my pops and my moms might as well be dead if I knew where she was. I've been in group homes since I was fucking twelve! How you suggest I replace them?"

The room tenses. Bean moves and I wonder if it can feel the years of pent-up anger trying to dig its way out of a shallow grave.

"So yeah, you right, China," Joi says, rolling her neck. "I wouldn't know nothing about her life!"

Ms. Veronica swallows, avoiding eye contact.

"You know what," she croaks. "I think we should end our session early today."

Joi huffs. "Don't you mean on time?"

There are two DMVs in Brooklyn. One downtown and one in Coney Island.

"Go to Coney Island," one of the cooks in the kitchen told me. "The lines there are shorter."

He lied. I waited forty-five minutes just to get a ticket number. That's when Ted walks in.

"What are you—"

"I overheard you talking," he says with a guilty expression.

Damn, I miss his voice . . .

The place is empty except for us, or that's how it feels when he talks to me. Like we're the only two people in the world. I want to stand here forever looking at him, hating him and still loving him at the same time. He still has my teeth marks on his arm. I walk away and he follows.

"Mary, come on, talk to me. You can't just not talk to me!"

There is one empty seat left between a grandma and some lady with a heap of kids playing around her. I wiggle into the seat and he stands in front of me. The pink ticket says D097. The monitor says D013. This is going to be a long wait.

"Please, baby," he begs. "Let me explain. About what you saw."

His shoes look brand-new and fancy. Not the shoes of a poor group home kid like me. He kneels down just to meet my eyes.

"Baby? Please," he whispers, hand pressed against my thigh.

"Don't touch me," I say.

"Yo, stop trying to push me away."

"I said, don't touch me."

"Mary, what you saw, it wasn't like that!"

The lady next to us with the kids is hanging on to every word of our conversation. Across from us, an older man in a construction jumpsuit watches, eyeing Ted like he wants to say something, but doesn't.

"Those are new," I say, a bite in my voice, nodding at the floor.

Ted peeps down at his shoes like he forgot he had some on.

"They were a gift."

Has Ted always been such a liar? Yes. I knew it all along. It never made sense for him to love someone like me, after everything I've done.

The old woman next to me is so deep into our business she missed her number. She jumps up and Ted moves to her seat.

"I know what you're thinking. And I just want to explain. I should've been honest with you. But baby, it was for us."

D027. Time and this line could not move any slower.

"The girl you saw . . . she's not my girl," Ted whispers. "She . . . I just live with her. Aight. There. You know everything now."

Ted is wearing cologne or something. He's never smelled like this before. Everything about him seems new. He's a whole new Ted. Or maybe I never really knew him at all.

"You live with her? For free?"

"Not really . . . sort of."

It hurts to look into his eyes. It hurts to be so close to him. To want him and not want him at the same time.

Feels like my arms are being pulled out from both sides.

"You sleeping with her?"

He exhales and doesn't look at me.

"Baby, I would've been out on the street."

A knife cuts me open from my heart down to my belly button. I'm bleeding to death and no one can see.

"But it's different, with you," he adds.

I turn away and stare at nothing. He must take me for an idiot.

"You don't believe me? Do you?"

He reaches for my hand and I snatch it away so fast I almost hit the lady next to me.

"Baby, I'm doing this for us. So we can have paper for Bean!"

I don't respond and he doesn't push me. We sit there silent, frozen, stubborn as boulders.

D038.

"I forget sometimes, how young you are," he says and slouches in his seat. "You just don't understand."

"You can't blame my age for your lies."

Ted raises an eyebrow. He wants to respond, but is smart enough not to. There's nothing he can say to save himself.

We wait in silence for another thirty minutes. Ted only moves to stretch his legs in his seat.

D072.

"Me and Leticia, we just cool. She's smart and knows how to work niggas. So we came up with this plan to,

241

you know, have her bun up with some of the dudes in the building and niggas on the block. They give her money, buy her clothes and all that shit, and she gives me a cut. We figured we could make more money if we brought in some of her friends that are like her. I link them, like I'm doing a homie a favor, and they hit me up too. But I'm not out spending the money like that. I've been saving the money for us. For Bean."

I look down at his shoes again. Bright green expensive laces. He kicks his foot out.

"I told you, these were a gift! Leticia gave me these. But I don't love her, baby, I love you. We're different. You know that."

Stop talking, Ted. Just stop.

D080.

"I didn't tell you about it 'cause I knew you wouldn't understand. I was gonna use the money to get our spot when the baby was born and dead all contact after that. I swear, baby."

"How many girls?"

"Huh?"

"Girls, Ted. You have more than just Leticia. You have more places to stay. How many?"

Ted winces and turns away. The number must be high. How long has he been pretending to be broke? How many times have we pooled our money together like he had none?

"Why didn't you tell me?" I ask.

"The same reason you didn't tell me."

For a moment, I forgot I told him about Alyssa. And then I understand. It wasn't shame, it was fear that kept him from telling me; fear of the reaction from the one person who matters more to you than anyone in the world.

We hear my number called and I scramble out of my seat. Ted follows to the window, hands in his pockets, sulking. The woman looks like she has been working at the DMV for over a thousand years, face sagging to her chin, hair dyed black with white roots.

"I need to get an ID," I say.

"Where's the paperwork?" she asks, smacking her lips.

I open my bag and hand her my birth certificate. She tips her glasses to the end of her nose, looking over my shoulder.

"Is this your guardian?"

"No. He's . . . my cousin."

She stares at him again.

"Then who is your guardian?"

"I'm . . . I don't know."

"Are you in foster care?"

I shrug. "Sort of."

"Then you need to come back with your guardian."

"But . . . I have all my stuff here."

"Do you have your MV45b?" she asks, losing patience.

"What's that?"

She sighs.

"I need your birth certificate, your social security card, and an MV45b form. You also need your legal guardian here with you with a proper state ID to vouch for you. We can't process you without it."

She shoves the paper back toward me and clicks a switch for a new number.

Another roadblock. It never ends.

I walk away, slipping my birth certificate back into my bag. Why wouldn't Ms. Stein or Winters tell me that? Aren't they my guardians? Did they know? They did know. They did this on purpose. It's punishment. They knew that I would have to tell them what I needed an ID for.

Ted walks behind me, rubbing my shoulders while we exit.

"It's okay, babe. We can get you a fake ID. I know a dude who . . ."

I squirm from under his hands and step away. He throws his hands up.

"Aight, Mary, that's enough! Quit being like that! I said I was sorry. I'm fucking here and not with them, aren't I? What, you rather me sleep on the fucking sidewalk? You want me to be a fucking bum on the street?"

His voice is loud and demanding, but his eyes are begging for forgiveness. I turn away to keep from being melted by them.

"I didn't ask for your help."

The words come out in a hiss, like a rattlesnake, poisonous and deadly. He steps away from me then sighs, all the fight leaving him. Torn, I quickly walk to the train before I have a chance to change my mind.

"Oh no! Oh no! Oh no! Mr. Giggles! Noooo!"

Ms. Reba's screams wake up the entire house. I'm not usually nosy, but when I hear all the doors open and the girls whispering, I follow the voices downstairs. And there's Ms. Reba, wailing by the doorway. Hovering over, from what I can tell, all that remains of her cat.

"Oh no! Noooo. Please, no!"

I never really paid much attention to that cat. You barely saw him but he was a quiet pain in the ass. His white fur covered the house like Saran Wrap and he hated using his litter box. He'd rather piss on the couch instead.

"Holy shit," Joi gasps. "Do you see that thing?"

The cat is a gory mess. Eyes carved out, holes throughout his body like he was jumped in the shower at baby jail, tail chopped off and hanging from his mouth. The hallway reeks of the bleach Ms. Stein likes using on the floor. He must be soaked in it. We all stand around, staring at each other. Why would anyone kill Mr. Giggles?

"Noooo . . . why! No no no no no . . ."

This all seems too familiar. Ms. Reba kneeling on the floor, wailing in front of her child. Reminds me of Mrs.

Richardson and Alyssa . . . I can almost feel the mud soaking through my pajamas.

I didn't mean to throw her . . .

The coldness sets in and the shakes start, violent as a seizure. I take a step back, bumping right into New Girl, watching Ms. Reba, her eyes cold.

Ms. Reba stands up, hands bloody, face dripping with snot and tears, eyes blazing in rage. The whole room stiffens.

"YOU! You . . . you little bitches! You little bitches killed my baby!"

My heart stops, hearing her hoarse voice echo almost the exact words Mrs. Richardson said that night. Feeling the stabbing pain of her blame. All these years, it's what hurt the most.

But I didn't mean to throw her . . .

Ms. Reba jumps up, arms swinging. The girls scatter and shriek. I'm so stuck in my past that I can't move and Ms. Reba is heading right for me, ready to kill. This is it. I'm going to die because I'm Alyssa-ing again. That hollow hole in my chest tightens. Ms. Reba lunges with a scream and I am ready to die, imagining her claws ripping me into shredded meat. But instead she snatches Kisha by the ponytail and shoves her against the wall by the throat.

"Who did it! You fucking better tell me!"

"I . . . I . . . didn't do it, I swear," Kisha screams.

"Tell me! You fucking tell me! Tell me NOW!"

"Reba, yo, calm down, man," China yells, trying to break them apart. "Kisha wouldn't do some shit like that, man!"

Ms. Reba spins around and backhand slaps China to the floor. Kisha coughs, beating against Ms. Reba's hand, fighting to breathe. Tara tries to save her while Marisol helps China to her feet. The rest of us are frozen in fear.

New Girl calmly takes my hand and pulls me up the stairs as Ms. Stein comes hobbling fast out of her bedroom.

"Reby! Reby! NO! Stop! You'll kill her!"

"I can't! No, someone else got to do this," Joi coughs, last night's dinner by her feet. "Y'all, I can't breathe. This shit ain't right!"

The eight of us are on the floor, cleaning up what's left of Mr. Giggles. Ms. Stein took one blue sponge, cut it into eight pieces, gave us a bucket of water, Ajax, and a trash bag, and then told us to get to work.

New Girl and Joi's job was to get rid of Mr. Giggles while the rest of us crawl around on our hands and knees, scrubbing puddles of blood seeping into the wood. But damn . . . the sight of that mutilated cat. Joi threw up twice just holding the bag open for New Girl.

"No, I'm not playin' y'all! I can't do this shit," Joi croaks, wiping her mouth with her sleeve. "This mad nasty. I didn't kill that fucking cat; one of you bitches did it!"

"Yo, shut the fuck up, Joi," China barks, losing her

patience. "Ms. Stein said if we don't clean this shit up we'll all be on house restriction for who knows how long!"

"I don't give a—"

China jumps to her feet and slams Joi into the door by her neck.

"I'm not gonna be on no fucking house restriction because of your dumb ass! We in this together so you better clean that shit up or I'mma put your fucking face in it!"

"Whoa," Kisha mumbles. China has never lashed out like this before. No one knows what to make of it so no one moves. Joi gasps for air, teary eyes shifting down to Kelly. For a change, Kelly doesn't come to her defense, thinking the same as the rest of us—no one wants to be on house restriction. No one wants to go back to life in a cage. China finally lets go of her neck and Joi slumps to her knees. Kelly glances at me, eyes narrowing. Without makeup, you can see her face is still a little scarred with red patches in the shape of random continents. I quickly look away.

"Yo, don't you have a man, Joi?" Kisha asks with a chuckle as China goes back to cleaning. "If you ever want to see him again, you better clean that shit up."

Joi's eyes widen, her lip trembling before she swallows up some air and picks up the garbage bag. New Girl sighs and grabs the cat bare-handed, tossing him into the bag.

"Damn," Kisha says, sucking her teeth. "I'mma mess up my nails doing this shit."

My back aches from squatting for what seems like hours. And I'm starving! We haven't had breakfast or even changed out of our pajamas yet. Bean moves, elbowing everything in its way. I try to hold in a whimper but the stench of bleached cat makes me dry heave. China glances over at me from across the room. She frowns, starts to say something then shakes her head, eyes falling back to the floor.

"You ever been pregnant?" China asks Kisha, scrubbing next to her.

"Yeah," she says like it's nothing. "Twice."

"Word? Why you never keep them?"

"'Cause I don't wanna get all fat like psycho! I like my ass the size it is," she says, slapping her butt with a smirk. "I made a little change though. Got them stupid niggas to pay for it. Tell them it's four-fifty at the clinic when it really be like two hundred. I got myself a nice little Coach bag from Macy's last time."

Kisha giggles, all proud of herself while China shakes her head and keeps scrubbing.

"Anyways, my moms wasn't gonna let me keep no baby," Kisha says, all the humor gone from her voice. "Real talk, she barely wanted me. She wanted my sister though. Pretty light skin baby girl, hair just like psycho. Bet she playing with that girl's hair now. She could never leave it alone." She pauses, face darkening. "But whatever, I don't need no kids. What I look like being some baby mama?"

China stops to look at her. Kisha zeros in on one spot

and scrubs harder, nails long forgotten. Even Tara stops to watch her dig her way to the basement.

"You ever want kids?" Kisha asks China, out of breath but focused.

"I got some already," China huffs. "A baby brother and sister."

"Where they at?"

"I don't know. Foster care, somewhere. Tried to get my aunt to keep them but she wasn't trying to feed any more mouths than she already got. But when I turn eighteen, I'm gonna get them back."

"They gonna let you do that?"

"Why not? They my blood."

Kisha looks doubtful but doesn't argue. Ain't that something? Everyone swears I'm stupid for even dreaming of keeping Bean and this girl thinks she's going to get some kids back that aren't even really hers.

"I got a couple of more months in here. Gonna get my certification, get a job, then I'm out!" China snaps then looks at the rest of us. "Ain't trying to fuck that up by killing some stupid cat!"

The room stays quiet while our sponges work against the floor, blood and gritty bleach powder covering our hands. New Girl ties up the bag of what's left of Mr. Giggles and puts it in the backyard. Ms. Reba probably wants to bury him, have a funeral or something. That's what you're supposed to do with the dead you love. I wonder where they buried Alyssa and what the funeral was like. Did they bury her with her favorite blanket? What does it say on her stone? Will they ever let me visit?

Damn . . . Alyssa-ing, even while covered in cat blood.

"I was pregnant once," Tara says and the whole room stops. The idea of Tara, of all people, being pregnant . . . I think it's an SAT word: *aghast.* It means to be horrified, stunned, disgusted, and confused. We look like every one of those words.

"So why'd you get rid of . . . it?" Kisha asks cautiously, sitting back on her heels.

Tara shrugs and rings out her soapy blood-filled chunk of sponge. "Daddy said the white man would never understand."

It's Sunday. Visitation Day. Two weeks since I last saw Momma. We've been on house restriction since the Mr. Giggles accident so I honestly don't mind her coming. I take a cold shower, have breakfast, and wait in the visitors' room for her this time. We need to talk. Things are getting serious. Ms. Cora filed the motion and we have a court date. That means there is going to be another trial, with more lawyers, doctors, and people in our business. I have to get Momma to see that the easiest way out of this is to tell the truth.

Two thirty rolls around. I'm real tired and ready for my nap. Bean makes me so tired all the time. I sit in one of the armchairs and try not to get too comfortable. Momma will be walking in the door at any moment. Thanksgiving was a week ago, but maybe she'll bring a slice of her sweet potato pie. She did one year, when I was still in baby jail. It was the best thing I had ever tasted.

Two thirty-five. I look out the window, expecting to see her parking, but the streets are empty. I tap my fingers against the windowsill, staring at the baby birds in the trees on the sidewalk. There's seven of them, flapping around, chirping.

Where's your momma, little baby birds? It's dangerous out there.

I look back at the clock. It's 2:45. Wait, where's Momma!? She's never late. Never.

I pace around the room, rubbing my stomach like I could rub right through to Bean's head. Something's happened. This isn't like her. What if she got in an accident? What if she's sick? Who would tell me? Troy?

What if she got hit by a car or something? Momma never looks both ways before crossing a street. And she's not taking her pills! She always gets lost when she doesn't take her pills. I don't even know where she lives! She never told me. Should I call the police? Maybe Mr. Jose. No, Ms. Cora. Maybe Ms. Stein might have her number . . .

Then it hits me, and this confusing type of relief wraps me up like a blanket, but I still feel cold. She's not coming.

She's just not coming.

chapter eleven

New Girl is writing a letter.

That's what she does now. We stay in our room, like the two unwanted guests we are. Me, studying, her, writing nonstop letters. I read one of her letters once when she went to the bathroom. They're to her sister, telling stories of how her mom used to make her scrub toilets, clean clothes, and iron on the hottest day of the year. Promising she would tell her the "truth" once she sees her in person, and that when she's free, she'll come rescue her. From what I can tell, her sister never writes back.

I'm on page 563 of my book and buy the *New York Times* every day now; two dollars and fifty cents on weekdays, five dollars on Sundays. It's a lot of money, but I read it cover to cover, circling words I don't know. Sometimes I go down to the Learning Center and look them up in

Ms. Claire's office, since her dictionary is way better than mine. I only average about two new words a day, but I'm reading faster and I know what's going on in politics, business, and sports. Ms. Claire says that will help me get into college.

All I have left now is Bean to take care of and the only way to do that is if I get my degree. I'll use the money people owe me from those stupid books about me to go to school. Then I'll find a job, make more money, and buy one of those fancy apartments I see in the real estate section. Someplace where it's safe, with lots of room for Bean to play. Because when Ms. Cora wins, I'm getting Bean the hell out of here, no matter what.

Ms. Stein busts into my room, unannounced as always.

"You have a visitor!"

I shoot up, dropping my book.

"Who?"

It's Wednesday. I'm not expecting Momma, no way, especially with everything that is going on.

"Hell if I know. Some friend of your mother's."

Troy. That's the only friend Momma has that would know about me. What the hell does he want? Maybe he's here to pay me off, like a bribe or something, to save Momma. I never thought about that. Maybe I could use that money to save Ted and he wouldn't have to live with those girls anymore. But what if he'd rather be with them?

Damn, I hate what he has done to us, making me question everything.

I run down to the visitors' room, fixing my hair, and stop short in the doorway. My stomach drops. It's not Troy. It's not even a man. It's a woman.

"Hello, Mary."

Alyssa's mother is standing in the middle of the visitors' room. The ghost of my past I was afraid of most. She's here to do it. She's here for revenge. She's here to finally kill me.

Everything is numb; I don't know what to do or say. If it wasn't for Bean, I'd let her do what she wanted all these years. But now . . . how do I talk her out of killing me? I guess I should start by being polite, like Momma always taught me.

"I . . . it's just . . . I mean, it's good to see you."

She snorts and rolls her eyes.

"Cut the crap, Mary. You were never a good liar."

**Continued Transcript from the January 4th
Interview with Melissa Richardson,
Alyssa Richardson's Mother**

Detective: Okay, let's step back here a minute and start from the beginning. When did you first meet Dawn Addison and her daughter, Mary?

Melissa: A little over a year ago. My husband and I are from Savannah, Georgia. Greg was transferred up here to New York. We thought it'd be a fun adventure. We were here a couple of weeks when a coworker of his invited us to his church. We thought it'd help, you know, since we didn't have any family or friends here. The pastor's wife invited me to their women's group meetings they have on Wednesday nights. That's where I met Dawn. She walked right up to me and introduced herself. Real sweet, very southern. It was . . . I guess . . . familiar. She's a little older, but we took to each other right away. And then I met Mary.

Detective: What was Mary like?

Melissa: Mary was always quiet. Real quiet, but smart.

Detective: How could you tell?

Melissa: I used to be an elementary school teacher. Sometimes I'd look over Mary's homework and the stuff was just too easy for her. I started giving her a reading list and extra math homework. Plus, Dawn wasn't too bright. Mary always had to help her with the bills and reading for her. I was over at their house once and Dawn was behind on practically all her bills and trying to figure out what she owed. Mary walked right over and did all the calculations, right in her head. She had just turned eight.

Detective: What's Mary's relationship with her mother like?

Melissa: They're inseparable. Never see one without the other. I thought it was a little strange, I guess, for a little girl to not have any friends or anybody her own age to play with.

Detective: Were you close with Dawn?

Melissa: I had just found out I was pregnant and Dawn . . . she helped me out a lot. Came over once a week with Mary. She cooked, cleaned, gave me all kinds of advice on what vitamins I needed to take and what to do. She even massaged my feet.

Detective: What happened when Alyssa was born?

Melissa: Alyssa . . . was a beautiful baby. She was . . . I'm sorry . . . I'm sorry.

Detective: Take your time.

Melissa: When . . . when we brought her home from the hospital, Dawn was there. She made us dinner and helped me the first night. I was having trouble breast-feeding. Alyssa wouldn't take right away. Dawn, you know, just knew what to do. Mary was there too . . . I let her hold her. I had never seen Mary smile so big.

Detective: Did Mary like Alyssa?

Melissa: Mary loved Alyssa. She brought some of her toys for her. She even helped me change her diaper.

Detective: So you didn't sense any animosity?

Melissa: No. Not at all. But she was so quiet. I never knew what she was thinking.

Detective: Was Alyssa a fussy baby, give you any problems other than the breast-feeding?

Melissa: She was colicky. I used to give her gripe water to help calm her down. I gave some to Dawn the night I left Alyssa. She said she didn't need it. She called it witch juice.

Detective: I'm sorry, I have to ask, did you ever drop Alyssa? Maybe something fell and hit her that could have caused the bruising before? Maybe your husband?

Melissa: No. Never. Not even once.

Detective: Just out of curiosity, when you arrived at the house, did you see anything unusual? Anything out of place?

Melissa: Just Mary. She was standing in the corner, staring. I asked her what happened. She said she didn't know.

Detective: How was this strange to you?

Melissa: Because you don't know Mary. Mary isn't a very good liar.

"Damn, you grew up beautiful. You don't look a thing like your mother."

She's here. She really is here, standing in front of me. I forgot how much Alyssa had her eyes. It almost hurts to look at her.

"Thank you," I mumble.

She strolls over to the sofa and sits with a heavy plop. I don't move, too afraid to do anything. The dreams I had of this day were always nightmares.

Momma used to call Mrs. Richardson a beauty queen, because of her tall, thin, perfect body, pink skin, big blue eyes, and long brown hair. "Chiclet Teeth," Momma would call her bright smile, but it never seemed like a compliment. She used to wear all kinds of colorful dresses, heels, and makeup. Now she's like a washed-up version of her former self, with a potbelly, thinning hair, jeans, and a T-shirt. No makeup. Not even grease for her chapped lips.

"Well, nothing to say?" she asks.

I shake my head.

"Hm. Are you in school?"

"Sort of."

"Do you still read?"

"Every day."

She stares at me for a long while. She is shorter than I remember. Or maybe I've changed.

"What are you thinking?"

She asked me this a lot when I was little. She would always laugh and sing, "Mary, Mary, pretty little lamb. What are you thinking up in there?" And I would always tell her the truth.

"You . . . you never visited me," I say, chewing my lower lip.

Alyssa's momma cocks her head to the side with a frown. "Come again?"

My throat closes up and I want to hide inside myself. Even after all this time, I still don't get how I can be so scared yet so desperate for her at the same time.

"Momma said that . . . you would visit me. After it was all . . . over. But you never did."

Mrs. Richardson cocks her head to the other side and studies me for a long while, like I'm some sort of strange painting. Oh God, what a stupid thing to say! I can tell by her reaction it was stupid.

She lets out a tired laugh and exhales.

"I'm going to kill your son."

She says it so matter-of-fact that I'm sure I'm hearing things.

"What?"

"You got a low stomach. It means you're having a boy. And when you have him, I'm going to kill him. Suffocate him with pills and beat him till he's black-and-blue. You'll have to have a coffin specially made just for his size, since they don't come mass-produced like the other ones do. You won't have many pictures to put in the funeral program, since he wouldn't have lived much. He'll just be a baby, three months old."

I'm going to throw up. I can feel it. My knees wobble and I sit on the floor.

"So yes, I'm going to kill your baby," she says. "And when they put me away, will you come and visit me?"

I'm so confused. At first, all I can focus on is Bean being a boy. A beautiful baby boy! Ted will love that, he wanted a boy. But then the rage building inside me takes over. A thick pill covered in hot sauce slides down my throat, making it hard to breathe or think straight. All I want to do is slice her face, throw a desk at her head, stab her with a pen, and run her over with a car, for even *thinking* about hurting my baby. My hands roll into sweaty fists.

A grin smears across her face.

"Yeah, didn't think so."

How could she even joke like that? How could I feel like this? This was the woman I loved more than my own momma. The woman I wanted to be my momma. Why is she being this mean? Because of Alyssa? But she doesn't know everything that happened.

I breathe through my nose, trying to calm down while she pulls a pack of cigarettes and a lighter out of her coat pocket. She never smoked before. It's strange to see her this way. Like a recovering junkie. The women in baby jail looked better. She lights a cigarette, slowly blowing smoke out toward the ceiling.

"Did you kill Alyssa?" she asks, without looking at me.

I can feel the weight of the question, built and held inside her head for years. She sounds exhausted from carrying it around for so long. And I don't want to lie. I really don't.

"No."

She sighs with her entire body. "Never thought you did."

The room stiffens, the house quiet. You can hear children playing up the street. She takes another drag from her cigarette, scratching her arm.

"So why did you say you did it?" She still isn't looking at me as the question rolls off her lips.

"I didn't say anything."

"Sure didn't. So why didn't you tell *me* the truth?"

"I . . . I . . . I didn't think you would believe me."

"How come?"

"The rabbit."

"The what?"

"The crystal rabbit," I choke. "Remember, I used to play with it and you always told me to put it down. Then you found it broke, but I didn't break it. And you told me no one likes a liar."

Mrs. Richardson's face darkens.

"Mary, those are two totally different things."

I bite my tongue. That is the second time she has made me feel stupid in a matter of minutes.

"I know that . . . now."

She blinks and flicks dead ashes onto the carpet.

"I forget how young you were. You really were just a kid," she murmurs, licking her lips a couple of times. She keeps rubbing her arms as if she is cold and I want to give her my hoodie.

"You just had this . . . old soul. I could see it in your eyes," she continues. "And the way you used to take care of your momma, without her even knowing. It made no sense."

She licks her lips again, staring at the stains in the carpet, and I'm suddenly embarrassed that she's visiting me in such a dirty home.

"You know, Alyssa would've been starting first grade this year."

"I know," I mumble. I think about that all the time. Alyssa-ing over everything that could have been.

She doesn't say nothing. Just sits there like one of the old folks in the nursing home, daydreaming about memories. Feels strange, having her here, but nice at the same time. It's never been just the two of us, even when I wanted it to be. I wish she would hug me, squeeze me tight like she used to. But I know she won't. Still, I'm happy being in the same room with her. The rest of the world feels invisible, like we are the only two people left on the planet. I hold back a smile, because it doesn't seem right to smile since she is so unhappy.

Please don't be mad at me, Mrs. Richardson. Please. I'm so sorry.

"So what's this business about wanting to dig up Alyssa?"

I blink.

"I don't know anything about that," I say. "Is that what they want to do?"

She smirks.

"Well, you're the one running this show, Mary Bell. What do you want to do?"

Mary Bell. I haven't been called that in years. Feels so familiar, so good. But there's not a bit of warmth or humor in her voice. She is as cold as ice pops.

"I don't know. I guess I just want to keep my baby."

Mrs. Richardson freezes like a picture, smoke swirling around her head, eyes locked on me. Then she snorts.

"You . . . want to keep *your* baby?" she says, as if it was the dumbest thing anyone has ever said. She puts her cigarette out on the heel of her sneaker and yanks on her coat. I jump to my feet.

Wait, what is she doing? Is she leaving me?

She mumbles and curses, my name coming up. I don't know what to do or say to make her stay.

Please! Don't go!

"YOU want to keep YOUR baby!" she screams. "Well, isn't that rich? We have something in common."

She walks out, leaving the house feeling haunted.

chapter twelve

"What number we at?" Winters says next to me, yawning big.

"D049," I say.

I'm D101.

He groans and rubs his eyes some more.

"Of all the damn days, you pick the busiest."

After trying twice to get an ID on my own, the DMV reported it to the state, which reported it to my parole officer. I guess he got in trouble or something, because early this morning he barged into the house, screaming "Get your damn coat! You're coming with me."

My heart dropped and I just knew I was heading back to baby jail, wondering how I could throw myself out of the moving car without hurting Bean. But once we were in his truck he screamed, "Why didn't you just tell Ms. Stein you needed a damn ID!"

It always surprises me how stupid he thinks I am. Like he really thinks I didn't try to ask her first and she kept saying no. Last thing I wanted to do was bring more attention to myself by getting Winters in trouble.

"Wish you would've just told me what you wanted to do in the first damn place," he says from his seat, looking up at the ticket counters. The line wrapped around twice.

"I told you, you just didn't want to listen," I mumble.

Winters glares at me.

"Well, ain't you the talkative one all of a sudden. Now we up here, on CHRISTMAS EVE, like I don't have shit else to do. I still gotta find my wife something. I'm not sleeping on the sofa like last year 'cause of you girls, I'll tell you that!"

I sigh. D061.

"She's gonna leave me one of these days," he says. "Months I go with peace from you, Addison. Months, and then all of this!"

Peace? Has he been to our house?

"Kelly is trying to kill me," I blurt out.

He laughs.

"Well, I wonder why? Couldn't be that pot of boiling water you threw in her face, right?"

Of course he wouldn't believe me. No one ever does.

"Yeah, I heard about it," he chuckles. "I thought you was one of the good ones Addison. Should've known better. And what in the hell do you need a license for so damn badly? Where you think you driving to and with what car?"

His story is just that, a story. Nothing about it makes sense. But since he never believes me anyways, I don't try to argue. Instead, I tell him the truth.

"I need an ID because I'm taking the SATs. I want to go to college and get my degree."

Winters falls silent, in a state of shock. His mouth drops, about to say something, but instead he blows out air and keeps quiet.

D084.

"Addison, I'm not trying to keep you from your dreams or nothing," Winters says in a lower voice. "Believe me, I'm all for higher education. But . . . getting into college . . . college ain't for everyone. It's hard, hard work. And a lot of money. Now I think it's great you're trying and all, but . . . well, hell, I don't know, Addison. Maybe you shouldn't be getting your hopes all up and stuff."

Words of encouragement from my parole officer, that is what I can always count on. I don't say nothing. I turn away, wishing I didn't wish Ted was here instead.

"Actually, you know what, I take that back," he says. "Because out of everyone, I think you'd be the one to do it. Shit, you've come this far."

Winters sort of smiles, like he's proud or something.

"I don't think there's a girl in your house right now

who would even know where to start. Some of them don't even know their ass from their head half the time. But you're different, Addison. I saw that from the very first day. Which makes me wonder . . ."

His last sentence falls dead, eyes conflicted. I'm sure it's not common for a parole officer to think one of their parolees is actually innocent. But there is a huge question mark floating above his head like a comic bubble I've seen in the paper.

Maybe I should tell him . . .

"I hear you . . . um . . . got a lawyer and stuff to open your case back up."

I hold his gaze, trying to burn the truth through his eyes and he fidgets. He is uncomfortable around me. Always has been.

"Now, I've read your case files cover to cover," he says cautiously. "And in every testimony you were either silent as the grave or couldn't remember a thing. Think they call it 'post-traumatic stress.' They talk to you about that?"

I shift away from him.

"Addison, people know you didn't mean to kill that baby. They know you got . . . problems. But you can't come back, years later, with a whole new story."

"It's not a story."

"You were so young. No way you could remember what really happened."

That's where him and everyone else are wrong. Because I remember every single detail that happened that night.

Interview with Anonymous #3, Inmate at Bedford Hills Correctional Facility

Yo, it's mad easy to get little niggas to do your dirty work. We do it all the time, son! All you gotta do is give a kid a buck, give him a piece, and tell him who to pop. Done, easy. And if that little nigga gets caught, he ain't gonna do no real time. Maybe a year or two in juvie, but that ain't nothing. Better than a real nigga doing a quarter to life. Everyone knows kids get off stupid easy. Kids can get away with murder for real.

Ms. Cora lives in a brownstone in Bed-Stuy, one bus and a train ride away. It isn't as fancy as the ones I'd seen with Ted in Fort Greene, but it's decorated real nice on the outside. The windows are framed with white lights and garland, and the door has one of those Christmas wreaths with a big red bow like I've seen in picture books. I stand at the bottom of the stoop, staring up at the door, ten minutes early.

Maybe I should wait. She didn't have to invite me to her party. It was really nice of her and I don't want to be a pain in the ass, but it's freezing. I can't feel my fingers and my hoodie feels like a thin sheet. At least my neck is warm, because of the scarf Ms. Claire gave me. The rest of my body is a block of ice.

New Girl gave me the present I'm wearing. A long-sleeved maternity dress, green as broccoli. It was on my bed when I got out of the shower, all wrapped up in red tissue paper with a card that said, "To my BEST Friend." I feel guilty. I didn't get her anything.

"I thought I recognized yuh," a woman's voice says behind me.

Oh God! From the book!

That's how people know me. The baby killer, the child murderer. I turn around, expecting someone to spit in my face, but it is much worse.

Ms. Claire stands there smiling, flanked by two small girls dressed in red peacoats, white tights, and black patent leather shoes.

"Happy Christmas! How yuh?"

I'm outside my lawyer's house and about to run away because I'm a baby killer and don't want you to know. That's how I am doing.

Her daughters stare up at me, all small and innocent, nothing like I was. Ms. Claire looks so warm, dressed in a gray wool coat, the color of a summer rain cloud with four big black buttons.

"Yuh live here? Dis nice!"

I back away, my legs stiff from the cold. She sucks her teeth.

"Gyal, you're always so quiet! Why yuh look at me so? Meh not gonna hurt yuh. It's Christmas! And yuh . . ."

The door opens behind us and Ms. Cora steps out on the stoop.

"Mary! You made it!"

She runs down the stairs in a cream sweater dress and tall brown boots, hair flowing like black water in the breeze. I've never seen it down before; I had no idea it was so long. I look at Ms. Claire, frowning at this beauty queen running down after me. What do I say to her? How do I make her go away? She can't know. She'll never speak to me again.

"I was afraid you wouldn't come." She tries to hug me and I let her. She smiles at Ms. Claire.

"Um, hello," she says.

They glance at me, waiting for introductions. And all I want to do is run away. Ms. Claire sucks her teeth again and holds out her hand.

"Hello, I'm Claire, Mary's SAT tutor."

Ms. Cora lights up, nodding at me proudly, before shaking her hand.

"Nice to meet you! I'm Cora, Mary's . . . um, counselor."

Ms. Claire raises an eyebrow.

"I see. Well, we were heading to church and bumped into Ms. Mary 'ere. Just saying hello."

"Oh, well, I'll give you a moment," Ms. Cora says and

nods at me. "Nice meeting you! Mary, just come on in when you're ready."

She smiles and heads up the stairs. Ms. Claire turns to her daughters.

"Go wait in di car. Don't touch nuthin'!"

The girls skip off and climb into a car parked on the corner. They seem so fun and playful. Something I never was as a child. Ms. Claire stares at me with this knowing look.

"So . . . yuh okay?"

"Um, yeah. I . . . ummm . . ."

She holds up a hand.

"Yuh business. Meh not interfering."

The frosted winds bite at my ears and my chattering teeth nip at my tongue. She looks at her scarf, wrapped around my neck like a noose. I can't tell if she wants it back, but I know I don't want to give it to her.

"Test in two weeks. Yuh ready?"

"Yes."

"Good. Well, don't be rude to dem people and have di gyal waiting on yuh," she says. "And what have I tell yuh about coming out di house without proper clothes! Chuh!"

She takes off her beautiful gray coat with the black buttons and wraps it around my shoulders, still holding some of her warmth.

"D'there. Better, right? Now, meh see yuh next week. Lata."

She rubs her arms and walks down to the car, without giving me the chance to say thank you.

The house is a warm stove, busy and loud, full of people that look like Ms. Cora. In a houseful of Indians, I look like the black sheep.

Kids are playing under a huge Christmas tree. I mean, this tree could be the big, big tree in Rockefeller Center. And it's real too; makes the whole house smell like sweet syrup. It's been years since I've seen a real Christmas tree, or even a fake one. They don't bother with Christmas stuff in baby jail.

"Hey, everyone, this is Mary!" Ms. Cora says, and the party waves at me. I try to smile back but it feels funny on my face.

"Mary, are you hungry?"

I don't think it mattered if I was hungry or not because Ms. Cora's family wasted no time loading up my plate with all types of funny-looking food. Curry chicken, rice and peas, fried plantains, shark, macaroni pie. When I was done with my second plate, they gave me something called roti. I ate everything, all of it delicious. I've never had so much food in my entire life. Bean was very happy.

The family danced to reggae music, drinking rum punch, talking in their funny accents. I huddle next to the tree with some eggnog and a slice of black cake, rubbing the pine needles between my fingers, the sap sticky like cement glue. The last Christmas tree I ever touched was Alyssa's. That's what Mrs. Richardson called it, Alyssa's Christmas tree. She let me help decorate it with big sparkly red and gold bulbs. The last bulb was one she made special with Alyssa's name on it and the words "Baby's First Christmas."

Ms. Cora makes her way over to the tree, grabbing a giant blue gift bag with a big white Santa Claus face on the front.

"Happy Christmas," she says and places it on my lap. It's heavy, like a bagful of laundry, a month's worth. Another present I don't deserve.

"I can't take this."

She sits next to me.

"You haven't even opened it!"

"I didn't get you anything."

"Don't worry about it. You as a client is better than any gift. It's nothing too fancy."

I really wish she hadn't done this. I set the bag on the floor and remove the tissue paper. It's clothes, all folded up neat like stacks of bricks. I take out the first layer, a simple navy blue long-sleeved dress. It looks almost too big for me.

"My cousin Cheryl had a baby two months ago and she had all these maternity clothes she doesn't need anymore. She's about your size, so I had them dry-cleaned. Good as new."

My eyes ache like I want to cry. I don't though.

"You really believe me. Don't you?"

She laughs.

"Of course I do!"

"Why?"

She smiles, as if she was expecting me to ask this all along.

"First year of law school, second semester, Criminal Law," she says. "I'm one of a hundred students in the room. The beginning of every class, our professor would read a headline and we would all discuss and debate it. Your trial came up. He read the facts of the case, the manner it was all handled, and then he agreed with the outcome. So did ninety-nine percent of the class. But not me. I raised my hand and challenged my professor, who happened to also be the dean of the school. Someone should have told me, never cross the man who can make or break you.

"He made my entire law school life hell. No one wanted to associate with a blackballed student. But we were being taught to uphold the law, and founding principles state that everyone is entitled to a fair and balanced trial. So how could they offer a plea without a thorough investigation in your case? There were so many holes and possibilities in the story, and so many disgusting people who wanted you, a child, dead. It just made no sense.

"Even though most of the case and verdict was kept confidential, I cut out every newspaper and magazine article I could find, saved every website. Every term paper I wrote was about you. Some of the adjunct professors noticed my passion for your case and I built a reputation. Both good and bad. But it helped land me a job right out of school. You were a highlight of my law education. It was no accident that you called me. It was fate."

She blinks back tears and smiles. I don't know whether to feel guilty or grateful. I stare down in the bag of my much-needed new wardrobe. Is Ms. Cora an answer to my prayers? I stopped praying so long ago that I can't even remember what I asked for.

"Mary, what are you thinking?"

Mary, Mary, pretty little lamb . . . what are you thinking up in there.

"I'm thinking that I'm scared."

"Of what? Losing your baby?"

"No. Yeah, but . . . I'm scared of everything. Scared of all this we're doing . . . of what it's gonna do. What's gonna happen to me?"

Ms. Cora's face turns real serious.

"Mary, you're not scared. You're brave. It takes a brave girl to stand up and come clean. You calling me was brave. You standing up to your mother, really brave. You trying to go to school, fearless. All you've got to do now is tell the truth."

I swallow a lump in the back of my throat. The truth? I don't even know what that is anymore. I've been living a lie for so long.

"Thanks, Ms. Cora. No matter what happens, thank you."

She looks a little nervous, but smiles.

"We're going to win. And when we do, you'll get to keep your baby. And you'll have a whole new world in front of you. Which reminds me!"

She wraps her arm around my shoulders.

"SAT tutor? Why didn't you tell me? I had no idea you were interested in going to college. What made you decide?"

The twinkling tree lights bring me back to Alyssa's living room. I can almost smell the sugar cookies in the oven, the baby powder, and pinecones. Mrs. Richardson, singing along to the Christmas carols on the radio. Me, sweating in my itchy red sweater and wool stockings, holding Alyssa under the tree, between the presents and toys, reading 'Twas the Night Before Christmas. Mrs. Richardson took a picture of us. I was smiling extra hard because I wanted it to be perfect. Wonder if she still has that picture.

"Someone told me when you go to college, your life gets better. And you can escape what you were before and find who you're supposed to be," I say.

Ms. Cora nods and smiles.

"Whoever told you that knew what they were talking about."

I don't mention that that someone was Alyssa's mother.

chapter thirteen

Excerpt from <u>The Alyssa Richardson Story</u> by David Simmons (pg. 213)

But no one was more devastated by the ruling than Mr. Richardson, Alyssa's father.

"Manslaughter. That's all they gave her. A fucking slap on the wrist. You know what's another word for manslaughter? A mistake. An accident. That's what they said happened to my little girl. They didn't see her. They didn't see the bruises all over her. She had a black eye, like she was in a fucking bar fight! She was just a baby! There was no fucking mistake about it! My little girl was murdered! I wanted that little bitch in jail for life!"

"Why are we here?" I whisper, since the halls in the court-house echo at the littlest sound.

"The judge wants to hear oral arguments based on the motion," Ms. Cora says without looking up from her papers. We are sitting on a bench in front of a giant window. You can see the thick snow clouds hovering low in the sky, threatening to soak my sneakers and freeze off my toes.

"But . . . why am I here?"

She gives me a serious look.

"Because I want you to see what we're up against for yourself."

I swallow, straightening my blue dress under Ms. Claire's coat. Ms. Cora stares off, not in a daydreaming type of way, more like she's concentrating, so I keep quiet. Her hair is in a tight bun, not like it was at the Christmas party. I feel special, knowing I've seen it that way.

I turn my head a little to sniff the coat collar. Smells like her; oranges and cocoa butter. Yesterday, I stopped at the dollar store to buy some cocoa butter. Five dollars and eighty-five cents. I remembered Mrs. Richardson used to rub it on her stomach when Alyssa was still in her belly. Momma said it was so she wouldn't get stretch marks. Momma knows a lot about being pregnant. I wish I could talk to her about it; I really don't know what I'm doing. And why hasn't she come by? I hope she's taking her pills.

As soon as he steps in front of us, I remember him. He has gained a couple of pounds in the face that evens out the rest of his hefty body and he still wears silver shiny suits that make him look like a nickel but his blond hair is exactly the same.

"Boy, you sure grew up fast," he says, glaring down at my stomach with a sly smile.

I don't move. I'm afraid if I move even an inch, I'll try to kill him. He reaches his hand out to Ms. Cora and I almost slap it away. I don't want him to touch her, not even a handshake.

"Michel Rabinovitch. I don't believe we've met, young lady."

She stands, raising an eyebrow.

"Cora Fisher. And I've heard a lot about you."

He laughs. I remember his laugh too. A disgusting loud cackle, mouth all open, spit flying out.

"I'm sure all good things."

He takes another look at me and smiles.

"Well, guess we should get this show on the road," he says, winking at Ms. Cora. "See you in there."

Mr. Jerk Face, or Michel Rabinovitch, is the man who put me away.

Now I know why judges wear those long black robes; because it's mad cold in this courtroom, like the seats were left outside overnight. I didn't want to take off my coat;

it makes me feel safe. But no one else had one on, so I figured it'd be weird if I didn't. I count nine people in the room. Last time I was here, they took me straight to baby jail. Ms. Cora says they can't do that today, and I'm trying real hard to believe her. I can't go back to the cell with the cement blocks and no windows. I can't have Bean on a prison floor. But there is nowhere to run if today goes bad.

The old redheaded lady sitting above us in her black robe and thin red glasses looks like a mean grandma. Papers and folders exchange between her and an officer, discussions and the same questions asked over and over in three different ways. Ms. Cora presents, then Mr. Jerk Face. Back and forth and back and forth . . . Judge Conklin doesn't look at me once. No one does.

And Ms. Cora and Mr. Jerk Face are talking about me like I'm not even in the room.

"Your Honor," Mr. Jerk Face says. "Alyssa's family wants to be left at peace. Why on earth would we want to put them through this again based on a story with no real evidence?"

Ms. Cora, standing with her hands folded in front of her like a church steeple, is real calm. Unlike Terry, who is sitting on the other side of me, fidgeting, flipping through files, and taking notes. Don't know why he's nervous. He doesn't have to go back to baby jail, I do.

"New evidence and testimony confirms findings from the original investigation. Further, Mary wasn't allowed a fair trial, especially when her mother, a possible suspect, had power of attorney and accepted a plea on behalf of her daughter to save herself."

Mr. Jerk Face laughs, that nasty cackle, reminding me of Ray. Speaking of Ray, I wonder why no one ever brings him up. He played as much a part in this as I did when it comes to Momma being crazy. I guess because he's dead. I know how, I just don't feel like talking about it.

"New evidence has emerged? You mean a new story has emerged. If Mary lied before, how do we know she's not lying now?"

"Mary never lied. She never said she murdered Alyssa. Conclusions were deduced based on the testimony provided by her mother. Mary told the truth. She didn't know what happened to Alyssa."

"She didn't know what happened then, but knows what happened now?"

"Mary was a child at the time. It was understandably difficult for her to articulate the events that transpired."

Mr. Jerk Face shakes his head. His two assistants, an older blond woman and a young black guy, pass him notes.

"Okay. Let's all cool our heads and think about this logically here. You're talking about opening up a case so a teenage convict can keep her baby? Am I the only one looking at the bigger picture here? What kind of life could she provide for the infant? No source of income, no education, no adequate living arrangements. She can't possibly raise her child in a group home."

"Women do it. All the time. But her current situation is not on trial here. Her parental rights should not be stripped because of a crime she did not commit."

Even though she said it, I hope she doesn't really think Bean and I can stay at the group home. I'd rather live on the streets with the rats and pigeons.

Mr. Jerk Face is confused and baffled. It's an SAT word I think, *bemused*.

"Dozens of psychologists confirmed she is unbalanced and needs lifelong psychiatric treatment. Her current situation is exactly what we need to focus on to determine her current mental state."

"Their findings were inconclusive. You have a dozen that say she's unbalanced, but there's another dozen that found her mentally sound and capable to stand trial, even as a child."

Mr. Jerk Face flips through his notes, punishing the papers.

"One of these psychologists concluded, and I quote, 'Mary could quite unfathomably suffer from an undiagnosed bipolar disorder, resulting in her manic break.' Then goes on to list the multiple medications, still prescribed to her this very day."

Ms. Cora swallows, face stiffening. We never talked about my pills. We never talked about my time at the hospital. I'm too embarrassed to. I hate anyone knowing I was like that.

"They also said she had ADHD," she snaps. "But none of the standardized approved evaluations proved that to be the case. On top of that, three doctors confirmed she was highly intelligent."

Mr. Jerk Face's eye bulges. He's really mad now.

"Eight months she went without talking. Eight months!"

"Which was the result of her traumatic experience! Every doctor, including the one that you so eloquently quoted, confirmed she suffered from an acute case of post-traumatic stress. She witnessed a murder, committed by her own mother—her sole provider and protector—and was then instructed to cover up the evidence, making her an unwilling and unknowing accomplice. At nine years old, she did not have the capacity to make her own decisions, especially in a frantic situation, involving a death. She was, as described in her testimony, doing what she was told by an authoritative figure."

Judge Conklin doesn't say a word. She just sits there, her lips in a thin red line, watching their Ping-Pong game.

"So what do you suggest, counselor?" Mr. Jerk Face asks. "How do you plan to prove this new version of events?"

Ms. Cora exhales. Maybe for the first time since they started.

"Based on the new testimony, evidence needs to be reexamined to confirm the findings. We need to exhume the body."

Mr. Jerk Face jumps like he's been hit by lightning.

"You can't possibly be serious!" Mr. Jerk Face yells. "Your Honor!"

Exhume is another SAT word. It means to dig something out of the ground. Usually a body.

Wait, she's the one who wants to dig up Alyssa?

The whole room spins faster. No no no no . . . I can't see Alyssa like that! Skin rotting, a pile of bones covered in dirt . . . my stomach heaves just thinking about it. I touch Ms. Cora's leg. She looks down at me, annoyed, mouthing, "Not now."

"Okay. I think I've heard enough," Judge Conklin says, organizing some papers in front of her. The room takes a deep breath. Mr. Jerk Face's black assistant is looking at me, sort of the way Sales Guy at the Duane Reade did before Ted threatened him. Mr. Jerk Face catches him and glares. Judge Conklin passively rearranges some more papers on her desk, sipping water.

"I'll consider your arguments while reviewing the motions and evidence before making a decision on how to proceed." She looks at Ms. Cora. "Counselor, I'm ordering another psych evaluation for Miss Addison. I'd also like to see all evaluations from the past six years and subsequent reentry treatment reports."

"Your Honor, the reports submitted include all that was documented," Ms. Cora says.

Conklin looks down, then back up quickly. Her frown

makes a deep *V* on her small face.

"There are only seven reports here," she says.

Ms. Cora nods. "Yes, Your Honor."

"You mean to tell me that in the last six years, she has only been evaluated seven times?"

Mr. Jerk Face jumps in.

"Your Honor, reports state that she refused to communicate with officials and—"

"That is no excuse, counselor," Conklin snaps. "Whether she talks or not, the final judgment was *very* clear that she should receive thorough treatment."

"Your Honor, we're waiting for any additional evaluations from social services and the group home therapist that were not ready in time for today's hearing."

She chuckles. "You mean, you're waiting for them to magically make up reports that should have been filed years ago?"

Ms. Cora smirks while Conklin picks up another file, reading it over again. Mr. Jerk Face glances at me, looking stressed and almost frustrated. Nothing like he was before. I almost feel sorry for him, for chasing a lie for so many years. He meets my stare and we share a moment. We're the only two people in this room that share a history.

"Young lady?"

Oh God, she's talking to me!

"No," I whimper, clutching my seat, and my whole body starts to tremble hard.

Ms. Cora snatches me up by the arm. Feeling too heavy for my legs, I sway forward. This is the part where she sends me away, back to baby jail, back to my cell. No no no no no!

Ms. Cora holds me steady while I try to pull away, whimpering and begging. She promised, she swore they wouldn't take me! She shakes her head and mouths, "It's okay."

"Relax, Mary," she whispers, rubbing my arms. "It's okay, it's okay. Deep breaths."

Conklin flips through her files, eyeing me.

"Miss Addison, did you ever talk to a . . . Dr. Yarsmin Kendrick?"

I shake my head, eyes on the floor.

"Dr. Kendrick is your state-appointed psychiatrist. Have you met with Ms. Natasha Charles?"

I shake my head.

"Ms. Charles is your state-appointed legal counsel. Were you at all in contact with Ms. Charles before hiring your present legal counsel?"

Huh? What is she talking about?

"What about April Madison? Maria Straves? Ira Howard? Or Anne Marie L'Faunt?"

None of these names sound familiar except Anne Marie. That sounds like Annie. She gave me a big book on space and *National Geographic* magazines. She was really nice.

"Annie," I mumble.

She sighs and closes the file.

"Annie was your first social worker. The rest are all the social workers after her that you have no recollection of meeting, yet your files have vague logs of their visitations."

Mr. Jerk Face is quiet. Ms. Cora smiles at me, as if to say "good job."

"Prosecutor, I want your office to do a thorough investigation into this matter," Ms. Conklin says to Mr. Jerk Face. "I'm interested in knowing why a direct court ruling was blatantly ignored. Per her records, she has been seeing teachers and psychologists every other week for the past six years, but I only see seven status reports. If you ask me, it appears that these visitation logs are either completely inaccurate or forged. I would hate to think the latter."

Mr. Jerk Face is red, steam blowing out of his ears.

"Also, prosecutor, I'd like to hear the mother's side of things."

I stop breathing and fall back into my chair.

Shit. They're going to talk to Momma?

"Don't forget, when yuh don' know the answer, eliminate at least two choices then guess," Ms. Claire says, putting some books away. She asked me to stop by her office to pick up some paperwork so I went right after court since it was close. Now that I'm here, I think all she wanted to do was talk, but my hands are shaking.

"And don' tink about di time. Just move like yuh have

somewhere to be. Get a good night's rest so yuh nah yawning and so forth. And don' be late!"

"Will you be there?" I ask, a tremble in my voice.

She smiles. "No. Meh only run di practice test. Don' worry! Yuh be fine."

But I won't be fine. Not without Ms. Claire. Not without Ted. Doing this was all for us. And now, I don't know if it's even worth it anymore.

"Eh eh, what's wrong wit yuh?"

I don't say nothing. I'm not ready to tell her the truth yet but Ms. Claire is the type of lady that gets stuff out of you with a stare.

"There's this . . . guy," I sigh, feeling mad foolish.

She frowns and waves me off.

"Yuh see me 'ere, don' even think about anything else but dis test! Dis 'ere is all that matter. Take yuh further than any ras-clat boi."

I smile. She sounds so funny when she's mad. She shakes her head with a grin.

"Swell belly gyal, yuh have more important tings to worry about than some boi."

My hands are still shaking as I walk into the house, but I'm not back in baby jail so that's all that really matters. Ready for check-in, I head to the back and see Ms. Carmen standing in Ms. Stein's office with some lady I've never seen before. She looks like she could be Kelly's older sister but dressed like Ms. Cora. Real official-like; must be another social worker or something. They talk in hushed whispers, none of them seeming happy about seeing each other. I stand off to the side, trying to stay out of sight. Ms. Stein squirms in her sweaty skin, two seconds away from puking. Why is she nervous? I'm so caught up that I don't even notice Joi standing behind me.

"Damn, psycho, you brought the heat on you now," she whispers, looking over my shoulder. "That's Leah. She's, like, the big boss at ACS. Used to visit the last group home I was in. And if she's here, you definitely in trouble. She sends kids to Crossroads mad quick."

I've heard stories about Crossroads. It's a juvenile detention center in Brownsville, the last stop before hell, purgatory. It's the place they return you to when you act up in group or foster homes. One night there and a kid can come out with cracked ribs, a broken jaw, and a hundred stitches. Ted stayed there. His hands were proof all those stories were true.

"Well, things have been . . . busy here," Ms. Stein says, all defensive, lips in a tight line. Ms. Leah shakes her head.

"You know, after everything you've been through, I figured you wanted nothing to do with kids," Ms. Leah says.

Ms. Stein shifts, squinting at her like she's the sun. "This is a little . . . easier than fieldwork."

"Is it?" Ms. Leah says, almost like a laugh. "You

complained about your caseload, but you can't even handle one girl!"

Ms. Stein fidgets, at a loss for what to say.

"I heard Ms. Stein used to work with her back in the day," Joi whispers. "But then Ms. Stein got fired 'cause one of the kids she was supposed to be checking for got beat by his daddy and died. Said she had too many cases and couldn't keep up."

My mouth drops. She used to be a social worker? Damn, no wonder she hates me. No wonder she don't want me to keep Bean!

"What? You didn't know?" Joi grins and walks away before I notice Ms. Leah nod in my direction.

"Is that her?"

Ms. Stein spins around and glares at me. "Yeah. That's her."

"You sure you can handle this?" Ms. Leah says to Ms. Stein, voice laced with a warning.

Ms. Stein's back straightens. "We got everything under control."

Something about the way she said that crunches fear right into my bones.

chapter fourteen

One wallet with picture ID, check. Three number two pencils, check. One pen, blue ink, check. One graphing calculator, check. One bottle of water, one bag of peanuts, one apple, one pack of graham crackers from the nursing home (in case I get hungry), check.

I'm ready.

I packed my book bag before dinner since I'm on kitchen duty this week and would be too tired to do it afterward. I set my alarm for 6:00 a.m. so I could get there early, like Ms. Claire told me to.

This is it. This is my chance to go to college. To get a degree so I can get a good job and find a safe place for me and Bean. The place I was supposed to have with Ted. Wonder if he thinks about me as much as I try not to think about him. In the shower, the cold water rides over my stomach. It's growing fast, a big ball attached to a thin stick. Bean, my baby boy. Baby Benson. I'd do anything for him and he doesn't even know it. I should start thinking of a middle name. Maybe after the test.

Pajamas on and ready for sleep, I'm at ease for a change as I walk into my room. Until I see Kelly, sitting on my bed, my SAT book in her hands.

"What's up, psycho!"

New Girl is a statue on her bed, hands folded in her lap like she is praying. Kelly smirks and throws the book on the floor. If she moves her hand a half an inch, she'll feel my knife under the pillow. I shuffle over to my right, hoping to make it to the stick hiding behind the door first.

"So, you're still trying to take the SATs? You really think you're going to college? With what money? And who is gonna hire you? They don't hire people with records, dumb ass. Didn't they tell you that?"

I swallow, inching over slightly, unable to ignore the twitch of fear that she is right. Kelly stands up slow with a satisfied grin.

"Good night, Sarah," she says, all pleasant-like. "Nice talking to you."

She strolls out, our eyes locked on each other. As soon as she passes the threshold, I slam the door shut and whip around.

"What the hell was she doing in here!"

"Nothing," New Girl stutters.

"Then why'd you let her in?"

"I didn't! I came upstairs and she was sitting on your bed and—"

"She was here by herself!"

I run to my side of the room, shift the nightstand, and feel around back. The money is still there.

The alarm doesn't go off. I think Jesus woke me up instead, twenty-five minutes before the test. I jump, slip on my clothes and sneakers, barely tying them. I can't believe New Girl is still asleep with me running around the room, bumping into furniture like a blind woman. Twenty minutes.

It takes Ms. Reba five whole grumbling painful minutes to check me out and open the door. I have to run. Run with Bean in my belly. I run four blocks in the early morning frost, my lungs about to pop out my mouth. Panting, I hail a gypsy cab on the corner. I tell him the address. He tells me eighteen dollars. Now ten minutes.

I eat an apple on the way, the tart juices drooling down my chin. I still can't catch my breath. How did my alarm not go off? I know I set it. I know I did.

With five minutes left, I get to the school and run to the end of the line, coughing and wheezing up air. I can't catch my breath in the time it takes me to get to the front of the line. Everyone is staring, waiting for me to die instead of offering me some water. The old white lady at the registration table takes my ticket. I miss Ms. Claire.

"Mary Addison?"

I nod, swallowing air in gulps. I'm hungry, which means Bean is starving.

"Mary Addison? Hmmm . . . why do I know that name?"

The room goes black and silent.

She knows!

My knees collapse like a bridge and I hold the table to keep from falling. She flips through her papers, glaring up at me, trying to place my face and name in her memory like a puzzle piece. She finds my name on the list and gives me a fake smile.

"Okay, can I see your ID?" she asks.

It takes a moment for me to move before I rummage through my bag, looking twice, then again in all the pockets. Where's my wallet?

Don't panic. Don't panic.

Old Lady pushes up her green glasses as I search again. My wallet . . . it's gone.

"I . . . I . . . can't find it."

"Okay, well, I need you to step aside until you can find it. Quickly now, you only have a few minutes left before we start," she says.

I rush to the corner and dump my bag out on the floor, pencils and snacks scattering. Old Lady is whispering to her friend, pointing at me, and I try to ignore her.

She knows. I know she knows. She read the book about me. She knows what I did.

A fly buzzes near my ear. I shoo it away and keep digging, but there is no wallet anywhere. Did I leave it in the cab? No, I took the twenty dollars out of my hiding spot and had it in my hand the whole time, even when I was running. Did I forget to pack it? No, that was the first thing I packed. Did it fall out somewhere? If it did, it would be long gone. No wallet would live on the streets of Brooklyn for five minutes. But I know I didn't drop it. I know it didn't fall out. I don't lose things. That is not something I do.

Blackout? No, I'm not having blackouts anymore. I remember everything now. But what happened to my wallet?

Kelly.

She was in our room, alone.

The lady looks dead faced with disgust as I return to the table.

"Did you find your ID?" she asks. Her entire tone and body language has changed.

She knows. And she hates me.

"No."

"Then I'm afraid you can't take the exam."

I don't attempt to beg. I just walk out.

● ● ●

A quarter after five, I walk in the group home, soaking from freezing rain, the mirror greeting me. The top of my ponytail looks like a coconut-shaved icy. I'm so tired that just the thought of stairs makes me want to sleep on the floor in front of them. Bean is making me weaker, my muscles turning into jelly. With every step I can feel the extra weight slowing me down. It'll make running from Kelly much harder.

Pots and pans clash in the kitchen.

"I told you to turn the chicken over! What are you, stupid? You're gonna burn my dinner! Put the cheese sauce on. Reby, why didn't you tell her to put the sauce on?"

My wet sneakers squeak on the floor as I slip them off. My ankle bracelet is a tight rubber band, pinching my skin. The first time Ted and I did it, our ankle bracelets clicked and clacked under the sheets like fighting Legos. I laughed the same time Ted did. I miss his laugh.

Maybe if I run away, I would be free. Free to live with Ted and Bean. The only life I really wanted. It's what I've been fighting for, trying to do the right thing for once. But every step forward I take is another two steps back. Today is a perfect example of that. Maybe if I just do wrong, I can actually get what I want.

"Damn it, Reba! You forgot my damn donuts! And where's Mary? Did she clean them bathrooms yet? I need to go!"

How did I wind up here? Why didn't I just tell the truth

from the start? But if I told the truth, Momma would be in jail. She'd forget to take her pills, hang herself or something. She tried it before. How could I live with myself if she did that?

But how can I live here?

My eye is twitching. Maybe I should start taking my pills again. No, that won't do me any good. And I got Bean, can't take pills with a Bean in my belly.

Joi strolls in with empty plates for the dinner table.

"We're having chicken and beans tonight."

I nod, wringing the water out of my socks. This is her version of small talk. This is what she starts with, meaningless information before she gets to what she really wants to say.

"Oh yeah! And New Girl's mom died," she adds with a grin, continuing her stroll to the dining room. I take a deep breath, looking up the stairs.

Damn.

My bare feet touch the top of the first landing. What am I supposed to say to her? She must be devastated and "I'm sorry" doesn't seem like enough. Not when you lose a parent. A mother. Maybe I shouldn't say nothing, just leave her to be in her feelings. Like I do best, mind my business. But New Girl is the only person in the house who believes me. If it wasn't for her, I would've never met Ms. Cora. They would have just taken Bean away. I owe her.

I make my footsteps loud so she knows I'm coming,

giving her time. That's what I would've wanted. A moment to prepare myself. To pretend I'm okay when I'm really not, inhale that last real breath before holding it all in, a pipe ready to explode.

The bedroom door is wide open. New Girl sits in a chair in the middle of the room, facing the window, stiff as stone. I stand in the doorway without a clue of what to say. I want to sound real and sincere, like Benson would, but the words are stuck in my throat like a mouse on a glue trap. I clear my throat and ask something basic.

"You okay?"

New Girl's wavy hair covers her like a blanket. I never noticed how long it was before. It reaches her lower back, coils and curls at the tips like snakes. She stares out into the gray sky, the rain hitting the window with a soft patter, her left knee jittering.

"Sarah?"

She's playing with something in her hands I can't see, twirling it around over and over. I close the door behind me and keep my distance, this time not out of habit, but instincts. The room feels strange, off somehow. Something's not right.

"Sarah?"

New Girl is breathing funny, like she just finished running twenty miles. Then her slumped shoulders straighten. She stands real slow, turning with the biggest grin spread across her face.

Satan's grin.

"I did it. I finally did it. I finally killed her!"

New Girl giggled all through dinner, quietly to herself, and only I noticed. Drunk on happiness, she inhaled her food, even licking the fork and asking for seconds. My stomach, filled with fear, had no room for food.

After an "emergency" therapy session, Ms. Veronica holds her back so they can talk alone. As soon as I see them together, I run up to our room. I need to prepare for my first night with this new New Girl. Maybe she isn't new. Maybe I never knew her at all and she's always been this way. How could I've been so stupid to let someone in so deep?

I switch the hiding spot for my money, then move all my secret weapons for easy access. All the plans I had in place for Kelly I now have to use on New Girl. It seems wrong, and not enough. She can kill me in my sleep without anyone knowing. I've got to stay awake because I finally realize what that feeling was when I first walked in the room and found New Girl in that chair. It's the same feeling I have whenever I'm alone with Momma. It's the feeling of danger.

New Girl opens the door as I shove the mattress back in place. Even with my knife snug in my pajama pants, I still don't feel safe. She stares at me, almost a glare, then takes in the room, her eyes falling back on me.

"What are you doing?"

Her voice is so innocent and childlike. Doesn't make sense with what I know is lurking inside her. Blackness, every organ in her body covered with it, running through her veins, seeping out her pores, suffocating us in this room.

"Nothing," I mumble, fluffing my pillow. I slip under the covers, pulling them up to my chin, wishing I could go back in my old room with Tara. It'd be safer than in here.

She gives me an uneasy stare then dresses for bed. I move my pillow in front of Bean, keeping my hand wrapped around my knife under the covers. Twenty minutes later, lights-out, the house quiets down. The moon glows through the window, turning the room navy blue. High on fear, my head throbs, drumming on my temples. I'm thirsty and hungry, but I can't move because New Girl is still up too. I can feel her eyes on me.

"You think I'm going to hurt you, don't you?"

"Doesn't matter what I think," I say.

She sits up, hugging her knees to her chest.

"You're afraid of me."

She said it as a statement so I don't respond, because she's right. I'm scared as hell. And I have so many questions. I want to know how and why, but questions get you into trouble. Questions make you involved, and I don't want to be involved with her.

Suddenly, she springs up from the bed and begins to pace around the room. Every time she comes close, my heart skips into my throat. I sit up and switch on the lamp so I can really see. The light bounces off her pale skin, eyes like firecrackers, smile so wide it takes up her whole face.

"I can't believe it," she says excitedly. "I did it! Took a little longer than I thought, but I did it! Ha!"

Is anyone listening to this? And if they are, would they help if she attacks? I doubt it. I don't have a friend left in this house. I clutch the knife under my pillow tighter.

"She was in a coma for so damn long! I thought she'd wake up or something. But she didn't."

New Girl is pacing fast now, bare feet slapping against the wood floor, chewing on her nails. I brace myself, imagining her lunging at any moment. She is playing with something in her hand again; it looks small and shiny, but I can't tell what it is. She notices me staring and opens her palm. It's a ring, with three big diamonds.

"Look! This was hers! I took it from her before . . . well . . . doesn't matter. She doesn't need it anymore."

Numbness comes over me quick. Did she steal it before she pushed her down the stairs or after?

"I . . . I gotta call my lawyer tomorrow," she says, mad giddy. "Oh, I can pay for him with this! I'm free now! Isn't this great?"

"Free?"

She cocks her head to the side and smiles at me, like parents do when their child asks dumb questions. It's a look I've been getting all my life.

"Mary, you got to believe me. She wouldn't leave me

alone. Kept making me do all their chores, go to church EVERY Sunday. Ballet lessons, music lessons, on and on. I NEVER got a break. I NEVER got to do anything I wanted!"

"Did she . . . beat you?"

New Girl stops pacing.

"Well, no. But it's just like abuse. That's what my lawyer says. Mental abuse. She called me names! She controlled me! I know about it. I've studied it."

I don't know anything about mental abuse, but I do know New Girl is definitely insane.

"Oh," I mumble.

New Girl gasps, looking like another SAT word: *incredulous*.

"After everything that's happened, don't you want your mother dead too? Look where you are! Look what she's done to you!"

Words fall dead in my mouth. She's right, why wouldn't I want Momma dead? It's her fault I'm in this mess to begin with. But wanting Momma dead and actually doing it . . . two totally different things.

"See, Mary," she says with a smirk. "You of all people should understand. You're just like me! And now we'll both be free! Together! Just you and me."

Yes, I'm an idiot for trusting anyone in this house, even innocent mousy-looking white girls like New Girl, but I'm far from her.

"I'm nothing like you," I hiss, eyes narrowing.

Her smile drops. She looks me up and down, then coughs up a gasp.

"Wow. You really believe that, don't you?"

"Okay, Mary, remember what I said. No beating around the bush. I want you to tell this woman everything you've told me. Matter of fact, more than you've told me," Ms. Cora says.

She walks fast through the halls of a plain office building somewhere downtown, her heels mute against the carpet, carrying her briefcase. I waddle fast, trying to keep up. She seems mad edgy and impatient today.

"Just be calm and tell her the truth."

The truth, the truth, the truth . . .

"And I mean it, Mary! Don't leave anything out."

"Have I before?"

"Well, you weren't exactly forthcoming about your medication, now were you?"

Damn, is that what this is all about? She stops midstride with a grimace, shaking her head.

"Sorry, Mary. I didn't mean that," she says. "Stress is getting to me. I just . . . hate surprises, that's all."

She gives me a fake smile that I don't return and continues down the hall while I follow, shaking off the sting of her words.

"Okay," she says as we reach the end of the hall.

"Here we go. Suite 1603."

She pushes the heavy metal door and we step into warm golden light. This office is not like a regular psychiatrist's office, or at least, not any I've been to. Cream walls with black Chinese symbols in thin frames, tan chairs with green leafy plants scattered around. On the coffee table, a waterfall pours over moss-covered rocks. It's beautiful and peaceful, like we're in the middle of a rain forest.

"Nice," Ms. Cora mutters, just as a side door opens.

A white lady with short silver hair and a long burgundy dress comes out, smiling. Her teeth perfect and bright.

"Hi, Mary," she says. "It's nice to see you again."

Ms. Cora does a double take as the woman extends her wrinkly hand. I want to slap it away. Who the hell is this and what does she mean by "again"?

"Wait a minute, are you saying you've met with Mary before?"

She frowns, staring as if she expects me to back her up. I don't say nothing.

"Yes. Twice, actually. And hello, by the way. I'm Dr. Cross."

Ms. Cora and I exchange the same shocked look.

What! She's lying! I've never seen this lady a day in my life!

The smoke from her incense floats into the room. Ms. Cora flusters, failing to contain her fury.

"Then . . . why was it never reported? I've never seen your name in any of her files!"

Dr. Cross frowns, glancing at me then back at Ms. Cora. I struggle, but can't place her face anywhere. This is a trick, set up by Mr. Jerk Face, I bet. We should go.

"I've submitted reports about Mary, on both occasions," she says defensively. "I have no idea why they wouldn't be in her files."

"Well, do you have a copy of the reports?"

She sighs. "Unfortunately, my older case files were all lost in a basement flood during the storm."

Ms. Cora snorts, crossing her arms. "How convenient."

Dr. Cross's eyebrow arches, her lips in a tight line. She glares at Ms. Cora before nodding in my direction.

"The color of the belt that made the scar on the back of your neck . . . it was brown, right?"

My mouth drops and I almost faint on the spot.

How did she know that!

Ms. Cora is motionless, eyes wide. Dr. Cross smirks.

"Some things you can't forget. Why don't we talk inside my office?"

She gestures to the door and I step back. No goddamn way I'm going with this mind reader anywhere! Ms. Cora touches my arm, her fingertips cold.

"Go," she croaks. With a gulp, I follow Dr. Cross into her office.

"Don't be afraid, Mary," she says, smiling. "We're just going to talk a little bit about your past."

That is what the last doctor told me too.

chapter fifteen

Six months. That is how far along I am; six months pregnant. Three more to go before Bean gets here. Time is running out and my problems seem to be getting worse instead of better.

I haven't slept in weeks since this new New Girl showed up. This new New Girl is becoming best friends with Kelly. The house seems smaller and smaller with both of them in it. And I'm getting bigger and bigger.

Momma came by yesterday, but she was as far away as the moon. She had that strange look in her eye, like she was going to try to swallow all her pills again and leave me. Having "a day." I don't think she noticed how big I was. I don't even think she meant to come by and see me. The part of her that is still there was just looking for something familiar.

The nursing home is also becoming a problem. Ted, for the most part, has given up trying to talk to me. But I can't hide my pregnancy as easily as I did in the beginning, and the staff is starting to notice. The same people that have seen me and Ted together all the time. Sooner or later, they are going to put two and two together. Still, I go, because it's ten times safer than the group home.

The pimp from 211 had a stroke last month. He's back from the hospital, but not the same. The right side of his body is paralyzed. He can't pinch butts or talk slick without slurring and drooling.

"Mr. Abernathy. How are you feeling today?" the nurse shouts. She is a tall woman, so he has to strain to look up at her. "You want your paper? You used to like reading every day."

He grumbles, tears in his eyes, and looks back at the TV. He doesn't want to be reminded of what he used to do.

"Well, here, just try."

The nurse leaves the paper on the tray attached to his wheelchair and nods at me before walking off. I wait until she is long gone and then take the memory of his past life from in front of him. He gives me a look that is neither friendly nor mean, more like relieved. The Sunday paper is like a thick and heavy book, which I love. I grab a pen and huddle with it in the corner, out of habit, I guess.

The first word I circle is in the business section,

appropriate. I know that word, I just like the way it sounds. Usually, I skip the entertainment section because it's nothing but fantasies, except this time, my name is in the headline . . .

Excerpt from the New York Times: "Lifetime Set to Film the Mary Addison Story"

Lifetime network has begun development on a new TV movie, The Devil Inside, *based on the novel by Jude Mitchell. The movie revolves around the death of three-month-old Alyssa Richardson, tortured and beaten to death by then nine-year-old Mary Addison. This is off the heels of Lifetime's success with their original movie slates based on the lives of Elizabeth Smart and Anna Nicole Smith.*

Addison, recently released and on house arrest, is currently being represented by the Absolution Project, claiming her innocence. The case has been set for appeal. Producers say the outcome of the case will have no bearing on the adaptation. Production will begin next summer.

Black ink smears under my finger. A book is one thing, but a movie? For hundreds of millions of people to see? People like Ms. Claire, the nursing home, the girls . . . all to watch and know.

Tears come, breath wheezing through a small pipe, and I explode. The newspapers are everywhere, weeds of my past, springing up in TV rooms, coffee tables, reception desks, and nightstands. I collect them all like flowers. Up and down the stairs, room by room, I gather. No one stops me. No one knows why they should. I carry the heavy stack of papers to the janitor's closet, shoving them to the bottom of a garbage barrel. But the problem still remains; I can't bury all the papers in the world, just like I can't bury my past. So no matter where I go, Alyssa will be there. I'll never be able to hide from the mistake that wasn't mine alone. I try and try . . . but she won't leave me. It's too much to bear . . .

I bite down on my arm and let out the biggest scream, so hard it ripples back down my throat and Bean stirs. I bite harder, tasting the salty sweat and blood, the pain no match for the hysteria inside. My eyes fill with tears, buckets of them. I bite harder, the scream stuck and muffled in my throat, straining my neck, until my whole body turns red, trembling like a seizure. I bite harder.

That's when I notice his sneakers on the floor in the corner, hiding behind the sink. The new ones, under a black duffel bag next to a pile of sheets and blankets, a makeshift bed. I dig around the bag full of his clothes, stuff my face inside, and inhale. His smell devours my pain.

Ted.

It takes one minute to process what is happening.

I find him mopping in the TV room on the fourth floor, a few patients asleep in their wheelchairs around him. It's been such a long time since I took a real hard look at him.

The hair on his baby face makes him look like a tired old man who belongs on the second floor. He notices me by the door, but doesn't say anything. He is used to me ignoring him now. I step on the wet floor.

"Stop," he snaps. "You'll slip and fall."

The floor is slick with water and generic Pine-Sol. I take another step toward him.

"Yo, I said stop! I'm not playing."

The floor is like black ice. I take another step and my foot slides a little farther than I wanted it to. Grabbing the air, I try to hold in a gasp. Ted throws down the mop and stomps over. He yanks me by the arm, dragging me to a dry patch of floor.

"What are you doing! You know what could've happened if you fell? You could've hit your fucking stomach! You could've hurt the baby! What the fuck is wrong with you?"

It feels good, this rough-handed shaking, the pinch of his fingers around my skin. It almost feels like love. I curl into his chest, breathing in his scent, wanting it never to end. He stops, letting me wrap around him tighter, stomach spacing us apart. His heart beats a familiar rhythm of calming music.

"Your feelings are showing," I whisper, knowing he wouldn't be this mad if he didn't care.

He presses his nose into my hair and inhales. The nerves return to his body as he defrosts and hugs me back.

"So you think Kelly stole your wallet?"

Damp of sweat, Ted and I hold each other for what seems

like a lifetime in a patient's bed on the fifth floor. The delirious cries in the background are like the comforting sounds of my childhood. I miss Momma. I shouldn't, but I do.

"I don't know anything anymore."

He presses his ear to my bare stomach, listening to Bean dance around.

"Did you tell the lawyer?"

"I don't know what to say."

He looks up at me.

"Say you have to get out of there. Now."

"I don't know," I mumble.

He smooths his hand over my skin.

"What about your moms?"

I swallow and hug him tighter.

"She's not any safer either."

Transcript from the February 2nd Interview with Mrs. Dawn Cooper-Worthington

Detective: Hello, Ms. Cooper, remember me?

Dawn: It's Mrs. Worthington.

Detective: I'm sorry. Mrs. Worthington.

Attorney: Detective, let's not play games here. Mrs. Worthington came here willingly and would like to speed this along if you please. She's an upstanding citizen, member of her church, with an impeccable record. She would like to be completely absolved from this matter once and for all.

Detective: Oh really? How kind of her to be here. How kind of you both. Well, we do have some questions.

Dawn: You asked me plenty six years ago. Lord only knows what's come up now that I haven't already answered.

Detective: Fair enough, I'll skip to the new stuff. Mrs. Worthington, are you a religious person?

Dawn: What kind of question is that?

Attorney: Speak plainly, detective, we don't have all day.

Detective: Very well. Mrs. Worthington, do you remember the types of toys Mary had in her room the night Alyssa died?

Dawn: Oh, it's been years.

Detective: Take your time. I'm sure you can remember a few.

Dawn: Didn't you ask me this before? You most certainly did ask me this before.

Detective: Refresh our memory. You're a smart woman, you know better than us, I'm sure.

Dawn: Well, alright. Okay, so there were dolls, lots of them. A dollhouse, blocks, those Lego things. Coloring books, reading books, writing books. That's 'bout it.

Detective: Did Mary play any dress-up games? What about jewelry? Any fake jewels or crowns? You know, those princess tiaras?

Dawn: No. Makes no sense dressing her up to be something she's not.

Detective: Maybe Halloween costumes?

Dawn: No, we don't celebrate that! That's the devil's holiday!

Detective: Do you remember what you were wearing the night you took care of Alyssa?

Dawn: Why yes, I had on my nice silk pajama pants and my red sweater. I was just getting ready for bed when I heard her crying. I didn't even get a chance to take my top off yet and change into my robe.

Detective: So you didn't take a shower?

Dawn: No.

Detective: Did you, forgive me, wrap your hair up or put it in those rollers, like women do these days?

Dawn: Ha, no, I didn't have much time for anything like that.

Detective: So it's safe to assume you had on all your jewelry, makeup, and such?

Dawn: I guess . . . I can't quite remember, but I suppose so. Well, yes.

Detective: What kind of jewelry do you typically wear?

Dawn: Well, my earrings. And my bracelet.

Detective: What about a cross?

Dawn: Oh . . . no, I don't have anything like that.

Detective: Really? 'Cause Mary mentioned you used to wear a cross all the time.

Dawn: Oh. Oh right, my cross. Well, yes, I used to. But . . . not that often. Not all the time.

Detective: Folks we talked to remembered you wearing it, almost every day. Said it was pretty distinct.

Dawn: Well, not every day. But yes. It was my mother's.

Detective: Do you still wear it?

Dawn: No. I lost it.

Detective: When?

Dawn: About a few years back.

Detective: Do you remember specifically when?

Dawn: No. Now, what's this all about?

Detective: There was a specific item we kept from the press . . . about something that was found inside Alyssa's throat.

Dawn: What's that got to do with me?

Detective: The jewel we found in Alyssa's throat matches the description of a jewel on your cross. The one people said they saw you wear all the time.

Dawn: Well . . . well, that's ridiculous!

Attorney: Those are some pretty big allegations there, detective. Able to back it up with proof? Evidence?

Detective: I'm hoping Mrs. Worthington can help with that. Because your daughter mentioned you were wearing the cross the night . . .

Dawn: I have no daughter! Never did. Still don't.

Detective: What?

Dawn: No daughter of mine would ever hurt a baby like that. No sir.

Detective: So what are you saying?

Attorney: What she is saying is that Mary is not her biological daughter.

Detective: So . . . okay. So whose daughter is Mary? Where did Mary come from?

Dawn: The devil himself.

I knew I couldn't be her child. What type of person lets her kid take the fall? The kind of person who lies to a child all her life, that's who. A sick monster of a woman, grown and birthed out of the devil. Ms. Cora reaches across the table in the conference room and holds my hand.

"I'm sorry, Mary. I hate being the one to tell you this."

Mrs. Worthington, or Momma, says someone gave me to her, but she won't say who that someone is or was. They didn't want me, so she found some way to forge documents and took me in like a stray dog. That has been the never-ending theme of my life, nobody wanting me. But why can't I shake the feeling that I still belong to Momma, no matter what everyone says? Why does it feel like me and Momma were always supposed to just be? It's like she got a hold on me, her blood beats inside my heart. Is that why I can't tell Ms. Cora everything . . .

I shake my head and wiggle out of Ms. Cora's hands. She nods like she understands, but she doesn't. Nobody understands. Terry pushes a box of tissues near me, but I don't need them.

"What did the police say . . . about Alyssa?" I ask.

Terry and Ms. Cora share a funny look. They're about to lie to me.

"Mmm . . . not much," she says. "There are a lot of unanswered questions. Everything is still a bit too circum-stantial."

That means they still don't believe me. Ice knocks around the pitcher of water, glass sweating on the table. This could end bad. Not only will I be a baby killer and a liar, but I'll also look like a girl who tried to blame her mother for something she didn't do. If Momma doesn't come clean, they could send me back to baby jail and I'll never see Bean. Not even once. They will just snatch him right out of me.

"Don't worry, Mary. We have a pretty solid case," she says, but sounds as if her thoughts are drifting out the door. Terry still looks nervous.

"But?" I ask.

Ms. Cora sighs, pouring herself some water.

"But . . . I just wish we had the smoking gun."

"What's that?"

"You know, that key piece of evidence, something that puts one hundred percent of the blame on your mother. Physical, tangible, direct, scientific evidence."

"Oh," I mumble and nibble on my lower lip.

"But I don't want you to worry. Your story is key here. It corroborates the autopsy and evidence. So let's not worry about that for now."

I'm not worried, but it looks like she is.

"How about some lunch! Terry, why don't we order a pizza!"

I nod and lean back in my seat. The truth is, I have the smoking gun. I just don't want to be the one to give it up yet. Police already think I'm shit for putting the woman who raised me through this; they might not even believe me. And if they do, they'll think I'm shit for being a tattle-tale. No, it has to be her. After everything she's put me through, I want Momma, or Mrs. Worthington, to be the one to shoot that gun herself and tell the truth. She still has so much pain left to feel.

When I get home and check in, I hear Ms. Carmen in the office with Ms. Stein. The two of them have been pretty quiet all week. They're up to something, I just don't know what.

"Mary! Come in here," Ms. Carmen says. "Sit down."

She closes the door behind me and grins. There are a few more empty Entenmann's boxes on the floor. Ms. Stein has been celebrating.

"We have some good news," Ms. Stein says, a sly smile spread across her fat greasy face.

"With all the . . . issues you've been having," Ms. Carmen starts. "And your condition, we feel it's best to find you a more suitable placement. So, there is a halfway house that will be a more appropriate fit you will be transferred to. It's for teen girls like you, pregnant and underage. They'll be able to provide you with safe, proper care until your baby comes to term. And then . . . well, we'll see."

Her last sentence hangs in the air like a threat. Nothing in life surprises me anymore. It's one unexpected thing after another, so I don't react. I don't say nothing. I just sit there, absorbing the words and what they will eventually mean. They glance at each other and smile. My silence is a victory in their eyes.

"Where is it?" I finally ask.

"Upstate," Ms. Carmen says. "About three hours from here."

That's why they look so damn happy. They've been trying to get rid of me, I mean *really* get rid of me, for months and they finally did it.

"And before you ask," Ms. Stein says. "Winters is on board with this plan. He'll be taking you first thing Saturday, so start packing."

"We'll submit your leave of absence papers to school, and the nursing home will find a replacement at another house," Ms. Carmen says.

Wait, no nursing home means no Ted!

Panic hits me like a car, my insides on fire. I leave the office in silence without being dismissed. I've heard about places upstate. No trains, no buses, no cabs, no corner stores. Just a deserted jungle. And Ted . . . I can't live without him.

New Girl isn't in the room, thank God. I lock the door behind me and plug up my phone, digging around for the paper I wrote Ms. Cora's number on until the thought of her makes me stop.

What am I doing?

Ms. Cora works hard, but not fast enough. She'll want to do this the right way, all the proper paperwork and stuff. But by the time she finishes following the rules, I'll be long gone, lost in the woods, never seen again. Every time I try to do right, things come out worse. I could try Ms. Claire, but would she even believe me? I don't know one adult who ever really has.

I dial the only number I know by heart and it goes straight to his voice mail. Maybe he's at the nursing home. I think. I hope. I call again to leave a message.

"They're going to send me away. We have to leave. Now."

That is all I can think to say. I put the phone back and button up my coat. My insides are still burning. I have to find Ted. We only have two days left.

I open the door and New Girl is a white wall in the door frame. We stare at each other, her lips in a tense straight line, which means only one thing: she's been listening the entire time.

"You have a phone?"

Her face is smooth, but her tone is deep. My heart goes missing, my voice too, all hiding from New Girl. She walks toward me and I back into the room.

"Where are you going?" she asks.

"Nowhere," I mumble.

She looks me up and down, standing so still, eyes cold as snow. Her fingers start tapping her thighs like she taps on the computer.

"You're going to leave me," she says.

"They're . . . sending me away."

"But are YOU going to leave me?"

The girl I once referred to as mousy feels larger than life, her anger filling the entire room like smoke. She glances down at Bean. A chill rips through my chest and my mouth goes dry. I've been living with the most dangerous person in the house and didn't even know it.

"Sarah . . . you're scaring me."

She smirks and walks back to the door, stopping to look over her shoulder.

"Good."

"You ready?" Ted asks.

"No. Not really."

Ted and I pick over Salisbury steak and potatoes in the cafeteria, for what may be the last time.

"Where are we going?" I ask.

"Virginia. Gonna stay with my cousin's family."

He reaches under the table and rubs my belly.

"What'll we do when we get there?"

"My cousin got a friend who's a cable guy," he says. "He's gonna hook me up with a job. And you, you're gonna take the SATs and take care of Bean. My cousin's girl works at the university down there, so we'll get you into school easy."

Sounds like a good plan. A very thought-out plan.

"What about money?" I ask.

"How much you got?"

"Six hundred. You?"

He gulps. "I got thirty-three hundred."

"What! How did you . . ."

Oh. The girls. Right. I poke at my potatoes and stay quiet. He slides an extra juice on my tray.

"You should go upstairs and get some sleep," he suggests. "We got a long night."

"You sure your boy can cut these off?"

I swing my ankle out and the tracker clanks against the table leg.

"Yeah, we'll be straight, babe. Don't worry."

I shrug.

"At least there won't be a storm this time," I say.

He snickers. "Yeah, we good on money too."

A nurse wheels out the woman from 408. Eyes wide, pupils dilated, hunched over in her chair, drool slipping down her chin. They found out. I tried to protect her as long as I could. And this is what they do to her, make her a vegetable, taking away her dignity.

"Did you tell your . . . friends, you were leaving?"

His face turns cold and serious.

"No. I haven't spoken to them in weeks. I told you, I'm all about you now. Us, I mean." He rubs my stomach under the table. I close my eyes, relishing the comfort he brings.

"You tell any of your friends?" he asks.

"I have no friends to tell."

"Maybe the lawyer lady?"

I thought about telling Ms. Cora. Even if she could get me out of the house like she said, I still may lose Bean. He could end up in a place with people worse than Ms. Stein. If I tell her where I'm going, she'll only try to stop me. This is the only way.

I walk over to 408 and wipe the drool off her chin. She looks at me with no recognition. It's a thankless job, taking care of the crazy.

Kelly and New Girl, sitting next to each other at dinner, never take their eyes off me. Like they know what I'm up to or something. Never have I been more anxious to leave anywhere in my entire life. Not even baby jail. The two of them together is like rival gangs teaming up, all to kill me.

"Mary! Eat your damn spaghetti!" Ms. Stein snaps.

My cup of water tastes like the kitchen sponge, old wet food and dish soap. I won't miss Ms. Stein or anyone else in this house. I won't miss the food, the lumpy beds, the scratchy sheets, or the dirty bathroom. This place is a dead body that the flies, roaches, and mice swarm to feed on.

"Mary, clean up your plate!"

Now or never.

I pick up the plate and launch it across the room at Tara. For someone with slow reflexes, she ducks quick, enough for it to miss her head.

"You crazy bitch!"

Her big bones couldn't move fast enough to charge after

me. She has to get out of her seat first, and that takes time. Ms. Reba jumps up to save the day while the table cheers.

"Get her, Tara! Get her!"

Tara slips out of Ms. Reba's hold and rushes for me. I run past China, who just stares with a raised eyebrow, and head straight for Ms. Stein's office, Tara a few paces behind me.

"Stop her, Reba, she's gonna kill her!" Ms. Stein screams, not because she is worried about me, but because she is worried about getting in trouble again.

Tara huffs behind me, her fat hand reaching for my shirt. And in one quick move I make a hard left into the bathroom, leaving Tara charging full speed into Ms. Stein's office door. The door cracks under the pressure. She screams, riding the door down like a falling tree into the office.

"Goddamn it, Mary! What the hell is wrong with you!"

Tara jumps up but Ms. Reba ropes her into a hold, calming her down.

And that's when I slip behind Ms. Reba, run into the office, and grab the extra set of keys to the front door off Ms. Stein's desk.

There isn't much of a punishment they can give a pregnant girl other than sending her to bed without dinner. And I went willingly, all so I could pack without New Girl lurking over my shoulder.

The only thing worth taking is my SAT book. Everything else would just remind me of the life I want to leave behind. Maybe when I get down to Virginia and take the test, I can send Ms. Claire my score, so she can be proud of me. Maybe send her a picture of Bean, when he is nice and big. I won't send Momma nothing.

Outside, it's snowing. A thin layer coats the cars like Joi's dandruff. Hope it stops; it would suck to walk through snow in my condition. I pack the two dresses Ms. Cora gave me, my favorite pair of jeans, my hoodie, a T-shirt, and my calculator. I tear the picture of Alyssa out of the book about us and fold it in my pocket with my savings, taking in the room once more. This is the end of my life here. I may never see Ms. Cora or Ms. Claire again and they're the nicest adults I've met since Mrs. Richardson. Maybe Ted's right, maybe I should tell Ms. Cora something. She shouldn't be left in the dark after everything she has done for me. I sit and write a quick note, thanking her for fighting for me, explaining that this is my only way out, hoping I'm right.

The door flies open, cracking against the wall as New Girl storms in. She doesn't say anything. Doesn't even look at me. She changes into her pajamas and slips into bed with her back to me. I exhale, tucking my knife under my pillow. I'm, no lie, more afraid of her than anyone in the world. She has more opportunity to kill me in my sleep than Kelly ever did.

Stay awake, Mary. Stay awake.

But all that running from Tara wore me out. Weights

are pulling on my eyelids. I all but blink and wake up to the dark stillness of the house. Oh God, what time is it? Two in the morning? Damn, I've overslept and only have an hour to meet Ted at the station! I sit up quick and glance across the room. New Girl's bed is empty.

Shit.

I throw my blanket back and slip on my sneakers, listening to the house breathe. The heat is off and the snow hasn't slowed. The house smells like the crispness of it. Maybe she just went to the bathroom or to go get some water.

Ted. I should call Ted. But if I don't move now, she may be back soon to kill me. The longer I stay here the more likely I am to die. I shrug on my backpack and slip a hand under my pillow. Gone. My knife is gone.

I've got to get out of here.

The door creaks like an air horn as I peer into the hallway. Nothing but blackness, an eerie graveyard, the stairs a million miles away. The keys in my pocket dig into my fingertips as I tiptoe into the hall. Tara snores through the walls, the fridge rumbles in the kitchen, and the wind slaps against the storm door. No New Girl. If I didn't know any better, I'd swear I was alone. But she's still in the house, somewhere. I can feel her, a ghost as thick as fog surrounding me.

Another step and my sneaker squeaks. No longer light as a feather, Bean makes me a heavy moving rock, each step causing the floor to buckle beneath me. My hand sweats around the keys as I pass Tara's room. A small sliver of streetlight beams through the bathroom window into the hallway. I can see the stairs now. Still no New Girl.

The prickling nerves creeping up my spine are now radiating over my entire body.

Go back! Go back! Call Ted!

But I can see the door. Freedom is so close I can almost smell the air . . . before it mixes with her lemongrass shampoo.

"Where are you going, Mary?"

New Girl comes out of Kelly's room just like a ghost, snow-white skin glowing. My breath hitches and I stumble back.

"You can't leave me, I won't let you," she breathes.

Run! Go back!

I spin around but Kelly is there, standing with a knife pointed at Bean.

My knife.

That is the last thought I have before taking two steps back in the wrong direction. And all it takes is one simple push from New Girl's wimpy little hand before I go flying down the stairs.

chapter sixteen

When I wake up groggy in my nice soft fluffy hospital bed, I find my throat still sore from the screaming. I've been in and out of sleep for the past two days but that's always the pain I notice first, the burning, like I ate hot peppers for dinner. Then I take in all my other injuries: sprained ankle, busted knee, broken wrist, and stitches over my eyebrow. The knot on the back of my head is the size of Jupiter.

Bean is still okay.

How did I survive that fall? Well, that's a good question. I know when I started falling I immediately thought to protect Bean, so I fell backward but still tumbled down the stairs like a Slinky, my backpack protecting my spine from splitting in two.

Knocked out cold at the bottom of the stairs, when I

first came to, the pain surrounded me like water, drowning me. Hands working on me, lights of the ambulance blinding, Ms. Stein yelling while I begged them to kill me. Because if Bean was dead, then I was dead too. I couldn't take the guilt of killing another baby.

But Bean is still inside me. Bean is okay, for now.

My room is bright white and spotless. Hospitals clean better than Momma, so I feel safe here. It's a lot like the hospital I stayed in before I went to baby jail, back when I wasn't talking.

A nurse rolls in with my lunch and Winters wakes up. He's been snoring in the corner for the past two days.

"You're up. Good," he grumbles.

He walks over to my bed, appraising me like a car. I must look pretty bad, because he winces like he got a paper cut every time he takes a good look at me.

"You're having a boy, they say. Congrats."

I want to smile, but it hurts my face when I do.

"I have five girls. Ages fifteen to twenty-four," he says, sitting in a chair closer to the bed.

"Latoya, my youngest baby girl, is turning sixteen next week. We're throwing one of those big sweet sixteen parties. Expensive as all hell. My wife's going overboard, as usual. The hall, the decorations . . . eight hundred dollars for a damn deejay, can you believe it?" He shakes his head. "You're about sixteen, right?"

I nod.

"I didn't have a party," I say, sounding like a smoker, voice aged by nicotine.

He winces again, rolling the newspaper in his hands.

"Right, right," he mumbles. "Well, I've always wanted a boy, but after five girls, we figure it wasn't in the cards. And even after all these years, I still can't understand you females and the way y'all think. Y'all be coming up with stuff, never saying exactly what's on your mind."

He sets the paper on my bed, pushing my lunch tray closer. Broth with a white roll and red Jell-O. He opens up my juice cup and slides in a straw.

"Y'all expect us men to be mind readers and shit," he grumbles like the miserable old man he is. "You know, my wife got angry at me the other night for God knows what now, and when I ask her 'Baby, what do you want from me?' she says 'You should know.' I mean, this woman can drive me to drink!"

Maybe it's because I'm not laughing, or that I'm just laying here like a dead slug, but he stops babbling and meets my gaze.

"But . . . I should've listened to you, Addison. You were trying to tell me something without saying it, and I didn't listen."

The softness in his tone makes him sound guilty. But I don't blame Winters for what happened. Who could've known New Girl would turn out to be exactly what her parents feared.

333

"I contacted that lawyer of yours. And . . . whew . . . she's something, that one. I ain't ashamed to admit she tore me in two. She'll be here in the morning. You got anyone else you need me to call?"

Ted. Momma. I think of them together, then apart. Ted would come here and risk getting caught. But would Momma come?

I'm hurt, Momma. Please come take care of me!

"Ms. Claire, at the Learning Center."

Winters looks at me funny, then nods.

"Well, I'm going to get some coffee. You should eat, get your strength up."

He stands and stretches.

"Social services will be here to question you . . . about the house . . . and Ms. Stein. I take it you'll be fair?"

He struggles with that last sentence and heads toward the door.

"And no need to worry about Sarah or Kelly. They've been taken care of."

"Winters?"

He stops at the door.

"Yup."

"You got a pen?"

He frowns, then takes one out his coat pocket. I claw at the newspaper beside me, opening to the first page. Winters watches like he wants to stop me, but doesn't. I circle the word *fastidious*.

"There's another test in May," I say, but he still seems confused while nothing could be clearer to me. "He's my baby. Mine."

Winters's face drops a little, and for the first time he seems to understand. Like he fully grasps what I am up against.

"Yup. I know."

Ms. Cora was a blue flame. That's how mad she was. The hottest part of fire, blue from the ends of her wavy hair to the tips of her heels. She stormed into the hospital, took one look at me, and said, "Start talking."

And that is when I told her everything. About the house. About Kelly. About New Girl killing her mom. About Ms. Carmen and Ms. Stein. Everything except the part about me trying to run away with my older boyfriend. I figured I might as well keep that to myself. She was already turning blue enough, and when Ms. Cora turns blue, the world gets quiet.

She cursed out Winters in the hallway outside my room. He couldn't even get two words in. I never heard anyone talk so fast in my life. And he just stood there and took it. Then she cussed out Ms. Carmen and that one was my favorite part. Ms. Carmen tried to put up a good fight, but then I heard Ms. Cora say something about getting her fired and she shut right up.

Then she was on the phone with friends, calling in favors

from all over. Ms. Stein's name was mentioned a couple of times. An hour later, two real police officers were in my room, taking a statement. And if that wasn't enough, when Ms. Claire came, she told off the nurses for not changing my gown when I peed on myself and demanded real food. Kings County Hospital was under Ms. Claire and Ms. Cora's control.

"Chile, what is dis? Why yuh circle dis word 'ere? *Fastidious*? Yuh know dis one!"

"I do?"

"Lawd, they box yuh head in good. Can't remember simple words. Chuh!"

Ms. Claire sits in Winters's spot in the corner, sucking her teeth. She turns the page, looking up the next word in her pocket dictionary.

"Boy, lemme tell yuh, dis country has di worst education system in di entire world! Don't teach basic words, don't teach nuthin' at t'all! No wonder everyone so blasted stupid around 'ere. Do yuh know I graduated from high school at yuh age and was already taking classes at the university? Come to dis country, land of opportunity, and find yuh three years behind everyone. Had to tutor grown men and women, older than me, in subjects I learned in secondary. Jesus blessed my soul wit the patience to be an educator cause dis country definitely needed some intelligence. Chuh!"

I can't believe she's staying with me, even after everything . . .

"How much do you know?"

She pauses for a moment, then puts her pen down to look at me.

"As much as yuh told me," she says plainly, face smooth and nonchalant.

"Do you know who I am? What I . . . did?"

She takes a deep breath, staring through me.

"What yuh may or may not've done is not di definition of *who* yuh really are."

That was all she had to say to make my soul calm, to ease some pain. Slowly, I swing my leg out from under the covers, feeling for the floor for the first time in days. I'm tired of using this pee pan. Every time, it just goes all over the place. Ms. Claire hops out of her chair.

"Aye, what yuh do? Yuh need the bathroom? Come, let me help yuh before yuh catch cold."

She bends and slips some blue socks on my feet that have little rubber tracks on the bottom.

"Oh boy, gyal!" She reaches up and smiles as her warm hands cuff around my belly. "Yuh popped!"

I wince a smile and for a change, I don't pull away. I let someone other than Ted touch Bean, because I know Ms. Claire wouldn't hurt him. She'd protect him as much as I would. She helps me off the bed and I limp into the bathroom, dragging along my IV. I lean against the door frame as she switches on the light.

"Someone's in here already," I mumble, turning away.

She must be my roommate, but damn she looks terrible. A bruised cheek, cracked lips, and a blackened eye. She looks like Momma the day after Junior died. Ray did a number on her that day.

"Huh? What yuh talking 'bout?"

"Someone—"

My knees give in. WHOOSH and the IV stand clatters. I fall forward, catching myself on the sink, hitting the mirror with the tip of my nose. A gasp fogs the glass. I freeze and the woman stares.

"Mary?"

There is no one else in here but me. I don't have a roommate. That face, it's mine. The battered woman . . . she is me. And my eye. My damn eye has blood in it. Not one drop of brown, just thick red blood.

"Mary? Yuh okay? Mary what . . . MARY!"

The piss runs out of me and my socks soak it up like a sponge.

I had a dream Herbert came to my room last night. He had big sparkly green wings the size of elephant ears and glowed like a lightning bug. He told me he was visiting from heaven. I asked him what it was like. He said it's just like I imagined. I asked him if he saw Alyssa there. He said yes. I asked him if she was mad at me, and he didn't say nothing at all.

"Chuh! One week in di hospital and they ready to kick her out. Dis what meh tax dollars pay for?" Ms. Claire shouts and sucks her teeth. "Is that house safe?"

They're talking in the hall about me while I finish dinner. Turkey slices with gravy, mashed potatoes, string beans, chicken noodle soup, and a pudding cup. Same type of food they serve in the nursing home. It makes me think of Ted. I lost my phone somewhere between the fall and the hospital. He has no idea what happened. Probably thinks I changed my mind.

"Kelly's been transferred to Crossroads and Sarah's at Bellevue," Winters says. "Psych evaluation."

"But is the house safe for Mary?" Ms. Cora asks. "It wasn't just those two tormenting her."

"She'll have a new placement by the end of the month," my temporary social worker says. She looks like she graduated high school yesterday. "With a facility that specializes in teen mothers, if she chooses to keep her baby."

"'If'? Who said anything about 'if'?" Ms. Cora says, voice rising.

"Well, there's a lot involved in that," Winters says.

"You still don't think she's capable of raising her own child?"

"I'm not one to say. But I think there's a lot of things

that neither one of us knows about her."

"And it's always going to be about the best interest of the child," Social Worker adds.

"I can't believe you fucking idiots!" Ms. Cora says.

"Hey! Watch it," Winters warns. "You know you don't really have any authority to make any decision here. You're not even family!"

"I'm speaking for my client, who's in the process of being emancipated from you assholes. I got enough damn authority to make your lives hell that's for—"

"Listen, I get it, okay!" Winters says. "All I'm saying is . . . she may not be in the best condition to raise a child . . . right now. Just for right now, not that she never could! She needs to be healthy for that baby and stand on her own two feet first. Think about it, she has no one to claim her, no money, barely has a place to live. And just a couple of weeks ago they reported she was hearing voices and—"

"You know what," Social Worker shouts. "Can we just focus on the immediate situation at the moment?"

Ms. Cora and Winters mutter to themselves.

"Honestly, it's the best place for her right now. Everywhere else is booked. No one can take the overflow of a girl in her condition. Now, the doctor said she must be on strict bed rest to avoid possible premature labor. So I don't think it's a good idea to move her to a new facility, one she's unfamiliar with, until she's well enough to walk on her own. Stein is under investigation, so she'll be on her best behavior. Mary will have her own room and we'll arrange for daily nurse visits."

They all fall silent. I wonder what that means, Ms. Stein is under investigation. Is she gonna be fired? I hope so.

"Okay, fine!" Ms. Cora barks. "But if one hair is out of place, so help me, I'll—"

"I know, alright!" Winters snaps. "Jesus, woman! Where'd she dig you up from?"

New Girl's bed is empty. No sheets or pillows. Just a green plastic mattress like no one has ever lived there before. But I'll never forget her. I'll never forget the look in her eyes when I went flying down the stairs. She was smiling, a big nasty grin. Wonder what they're going to do to her?

"I can't believe they pushed her down the stairs and that crazy bitch lived!"

"Yo, shut up, Kisha," China says. "That shit was fucked up, she could've died. She almost lost her baby."

"Well, what she do to them to make them do that?" Kisha asks. "You know she always starting something!"

"Nothing," China barks. "She didn't do nothing! And y'all know that."

"Nah, that bitch is loco," Marisol says.

"China, you even said you caught her walking around the house naked," Kisha says.

"But yo, did you see her eye though? That shit is nasty!" Joi giggles.

My interaction with the rest of the house is limited. I stay in my room, an outcast among outcasts. Other than a nurse who stops by to check on me and Ms. Reba bringing up my meals, I don't see anyone else. Ms. Stein is smart enough to keep her distance.

The doctors were very serious about bed rest. Too much movement and Bean could die. So I keep my feet up and if I'm not sleeping, I'm staring at the ceiling, daydreaming about Alyssa.

Ms. Claire came by to visit. She brought me some SAT flash cards and a new book on how to get into college.

"For when yuh get back on yuh feet."

Even back on my feet, I'm not sure if it will help or if it was even worth it. Winters is right. I can't raise a baby like this. No money. No job. Not even a place to live. And the way the case is going so slow, I'll be seventeen or older by the time they make a decision. Bean will be born. They'll take him. Put him in a home with some strangers. Strangers like Ms. Stein; that's what scares me most. There are thousands of Ms. Steins out there, thousands of Mommas, thousands of Rays, all waiting to take Bean and repeat history. No one will believe him. He'll cry for me, his real momma, and I won't be able to help him. I won't know where he is or how to find him. So many ways he could be hurt. I won't be able to protect him once he is out of my belly. So I keep my feet up, trying to stop him from coming too quick.

But then there is Alyssa. If I wasn't in her life at all, she'd still be here. I don't blame them for trying to take Bean. Maybe Bean would be better off without me. Maybe the greatest gift I can give him, the only way to keep him safe, is to keep him away from me.

And then I'll be alone. Forever.

My knee still hurts a little but my ankle is much better. I can flex it more than I could two weeks ago. The broken blood vessel in my eye is starting to clear up, but I avoid mirrors to stop scaring myself. I'm healing slowly on the outside, but inside, all that's left that matters is Bean. Everything else is dead.

The doorbell rings. It's one of two people, the nurse or Winters. He comes to check on me almost every day now. Brought me a piece of his daughter's birthday cake after the party. It tasted like nothing.

"Where is she?" I hear him scream downstairs. Bean jumps at the sound of his voice.

Ted?

"Whoa there, young man," Ms. Reba says. "Who are you here to see?"

I hear China walk into the foyer.

"Oh, I know you. You're Kisha's boyfriend, right? She's upstairs."

"What?" Ted snaps. "Kisha? Nah. Where's Mary?"

"Mary?" Ms. Reba and China say together.

"Yo, Mary!" he calls.

"Hey! Cut that out! It's time for you to go."

"Mary! Mary, where you at!"

My heart cries out for him, hands trembling, mouth fixed to say his name but locked tight. Should I go to him? No, I can't.

"I'm calling the police!"

"Wait, Reba, see what he wants first."

"I want to see Mary! Where she at?"

I wish the floor would swallow me up, straight down to the basement. He can't be here. They can't know.

"Hey! What's going on?" Kisha says, running down the stairs. "Who called my name?"

"I want Mary. Where is she? Is she dead?"

No one responds. Everyone is at a loss for words.

"Which one of you bitches did it? Huh! Which one of you killed her?" Ted's voice cracks, and I want to run and comfort him. But I can't. He can't be here.

"Now just calm down, alright! What do you want with Mary?" Ms. Reba asks.

"Mary's my . . ."

No Ted. No! We're gonna get caught.

Joi busts into my room.

"There's a boy here to see you!" she grins. "Is that your baby daddy? He's cute!"

I don't move or say a word. Ms. Reba comes upstairs.

"Mary? Ummm . . . some boy downstairs is here to see

you. Says he knows you. You know you can't have male visitors here. No one except Winters."

I roll away from her. This is stupid. Ted is risking getting caught, throwing our business out in front of the people I trust least in the world.

"I don't know him," I mumble.

"Mary!" he screams from downstairs. "I swear I will light this motherfucker up, if you don't let me see her!"

Ms. Reba clears her throat. "Uhhh, Mary?"

Ted won't go away till he sees me. I know him. He'll tear the house apart.

"I can't walk downstairs."

Ms. Reba looks at Joi, then at me.

"Well, he can't come up here. You know you can't have boys in your room!"

"Just give me five minutes," I say.

"No way! No!"

"Please," I beg. Because it's Ted, it's the only time I'll beg Ms. Reba for anything.

"Where is she?" Ted shouts, sounding louder now that the door is open. "I'm not fucking playing with y'all!"

Ms. Reba looks torn, scratching her graying dry hair.

"Come on, Reba!" Joi says, grinning. "Ms. Stein ain't even here. Who's gonna know? Live a little!"

Ms. Reba hesitates, then sighs.

"Okay, fine. But *only* five minutes."

Once they're gone, I straighten up in bed, pulling my

shirt down over Bean. I tie my hair back, licking my hand to smooth down the edges, wishing I had some of Momma's makeup to make me look pretty.

Ted rushes in the room. Just the sight of him and my body eases out of a tense hold. It's been so long, I can feel every muscle melt down to normal. One look at me and his mouth drops. My eyes water up, ready to tumble over. Didn't think I was that bad. He eases near me and tips my chin up, staring into my bloody eye. Anger radiates off his body like a heater. He doesn't say nothing for a long time, just stands there, hands trembling, until they ball into fists. Then he turns to the crowd of girls standing in the doorway.

"Which one of you bitches did it?"

"Who you calling a bitch!" Kisha snaps.

"It was the new girl," Joi says. "She pushed her down the stairs. But she ain't here no more."

Ted stomps over and slams the door in their faces, locking it. He sits on the edge of my bed, staring at me, looking over and over again at my injuries.

"I thought you . . . changed your mind."

There's so much I want to say, so much I want to tell him. But all the emotions I've held back the last few months come tumbling out my eyes as I crumble.

"Damn, baby," he says, scooping me up into his arms. I melt into him, hissing away the pain in my knee. He's the most powerful pain reliever I've ever known. My arm doesn't hurt and my ankle feels fine.

We sit for a long time with me crying into his chest. Crying like I've never cried a day in my life. Finally, my senses return.

"You can't stay." I sniff. "You're not supposed to be here."

He rubs his nose in my hair and inhales.

"We should have left a long time ago," he says, so much regret in his voice.

"It's not your fault."

"You could've been killed. And Bean."

He holds me tighter, kissing my eyelids with his soft lips.

"Social services called the nursing home yesterday," he says. "I overheard them talking about you. I didn't know what happened! I was waiting at the train station for mad long."

He rubs his big hands around my stomach. I clasp my little ones over them. We look like night and day, black and white, my skin so light compared to his.

"Ted, you can't be here. They'll—"

"I know, aight? Don't worry about them. But how we gonna get you out of here, baby? You can't even walk right."

He still thinks we're running away. He still thinks we have a chance.

"Ted, I'm . . . leaving."

He pulls away from my neck to look at me.

"What you mean?" he asks.

"When I get better, they're sending me to this place upstate. For girls like me."

"Upstate?" he says, like it's a foreign country. He mulls the idea over for a bit, stroking my arms. "Aight, I guess I'll just visit you there. Gotta be on the weekend though, at least till the baby is born."

For Ted, it's just that simple. He's a man of action. Something needs to be done, he never asks questions or complains or worries about the consequences. That, unfortunately, is my job.

"No. You can't. They'll ask questions. And then they'll know about you. About us."

Ted frowns, his body tense but his arms still wrapped around me like a warm blanket.

"What are you saying?"

"I'm saying . . . I can't see you . . . for a while."

This doesn't settle with him well. He jumps up and I pretend the movement doesn't cause me to suck in a breath and see stars at the pain. Then he starts to argue all the ways it could work, yelling and cursing. I let him vent, but the facts are not going to change. Ted is now nineteen and I am sixteen. We're both parolees, both on our last life.

I've been thinking a lot, on my back staring at the ceiling, and the truth is we may not win. All Ms. Cora's hard work may be for nothing because we may still lose one way or another. They'll take away Bean and throw me back in baby jail for being crazy. But if they know about Ted, not only will I lose Bean, but they'll take away the only person that has ever really loved me. It sucks, but I have to do what's best for both my boys.

"You've already done enough just coming here," I say. "They know your face now."

He curses again and sits on New Girl's bed, the stress making deep wrinkles on his forehead.

"So when then?"

"When what?" I say.

"When can I see you again?" he snaps.

It's hard to lie to those big brown eyes. So I tell him the truth.

"I don't know."

Ted glares at me, like he wants to be mad. He knows I'm right and he wants to hate me for it. But Ted can't hate me, it's impossible for him. That is how I know it hurts him more. He can't hate me but he can't have me. He runs his hands down his face, falls on his knees in front of me, and buries his face into my stomach, holding and kissing Bean like his life is ending. In a way, it is.

There is a light rap on the door. We ignore it until it becomes a badgering knock.

"Mary! Time's up," Ms. Reba shouts. "He has to go! Now!"

Ted looks up at me. His eyes. That's what I'll miss the most. Maybe Bean will have his eyes. But it will be years before I ever know.

"It's a boy," I say, and try to comfort the blow with a smile. Ted bites a trembling lip, eyes watering. He exhales and kisses me. His lips, I'll miss those too.

"Yo, promise me you'll fight," he says. "That you won't give up. And if you get to keep Bean, you'll tell me."

"I promise," I lie and hug him one last time.

Excerpt from The Devil Inside: The Mary B. Addison Story by Jude Mitchell (pg. 223)

When talking about Mary as a baby, Dawn Cooper once said, "Most folks think I named her Mary after Jesus's mother. But no, I named her Mary Beth, as in Mary of Bethany. Mary sat by Jesus's feet and listened to his words instead of helping her sister with preparation for dinner. She knew that nothing should ever come before the Lord!

"Jesus also brought her brother back from the dead.

"But really, I named her Mary Beth after my mother, Miryam. It means 'a wished-for child.'"

My knee and ankle are a lot better now. I can walk to the bathroom without a crutch. Major improvement, the nurse told me yesterday. That means no more visits, which is fine by me. I have bigger things to worry about. At least now I'm allowed out of bed.

I take the bus to the Q train, then walk three blocks to her apartment building, up the shiny elevator with the big mirrors. I remember fogging the mirrors with my nose while Momma straightened the ribbons in my pigtails as we rode up. The bell dings on the sixth floor and I knock on the last door to the right. She is not even surprised to see me. She just lets me right in.

The apartment is the same, but seems so much smaller and darker with this thick layer of dust covering everything in sight. I mean, one good sneeze would clean up the whole place. Smells mad stale too, like the windows haven't been opened in years, maybe longer. Stacks of newspapers and magazines tower on every surface, overcrowded ashtrays sit on sofa arms. And the Christmas tree—the one with the white lights and red and gold bulbs—is still there, in the corner by the window. She put it there so everyone could see how beautiful her tree was. But now, the tree is a bare stick, dried up pine needles surrounding it like ashes, ornaments rusted. The gifts underneath, once wrapped in green glitter paper, are faded almost to yellow.

Wonder if my gift is still there?

This is not how it used to be. Before, it was roomy and light. Always smelling like fresh laundry and cinnamon sugar from the apple pies she used to bake.

"Do you want to see it?" Mrs. Richardson asks with a sniff. She's wearing bleach-stained sweatpants and a wrinkled T-shirt. No more fancy dresses.

I nod and she opens the first door on the left. Alyssa's room.

It's exactly as I left it. Candy-pink walls, with yellow elephants and giraffes, a dark wood crib with pink sheets and a changing table. Baby books. Toys. A picture hung over the crib of Alyssa, one day old. Another picture, her in a red romper, the same picture on the cover of the book about us, sits on the dresser.

"Why do you keep it this way?"

She interlocks her fingers—her eyes watery, face tired— but doesn't step a foot in the room with me in it.

"Would you want someone to forget about you?"

Guess that makes sense. I look around at Alyssa's memorial, a frozen day in time, and inhale deep.

"It still smells like her."

Mrs. Richardson's face sort of crumbles. Her bottom lip twitches and she stutters out of the room. I follow, closing the door behind me.

The living room is dry, the cushion seats sunken in. I wait, letting her have her moment in the kitchen, gasping for air between her sobs. Glasses clatter, cabinets slam. It's not like the way she cried when she got to our house that night. She let out the longest scream ever, mouth frozen open with a sob that even made some of the police officers in the room tear up. I'll never forget her scream.

She returns with two glasses of iced tea. Hers looking

much lighter in color than mine. I glance at the mat by the door. His shoes aren't there.

"Where's Mr. Richardson?"

She passes me a glass and chuckles.

"He's long gone."

"'Cause of Alyssa?"

"No, 'cause of you," she says with a snort.

I don't understand. What did I do to him?

"We . . . had a difference of opinion when it came to you," she says. "He never forgave me for agreeing with the plea bargain. He thought you should have gone to jail for life."

"You didn't think so?"

She shakes the ice around the glass a little and takes a sip.

"Oh, trust me, I had a lot of dark thoughts about you. I wanted you dead."

She is staring at me so hard, so angry. She'd kill me right now if she had the chance. Maybe I made a mistake coming here. I hold the iced tea with both hands.

"But," she says with a sigh. "It all just didn't make any sense. I didn't want another child to lose her life."

She knocks back her drink like it's water.

"Then, they wouldn't file charges against your mother, and that really put him over the edge. 'She was supposed to be taking care of my little girl!' he screamed at the DA. After that, he wouldn't look at me anymore. He blamed me for leaving Alyssa with you and your momma. He never said it, but he did."

I can't believe Mr. Richardson left her. They were so perfect together. I thought he loved her. He didn't treat her anything like the way Ray treated Momma. And he was a good daddy.

"Your mother came by here once after . . . it happened. Unannounced as usual. Walked in here like it was nothing. Even brought a shepherd's pie, talking nonstop about the lines at the grocery store. We'd just buried Alyssa not even a week before. Guess I was so in shock when I saw her . . . I lost my wits. She went into the kitchen like she used to and I just stood there, couldn't move. Then Greg came home . . . he was so mad."

My bladder is about to explode. Can't drink another drop of this tea.

"Can I use your bathroom?"

"Go ahead. You know where it is."

I head down the hall, passing her bedroom. An unmade bed with a single sheet dangling over the side, newspapers scattered on the floor, empty glasses and bottles of vodka on the side table. It doesn't seem like one woman lives here, but ten homeless women instead.

Black mold lines the tiles around the bathtub. I finish my business and wash my hands, drying them on bleach-stained hand towels. On the cabinet by the toilet are a bunch of pill bottles with long-name prescriptions. One

I recognize because Momma used to take the same. But whatever those pills are supposed to be doing, don't seem like they working.

Back in the living room, Mrs. Richardson is standing by the tree, blowing smoke out the window. She looks so much older now, eyes far-gone like Momma's, foot tapping like New Girl's used to. She turns and stares down at my stomach for a long time, not saying nothing. I put my arms over it, protecting Bean.

"It's a boy," I say, noticing my own nervousness.

She grins and pulls out another cigarette.

"I told you it would be."

She tosses the pack on the coffee table by her new drink that she didn't bother mixing with iced tea this time. She offers me a cigarette and I shake my head.

"What happened to you?" she asks.

I touch my cast and shrug.

"Had an accident."

She raises an eyebrow, laughs, then kicks one of the yellowing gifts by the tree.

"This was for you. I bought you some books by Judy Blume. Remember I told you about her?"

"Fudge?"

"Right. Those Mary Higgins Clark novels were just a little too grown and dark for your age."

One of the old ladies Momma used to clean for gave her a shoe box of old books for Christmas. Momma was so mad ("Old bitch couldn't give me a real tip!") but I loved them.

On the bookshelf next to the tree, there are three framed pictures of Alyssa. She looks so tiny in them. I remember her being so much bigger, heavier in my arms.

I didn't mean to throw her . . .

"You know, that's my greatest regret. Not taking enough pictures." She sips her drink, desperately. "Should've taken more pictures."

She falls back into her chair, rotating a lighter around her fingers.

"I just miss her . . . so much," she says, her voice cracking. "I only had her for a second and I miss her so much. How do you miss someone you barely knew?"

She doesn't sob. She doesn't cry. Maybe she's like me. Maybe she's all cried out.

Below the pictures of Alyssa is a long row of black books with gold writing down the seams. Her encyclopedias always seemed so expensive and regal; I remember being afraid to touch them. They had the same ones in baby jail, except they were worn down, beaten, pages ripped and whole books missing. But I would read them, over and over, hearing Mrs. Richardson's voice. Whenever I didn't know something, Mrs. Richardson would make me look it up and read it out loud. "Do you know where diamonds come from Mary?" I'd shake my head and she'd smile. "Well, look it up. Tell me about them."

My knee is starting to throb. I also can't breathe right, and the smoke isn't helping. Maybe I shouldn't have pushed myself so soon.

"Why didn't you have more children?" I ask, sitting back down.

She sighs and takes another sip.

"Greg never thought he'd be a good father. He sorta did it 'cause he knew how badly I wanted a baby. Then Alyssa was born and boy . . . I've never seen a man fall in love so fast. He talked about having more children right away. He wanted two boys and another girl. That's why he . . . wanted to go out that night. Wanted to get me alone, get me relaxed, so he could get me pregnant again."

She laughs.

"Men are so stupid," she hiccups. "Think a little liquor and the sperm will go straight to the source of life."

I just stare, because I don't really know what she is talking about.

"You know, I never told the police this, but that night, I knew something was wrong. I felt it. I kept telling Greg I wanted to check on Alyssa. He kept telling me to stop worrying."

She looks at the door to Alyssa's room, as if she was about to walk right out. When she doesn't, I exhale.

"After . . . it happened . . . Greg was just a different person. He couldn't handle it. Who really could?"

No one could, it seems. No one could handle a dead

baby. Not Mr. Richardson, the mob outside the court-house, Mr. Jerk Face, the COs, the social workers, Ms. Stein, Momma, her, or me. I swallow and finally identify the stale smell, reeking and suffocating the apartment. It is six years' worth of pain, soaked in gasoline, set on fire. The smoke is smothering, which makes asking her for this one favor that much harder.

"Mrs. Richardson . . . I'm sorry. For everything that has happened."

She nods her head. "I know you are."

"And I know . . . I don't have the right to ask you this . . . but . . . can you adopt my baby?"

Mrs. Richardson's foot stops tapping. She just stares, her face turning dark. I don't know what to think, so I just keep going.

"They are gonna take my baby away. But if they do, I'd rather you take him than anyone else. I'd rather him be in a good home. With a good mother, like you. You're a good mother."

She huffs. If she squeezes her drink any tighter the glass will shatter.

"I'm nobody's mother anymore, Mary."

I shift in my chair.

"I'll be free . . . I think . . . by the time I'm eighteen," I push on. "And then I'll come back for him. I promise. He won't be any trouble. He'll be a good baby."

Mrs. Richardson sighs and looks out the window, the sun setting.

"You know the other thing that happened when your mother came to visit. She talked about you. Went on and on about her baby girl. How she was going to put you in dance classes when you get out of the 'hospital.' Beauty pageants or something. Went on and on then says, 'It's so much work having a girl.' Alyssa wasn't even dead three weeks yet."

That sounds just like Momma, foot all in her mouth.

"Please," I whisper. "You're my last hope."

"I'm a mess, Mary. Just a mess—"

"But you can get better. I know you can. You can teach him all kinds of stuff so he'll be real smart. Please."

She sighs and doesn't meet my eye.

"Mary . . . I can't. And I'm not even sorry that I can't."

chapter seventeen

"The prosecution is bringing up new evidence, which could, in layman's terms, be a problem."

Ms. Cora walks in, closes the door, and sits on New Girl's bed, very serious-like. She even has a suit on today.

"I need you to tell me what happened with your brother," she says slowly.

All the air leaves me in one quick second.

No, Momma, you wouldn't . . .

"Why do they need to know about Junior?"

She scratches her eyebrow, then takes off her raincoat, pulling some files and a notebook out of her briefcase.

"Because . . . your mother is claiming that you might have had something to do with Junior's death too."

I stare at her, wishing it all away as my eye starts twitching. There is a buzzing in my ear, like a fly. Herbert? No, he's dead. Just like Alyssa.

"I know, I know," she sighs, rolling her eyes like the whole thing is foolish, a waste of time. "But the circumstances surrounding your brother's death are . . . very, very similar to Alyssa so we need to have our story straight. We're trying to win the war, not these silly battles."

"Junior died in his sleep," I say, my voice cold. Her face tenses up.

"Your mother . . . she doesn't believe that's the case. She says she left him alone with you when he died. They are considering opening up an investigation. You were too young when it happened to be tried as an adult, but if they find probable cause, they can arrest you. You could face another ten years. Plus, the DA could use this as evidence . . . when it comes to Alyssa."

For the first time I feel like New Girl and I really could kill Momma for this.

"I didn't kill Junior. He died in his sleep. I found him. That's all."

She pauses and there it is. Doubt. It sweeps across her face quick like the shadow of a moving car. She nods and writes in her notebook, not meeting my eyes.

"Was your mother there at all?"

"I was home alone."

She blows out air and continues writing.

"Do you think Ray or maybe some of his friends or family would have any—"

I give her a look that shuts her up.

Ray is dead. I know how, I just don't feel like saying. I don't feel like talking about it. We didn't go to his funeral. His real wife wouldn't let us. He had a son, a little older than me.

His name was Junior too.

From the February 13th Deposition of Carmen Vaquero—Ramon Vaquero's Widow

I tell you, I know for true. That crazy bitch killed my husband.

My Ramon, he couldn't just be with one woman. I know for true. Men are never satisfied with just one. But no matter what he did with those other women, he loved me the best. We been together forever, since we were fifteen. My Ramon was a good father and took care of his family. So, why chase him? I let him do what he wants, 'cause he always gonna come home to me.

Then he meet this woman, she was crazy. He told me about her. That she would sing all kinds of crazy stuff in the living room, all kinds of things. I told him, stay away from that puta, *she crazy, she'll put something in your soup! He say,* mi amor, relaaaaaxxxx. *I have her under control.*

One day she come to my door, looking for my Ramon. Had a little girl with her. She was yelling and screaming that he beat her. I say, Ramon! No way, he would never hit a woman. And Ramon told me she used to hit herself when she sang those crazy songs. She crazy, I know for true.

Then she said he tried to sleep with her little girl. I punched that puta *right in the eye. My Ramon would never do something like that. Ever!* Qué asco! *Her little girl don't say nothing. Just look at the ground the whole time.*

When my Ramon didn't come home for seven days, I knew something was wrong. I called and she said he was dead. I say, how? How no one call me? I go to hospital, they say he die of stroke. I say, stroke! No way. He was healthy as a horse. Then they cremate him. I say why? He didn't want that. He wanted to go back home to Santa Domingo to be buried next to his mami. I tell you why, 'cause that crazy puta *kill my husband, I know for true. And you wait all this time to talk to me now. Ha! I could have told you years ago about that crazy* puta *and that little baby would still be alive today.*

Ms. Reba knocks on the door and pokes her head in.

"Umm . . . Mary? Your mother is here to see you."

I limp into the visitors' room, thinking Ms. Reba was lying. No way she'd be here, she ain't have the nerve. But there she is. My momma. Or whoever she is, sitting in a dark purple church suit. No hat this time.

"Baby! How you doing?"

Bitch is nuts.

"So NOW you want to see me?"

"Of course, baby girl! You know I will always be your momma."

"But you're not my momma."

"Yes I am! Now, I know you're mad, but Momma can't take the fall for your mistakes all the time. Not my fault the devil's inside you. I've been trying to help you for years."

She tries to touch my hair and I slap her hand away. It stings my hand to do it, so I know it hurt hers too.

"'YOUR mistakes'? How could you tell them I killed Junior!"

"Baby, I didn't!"

"I didn't do it. You know I didn't!"

She rubs the burn on her hand and huffs.

"You know what, I'm just about tired of all this nonsense. After everything I've done for you, you couldn't just keep your mouth shut. Your legs neither."

"What you've done for me? Momma, I'm in jail!"

"Oh, you in a home," she says, waving me off then checking her nail polish. Red, chipping like school paint. "You're not wearing some orange jumpsuit in chains no more. They've gone easy on you, just like I told you they would. You know what would've happened if it was me? I would've went away for life. Then who would've taken care of you?"

"You're not taking care of me now!"

She waves me off again like I'm a pestering fly, as if the idea is as crazy as she is.

"You had your whole life ahead of you. A couple of

years, ain't nothing. But me, I would've died in that prison. And you know it's true."

That is true. The COs wouldn't have done anything to help her besides beat her and throw her in the hole until she goes mad. That's if the other women wouldn't have gotten to her first, slicing her face or raping her in the shower for killing a baby. She would've been on her deathbed in less than five years.

"And it's so dangerous in those prisons. Fighting and carrying on. Them girls turning other girls into lesbians. Oh Lord, child, I just couldn't do it."

She waves me off again until something dawns on her and she spins quick.

"And what's all this stuff you been telling them about me! About Ray. About me trying to bring Alyssa back to life? Some type of witchcraft or something? You know I don't do that type of stuff. Why you tell them that?"

I don't say nothing. I'm tired of answering questions. Feels like all I do is answer questions nowadays.

"I told you to get those pills for you," her voice cracks. "Not for Alyssa! You were supposed to take them. Them pills were supposed to calm you down!"

She's right. She did tell me to get my pills. She did tell me to take them. But I didn't.

"It was just better this way, baby girl. It ain't all that bad, right? You not even in jail no more. I told you, they take it easy on little girls."

I snort. Easy? Nothing about this life is easy.

"You know I've always prayed for you more than I've prayed for myself. I visited you, just like I said I would. Then you go get pregnant and screw everything up! Why you doing this to me, huh?"

I cross my arms, leaning them on Bean, watching her come apart at the seams like a cheap dress. She starts pacing in a small circle in front of me, thinking hard, hands and lips shaking. By the fifth circle, she snaps her fingers with an eager smile.

"I know! How about this? I'll adopt your baby. Yeah, I'll raise him and when you're old enough, I'll give him right back."

Her head nods nonstop, as if it's the best idea in the world, which makes me think this is what she had in mind all along. To take my baby, to start all over again. Another SAT word pops into my head: *audacity*.

"What . . . in the world would make you think I would EVER let you near MY baby?"

Momma looks downright stunned. She clutches her chest and takes a step away from me, like the words could give her a stroke any minute.

"Well, I—"

"You have to tell the truth, Momma."

"The truth?"

Momma straightens, bravely remembering who the parent and the child is. Or who she thinks the parent and the child is, because she was always too oblivious to be the parent.

"Don't you tell me what to do! I didn't touch that child but to save her after what you did. I don't have to do nothing!" she says.

God, she is always trying to save somebody! She can't just let people and things be? Nobody asked her to save nobody. She grumbles something about me being crazy and starts toward the door. I let her pass and smile before shouting after her:

"I have the cross, Momma."

Her entire body jumps, a lightning bolt striking through her. She turns so fast I think her head might never stop spinning.

"You what?"

"The cross you stuffed down Alyssa's throat, trying to get the pills out. The one you tried to 'save' her with. I kept the cross, Momma. It's what they couldn't find."

She stares at me for a long minute, thinking it through.

"And I never touched it," I say.

Momma is frozen, eyes blank and far away. It's the face she wears when she has absolutely no idea what to do. I know the look well.

I've got to hand it to myself. Not many nine-year-olds would be smart enough to grab the cross with their night-gown so they wouldn't get fingerprints on it. Not many nine-year-olds would be smart enough to dig three ditches, one by the house, one in the neighbor's backyard, and a third one—one no one could find. Or maybe I should be thanking Momma. For all the nights she left me home alone with *Law & Order* and mystery novels.

Momma swallows, trying to relax her face.

"Give it to me," she says plainly, putting out her hand. "It was my momma's."

I look at her hand and chuckle.

"No."

"No? Young lady, give me that damn cross! You got no business with it!"

"Tell them you did it, and I'll give it to you."

She throws up her hands and stomps her foot.

"Jesus, Mary! What do you think you're doing, huh? What do you want? I took care of you, didn't I? Didn't I?"

What's crazy is, she really thinks she did. She really thinks she took care of me.

"No. You didn't. Not like Mrs. Richardson did."

The mention of her name hits a nerve. Momma takes a deep breath, eyes narrowing.

"Well, it made no sense for me to take the blame for killing that bitch's perfect fucking baby," she says in a husky voice, her neck rolling. "You the one who threw her."

"I didn't mean to throw her! You wouldn't let go!"

"Don't make no difference."

She really believes this. I guess that explains why I used to too.

"But you wanted to, didn't you? You never liked Alyssa. You were glad she got hurt."

Her lips pinch together in a tight line. She crosses her arms and the sharp, sticky scent of envy pours out of her skin. I know her and I know she thought about hurting Alyssa before I ever did.

"Well . . . it don't matter what I wanted. I didn't kill that baby, but I know you sure did."

"Well, I didn't kill Ray but I know your pills sure did. You want to talk about that?"

Her whole face drops, eyes big as golf balls. She wasn't expecting that. But how could she *not* have thought it would go there, when I was the one standing next to her as she put the pills in his soup? I was the one sitting next to him while he ate it. I was the one who watched Momma serve him seconds and thirds.

"How you . . . but . . . I did that for you."

"You did that for yourself, Momma. Just like everything else."

Her eyes get real cold.

"I should have left you where I found you. You ain't been nothing but trouble from the very start! You stupid, crazy little bit—"

Something clicks—the gas, the rage—and I charge like a bull ready to railroad her over. I stop close to her face, close enough to see her pupils widen, her mouth drop with a dead tongue. It's the same look she used to have when

369

Ray was about to hit her. But I'm not gonna hit her. That's too easy. I want to win the war, not the battle. And that's when I realize the great power I've always had over her.

"Fine, Momma. You win."

Frozen stiff, she exhales and relaxes her shoulders, relief coating her face. But I'm not done. I know what I want. What I've always wanted. I want to hurt her. The way she hurt me. And there is only one way of doing that.

"You will never see this baby and you will never see me again. This is your last visit. There won't be another."

Momma leans away, the words slapping her like a belt. We stand there, inches apart, in silence. I want to make sure she knows that I really mean it. She lets out an uneasy chuckle.

"But, baby, I—"

"You will never see me again. This is your last visit. There won't be another."

"Listen here, young lady, I said—"

"There won't be another!"

She shuts her mouth and swallows back whatever she is thinking. It must taste disgusting, because the bitterness turns up every wrinkle in her brown face. Her bottom lip starts to quiver and she tries to hide it with a fake smile. But I know Momma. I know the thought of losing me, really losing me, scares her more than a dead baby. More than Ray. More than anything. I'm her world. Without me, she has nothing. Not even God. I am doing the only thing that can hurt her—taking me away.

"But, baby . . . I'm your momma," she says, reeking of desperation.

Her trembling hands reach for me, ashy and dry. She is right. She is my momma. My protector. My best friend. But I'm somebody's momma too.

"Good-bye, Momma."

I don't look at her as I make my way out the door, not stopping until I get to my room. Not even when I hear her crying.

Notes from Dr. Jin-Yee Deng, Psychiatrist at Bellevue Hospital, NY

Is she capable of murder? On paper, the easy answer is no. There are no indicators of mental illness. Her records are impeccable. So one must look at Mary, the child, versus Mary, the child she wants you to believe she is. But I believe her relationship with her mother, her sole provider, is key to that discovery. This is where our assessments fail, as we may never know the dynamics of their relationship past what is reported and analyzed.

We may never know the real Mary.

"Today, I want to talk to you guys about letting go and grief," the perky little Staten Island trash says. The circle is smaller without our resident crazy girls, but she pretends not to notice. Ms. Veronica is the worst therapist ever. How come she didn't see that New Girl and Kelly were crazy? They didn't even try to hide it. Not like me. I'm good at hiding things. But you'd think I'd recognize it or something because real recognize real. Maybe that's why New Girl wanted to be my friend.

"The most powerful emotion we have in this world is forgiveness," she says with a grin. "Forgiveness is the ability to let go of the pain, bitterness, and resentment of others, and most importantly ourselves. We sometimes can be our biggest enemy. But when we forgive, starting with ourselves, a whole new world opens for us. Our conditions, our world, begins to change. We may even start getting everything we've ever wanted."

I almost fall out of my seat. That is the most profound thing she has ever said, ever. I look at China, mouth hung open and speechless. Ms. Veronica giggles.

"I was watching Oprah last night."

Well, that explains it.

"Now, who wants to share? You'll learn that once you let go, you'll feel free. And it's an amazing feeling."

I've never felt free. I raise my hand.

"Mary! Great!"

I think it's called stage fright, because once all eyes are on me, I forget how to talk.

"Go on, Mary. Let it out. It will feel good once you do."

I take a deep breath and stare at the floor. Alyssa's face comes to mind.

"Her . . . her name was Alyssa. Alyssa Morgan Richardson. She . . ."

My throat closes a little and I cough to clear it. Alyssa-ing.

"She was . . . beautiful. The most beautiful baby in the world. People say that about every baby, but Alyssa was different. She really was beautiful. She wasn't my sister, but I wanted her to be. So bad. So we could always be together. I loved Alyssa. She was everything to me. That's what hurts the most, that all these people think I hated her. Write all these things about me that aren't true."

The room is staring. Kisha's eyes water.

"They wouldn't let me go to the funeral. I wanted to see her one last time, but everyone was so mad at me. It was an accident. I didn't mean to . . . I didn't want anyone to get hurt. Things went too far . . . and saying sorry . . . sorry just didn't seem to help."

I didn't mean to throw her. I didn't mean to throw her.

"I had a brother that died too. Just died, no one . . . did nothing to him. He used to wake up in the middle of the night crying and I'd give him his bottle, 'cause we shared a room. One night, he didn't cry, and that just wasn't like him. I waited and waited, felt like I was waiting forever. I thought maybe he overslept or something. So I went to wake him up . . . he was cold, stiff, and his lips were all purple. Momma was out, somewhere. I was alone with Junior for hours. It was like sitting next to a coffin in the dark. I was five years old."

My face is wet but I don't try to dry it.

"Momma was . . . I guess there's no word for it. She blamed herself, but it . . . it just happened. It was nobody's fault. It was an accident. These things just happen . . . that's what they said, the doctors. But she was different after that. She was no longer my momma, just this shell of a woman I had to take care of. I had to feed her, wash her, make her eat on some days. And when she was having 'a day,' I'd be the one to make her take her pills. I'd put her to bed. 'Cause she didn't have anyone to take care of her. Just me. It's not her fault."

Even now, it's not her fault. She just didn't know any better. Not that it makes it right.

Everyone is leaning forward, faces pale and they can't get enough, even though it turns their stomachs to hear. Well, everyone except Marisol. She just crosses her arms and leans back in her chair.

"So you're trying to send your mami to prison now? Why?"

What the hell kind of question is that?

"Why?" I cough out the words. "'Cause they trying to take my baby."

She glares at me through her thick lashes, skeptical.

"So what?"

374

I stiffen, her attitude confusing . . . and out of nowhere. Where is this coming from?

"So what?" China says. "Man, do you hear how you talking right now?"

Marisol glances at her then back at me like she never said a thing.

"What you gonna do with a baby when you a baby yourself?" Marisol says. "You can't take care of no baby."

The words swirl around my head. I'm hot and the buzzing in my ear won't go away. I wish Herbert would go away.

"But I didn't do it."

She looks right through me, like I was made of glass, and calls my bluff.

"So?"

The chill of her stare goes straight to my bones, freezing the air inside. Feels like we're the only two people in the room.

"So?" Kisha scoffs. "Bitch, she's been in jail all this time 'cause of what her momma did!"

"Yeah, who sends their kid to do a bid for them? And let them take all that heat?" China says. "She was in all them newspapers and TV! That was some fucked up shit!"

Marisol never takes her eyes off me. I can't seem to look away either. She knows. I don't know how, but I can feel it. The fire in her eyes is scorching my bones black.

"So you did a bid for your mami. Big deal! How much

has she done for you? She give you life, raise you, feed you, washed your ass, kept you clean and safe. And she visits you. None of these other *puta's* mamis come visit them!"

The room goes cold, everyone sharing the same shame. She's right; Momma was the only one that came to visit me here. Everyone else is unwanted.

"Don't you love your mami?"

I just stare. She smacks on her gum, throwing back her hair.

"I'd do a bid for my mami, *Dios la bendiga.* No matter what she do, I would do anything for my mami. *Coño puta,* you gonna send your mami to jail! She too old to go to prison! You kill her if she go there. That what you want?"

No. I never wanted to kill Momma. I'm not New Girl.

"You already fucked up like the rest of us. It's too late for you," she says. "Your life is already over. Why go fuck up your mami's life now?"

I look around the room. A group of girls, a rainbow of colors, all in for different crimes, but somehow we all look the same. We have something in common: we're all too broken to be fixed. The girls avoid each other's eye contact, hating Marisol for saying all the things we already think about ourselves. Now would be the time for Ms. Veronica to step in and say no, that we have a chance at a happy life, that we can change. But she doesn't. She knows our future is grim. She knows that when at least three of these girls turn eighteen this year, they'll be out on the streets, probably doing something stupid and getting sent back to jail. Or they'll become the female versions of Ted, sleeping with men just to keep a roof over their heads.

"You hate your mami?"

The guilt burns through me. I want to hate Momma. I want to, but I can't. No matter what she has done to me, I can't hate her, even when I try to.

"No. I don't."

chapter eighteen

"You want to do WHAT?"

Ms. Cora stands up so fast the chair falls behind her.

"Just drop it, Ms. Cora. Drop the whole thing."

"Why? And this better be a damn good reason."

Her hands jump on her hips, almost knocking the laptop off her desk. I shrug.

"Nothing good will come of it."

"Nothing good? Are you . . . I just . . . are you crazy?"

She closes her eyes as soon as she says it.

"Jesus, Mary, I'm so sorry. That's not what I meant!"

I don't say nothing, because that is exactly what she meant. I don't take offense to it though. I am crazy. I let a baby die and lied about it.

Poor Ms. Cora, she worked so hard. She believed I was innocent from the very start, before I even knew her. Feel kind of bad for putting her through all of this. She is a good person. Not like Momma and me. Look at all the plaques on her walls, her degrees, and pictures of her family. She doesn't deserve this. But neither does Momma. She is already stuck in her own prison, for life.

"It's just not worth it. They're still going to take my baby away. They're gonna look up Junior and blame me for it like Alyssa. And Momma—"

"No, Mary! They can't blame you for Junior. The coroner's report proved it was sudden infant death syndrome. You had nothing to do with it. And your momma shouldn't have left you home alone with him. What kind of mother does that? Leave a child to care for a baby. It speaks to her character."

There is an ache inside when I think of Momma. The crushing look she gave me when I said she will never see me again. But just because I get to hurt Momma, doesn't mean I want anyone else to. Even if every decision she ever made was self-serving, she is the woman who raised me. All that I am is what she has molded. All that she has become is what I allowed, letting a lie grow from a mustard seed to a giant tree, casting a shadow around the world. Guess me always feeling sorry for Momma will never go away.

"She's my momma, Ms. Cora. No matter what, she's still my momma."

Ms. Cora's face softens at my plea, her arms unfolding.

"But, Mary, I just don't think . . ."

My stomach twists up. A cramp, starting from the tip of my spine down and around my downstairs in a circle. It's been coming and going all week. I breathe through it until it goes away.

"Mary? Are you okay?"

She sprints around her desk, bending near me.

"Just make it go away, Ms. Cora," I manage to moan. "Can you do that?"

Ms. Cora is super upset now. She can barely get her words together.

"Mary, I just can't drop the appeal. I can't make all your testimony go away! Even if I don't pursue it further, the state will probably pick up where I left off and investigate your mother. The allegations and the evidence are enough."

"But they don't have the smoking gun, right?"

Ms. Cora straightens. And there is that doubt again, painted on her face like makeup. This time it's mixed with realization.

"Do you?"

Her tone is a bit accusatory, but it doesn't bother me. I take another sip of water and hold back a smirk.

Mr. Charles Middlebury still lives in the same house on East 18th Street. His car is still the same, his hair is still the same, even his clothes are still the same. He has the same job at the insurance company and leaves for work at the same time every day. So as soon as I was out of baby jail, it was easy to go to his house after he left for work, walk in his backyard, and find the hole I dug by his hydrangea bush, where Momma's cross was in the same place that I had left it.

"No. I don't."

Notes from Dr. Lydia Cross, Children's Clinical Psychologist

Many of the previous reports focused solely on Mary's mental state during the night of the murder rather than on the full scope of the environment and circumstances surrounding her life beforehand. There were several key events in Mary's life that could have led to a psychotic break, but none so significant as the loss of her infant brother. At the time of his passing, there was an acute role reversal between her and her mother, triggered by survival.

Her love and loyalty to the mother she once knew transformed her into an unconscious guardian. Hiding the evidence of abuse and molestation was sympathetic in nature. Her coping mechanism manifested into blackouts, periods of intense rage, and memory suppression. Thus, her reaction to the murder from then to present day is that of preservation. She went into crisis management mode, much like the adult she has been forced to be for most of her life, continuing to hide and protect her mother, because in Mary's mind she is the mother, and her mother is the child.

And a mother always protects her child.

The end is much like the beginning. That is what they call the circle of life, like in *The Lion King*. My circle isn't smooth though. It's bumpy, full of hills and valleys, on repeat. But one thing remains constant: there was a baby at the start and there will be a baby at the end. New life has a funny way of changing your old one. Whether it wants to or not.

And so here I am, on bed rest. In a couple of weeks, there will be a baby. Ms. Cora didn't drop the case, and I don't blame her. No one wants to give up on their dream. Even if that dream is a nightmare like me. She may win, so I don't know what is going to happen to Momma or me. Maybe it's better we both be locked away. The world doesn't deserve to have us in it, screwing it all up for poor people like Mrs. Richardson. I can't believe I'm not from Momma's womb. Maybe I was born from her soul. That would explain so much.

I'm reading *The Great Gatsby*. It's on Ms. Claire's reading list. I've decided to switch my major to pre-law, so I can be a lawyer like Ms. Cora. Then I'll represent all the kids like me, after I get Bean back. I know they're going to take him. They're not even going to give me a chance.

And that is okay, because I need to get on my feet first. I need to take my pills, so I don't turn into Momma. I don't want to hurt Bean the same way I hurt Alyssa.

Allegedly. Well, sort of.

I'm not lying when I say I have no clue what happened that night. My blackouts are like blank pages in the middle of a book. All I remember is checking on her the same way I used to check on Junior, but she wouldn't keep quiet. So I gave her my pills. Ray used to say them pills were to shut me up so I figured they'd actually work on her. But she wouldn't stop . . . she wouldn't listen . . . next thing I knew Momma was fighting me. She wouldn't let go of her . . . she tripped over my pill bottle . . . I wasn't holding on tight enough and Alyssa flew. I didn't mean to throw her! But damn, if Alyssa would've just kept quiet, like a good baby supposed to, then I would've proved I could take care of her. Then maybe Mrs. Richardson would've wanted me and would've taken me away from Momma. She always said she wished she had a daughter like me. She meant that, I know she did.

But Momma . . . she was calling the police, snitching on me to Mrs. Richardson. After everything I'd done for her! I was already in trouble because of that stupid crystal rabbit she broke. Always saving her, she couldn't save me just once! So I hid the cross and didn't say nothing. I was waiting for Mrs. Richardson to come, so I could tell her all the awful things Momma had done to me. And she'd forgive me, because after all, Alyssa wasn't being a good baby. But she never came to baby jail like Momma said she would. My heart, all big and swollen from her love, shrunk down to a raisin. There was nothing left to live for. Until now.

But I didn't mean it though. No one misses her more than I do, they couldn't. I loved Alyssa like a sister and . . . ah, there I go again, Alyssa-ing. I shouldn't feel guilty. Alyssa was being a bad baby and I deserved to have a momma like Mrs. Richardson. Doesn't everybody? Because that's all this was about at the end of the day, doing anything to get away from Momma.

Even killing a baby.

There is a knock on the door. Winters walks in, glancing at my backpack and the bag of clothes Ms. Cora gave me in the middle of the floor.

"You ready?"

I nod and close my book, leaving it for the next girl. Maybe she'll be different, smarter than me.

"How long is the drive?"

"About three hours," he says. He looks confused and a little disappointed. He doesn't think I killed Alyssa. No one does now. That's what happens when you're a good liar.

I slip on Ms. Claire's coat, still smelling like her. Winters carries my bags out while I thump slowly down the steps. The girls, Ms. Reba, and Ms. Stein are huddled in the living room, watching TV, pretending they don't know this will be the last time they'll ever see me. They don't say nothing. Am I really supposed to say bye to these people? My tormentors, cheerleaders for the devil? No. It's not necessary. In a houseful of convicts, no one is capable of emotional good-byes. We'll just consider each other dead, killed off somehow. It's easier that way, familiar circumstances.

I slam the door behind me, letting it be the last thing I say to them.

The sky is dark gray and misty. Fog so thick you can barely see the houses up the street. Winters helps me into his truck and I look at the house for the last time. The same way I did when I left baby jail. I want to remember the details. The scuffs on the walls, the creaks in the floor, the bars on the windows, the stench of corn chips and bleach. The same bleach I poured into Ms. Stein's coffee this morning. I want to remember it all so I'll never miss it, wherever I go next.

"We got to stop at the precinct first," he says.

"Why?"

"Detective Rodriguez wants to take a DNA sample. Match it against any missing children in the database. You know, just in case."

They're still looking for answers to questions that no longer matter.

"Just in case," I repeat, and hold on to Bean.

He clears his throat.

"And I . . . I spoke to a Mrs. Richardson. She contacted that lawyer of yours. Said she is going to write a letter on your behalf . . . for the baby."

Nerves twitch a smile on my face as he starts the car. Mrs. Richardson. She still loves me, I knew she did! Yeah, I may never see Ted again, but I would trade the love of a thousand Teds for one Mrs. Richardson. Funny how things don't always work out the way you want them to, but so long as you get what you want in the end, the other things don't seem all that bad.

Winters drives off and I watch the house disappear in the side-view mirror. For the first time in months, I relax, knowing it's behind me.

"Also, I talked to the director at Brinwood. She said they are going to give you your own room . . . with a crib. You know, just in case."

"Just in case," I say with a smile so big it hurts my face to hold it. He huffs and turns down another street.

Mrs. Richardson is going to help me keep Bean. And this time, I'll prove everyone wrong. I'll show them that I know how to take care of a baby. This time I'll do everything right because Bean will be a good baby. He'll never cry and then everyone will see how good I am, especially Mrs. Richardson. She'll remember who I used to be, the little girl sitting under a Christmas tree, reading to a baby. She'll remember when she told me she loved me and said she hoped her daughter would grow up to be just like me.

I'll be the daughter she lost. She won't miss her or anyone. Bean and I, we'll be her new family. It's what I wanted. It's all I wanted. I'll take my pills too, like a good girl. I'll be good. I'll be better. She'll see. You'll see.

The mist turns into heavy raindrops and Winters clicks on the windshield wipers. BUMP BUMP. BUMP BUMP, the sound of my heart coming back to life.

"You thought about names yet?"

"Benson."

He nods with a small smile.

"Benson. Good, solid name for a man."

"What's your first name?" I ask.

"Kain. With a K."

"Benson Kain Addison. That'll work. For now."

acknowledgments

Be prepared. This is my first rapper's award speech.

First, I want to give thanks to God for this adventure called life.

To my amazing agent, Natalie Lakosil, thank you for picking me out of the slush pile, for easing my fears and insecurities, and for fielding my endless questions.

To my editor, Benjamin Rosenthal, who stepped up and took this challenge (the challenge that is me)! You were kind and nurturing throughout it all. I am immensely grateful for your patience. Harper is a lucky little girl.

To Anica Rissi, thank you for choosing this book and seeing my potential. Sad we didn't have the opportunity to work together but so happy you're following your dreams.

To Raquel Penzo, my writing sister, the one who reads through the first drafts and fields my monthly meltdowns without being stank, I share this success with you completely, *mi amor*. (That's the extent of my Spanish, no thanks to you!) To Leah Campbell, you helped shape this book when I was about to throw in the towel. Thank you!

To my parental unit: Mom, thank you for loving me so unconditionally. You were born to be my Mother. Dad, thank you for being Daddy. Nothing I could do could ever repay you both for supporting me, your weirdo daughter. To man-child brother, Duane, I am beyond proud of you. To my extended family, my aunts Kacy and Peaches, Godmother Justice, uncles, cousins, and all honorary members . . . it takes a village. To my loveable pup, Oscar, for forgoing walks and playtime so Mommy could finish her novel. Everything I do is to keep food in your bowl.

Big ups to Brooklyn, Jamaica, Howard University, my blueberry sister Tara, Malik for being my person, Jihaad for sharing your Grandparents, Mount Olivet Baptist Church, P.S. 261, Ms. Fulford, the Brooklyn Writers' Crew, and all the friends that have encouraged my madness. Big ups to my girls—Bison Babes, Travel Baes, Crazy Ladies, High School Crew— MY GOD! What would I do without our group texts, shenanigans, and unconditional love? Thank you for being a friend!

Lastly, to the girls from juvenile detention centers, group homes, and foster care willing to share their experiences with me . . . I am in awe of your perseverance. You are not forgotten; you are not a lost cause. Keep pushing.

JOIN THE

Epic Reads

COMMUNITY

THE ULTIMATE YA DESTINATION

◀ **DISCOVER** ▶
your next favorite read

◀ **MEET** ▶
new authors to love

◀ **WIN** ▶
free books

◀ **SHARE** ▶
infographics, playlists, quizzes, and more

◀ **WATCH** ▶
the latest videos

www.epicreads.com